FEB 2018

SF

ALSO BY SUE GRAFTON

H Is for Homicide

A Kinsey Millhone Mystery

SUE GRAFTON

St. Martin's Paperbacks

This is a work of fiction. All of the characters, organizations and events portrayed in this novel are either products of the author's imagination or are used fictitiously.

H IS FOR HOMICIDE

Copyright © 1991 by Sue Grafton.

All rights reserved.

For information address St. Martin's Press, 175 Fifth Avenue, New York, NY 10010.

Library of Congress Catalog Card Number: 85-24652

ISBN: 0-312-94565-5
EAN: 978-0-312-94565-7

Printed in the United States of America

Ballantine Books edition / May 1992
St. Martin's Paperbacks edition / December 2007

St. Martin's Paperbacks are published by St. Martin's Press, 175 Fifth Avenue, New York, NY 10010.

10 9

For the Women's Group in all its incarnations:

Florence Clark
Sylvia Stallings
Penelope Craven
Mary Lynn

Caroline Ahlstrand
Mary Slemons

Susan Dyne
Joyce Dobry

Margaret Warner
Georgina Morin
and Barbara Knox

sharing tears and triumphs, rage and laughter,
for the last five years of Monday nights.

The author wishes to acknowledge the invaluable assistance of the following people: Steven Humphrey; Ron Warthen, chief investigator, Fraud Division, California Department of Insurance; Robert Chambers, regional manager, and Michael Fawcett, special agent, Insurance Crime Prevention Institute; Lt. Tony Baker, Lt. Terry Bristol, Sgt. Tom Nelson, and Carol Hesson of the Santa Barbara County Sheriff's Department; Sgt. Dave Hybert, Santa Barbara Police Department; Traffic Officer Rick Crook, California Highway Patrol; Lucy Thomas, Reeves Medical Library, and Tokie Shynk, R.N., nursing director, Coronary Care Unit, Santa Barbara Cottage Hospital; Judianne Cooper; Joyce Mackewich; Irene Franotovich; Steven Stone, presiding justice, Ventura County Court of Appeals; Eric S. H. Ching; Austin Duncan, Gold Coast Auto Salvage; and Carter Blackmar.

The author also wishes to extend a special thank-you to Adam Seligman and to Muriel Seligman, national publicity director, Tourette Syndrome Association.

1

Looking back, it's hard to remember if the low morale at California Fidelity originated with the death of one of the claims adjusters or the transfer of Gordon Titus, an "efficiency expert" from the Palm Springs office, who was brought in to bolster profits. Both events contributed to the general unrest among the CF employees, and both ended up affecting me far more than I would have imagined, given the fact that my association with the company had been, up to that point, so loose. In checking back through my calendar, I find a brief penciled note of the appointment with Gordon Titus, whose arrival was imminent when Parnell was killed. After that first meeting with Titus, I'd jotted, "s.o.b. extraordinaire!" which summarized my entire relationship with him.

I'd been gone for three weeks, doing a consumer investigative report for a San Diego company concerned about a high-level executive whose background turned out to be something other than he'd represented. The work had taken me all over the state, and I had a check in my pocket for beaucoup bucks by the time I wrapped up my inquiry on a Friday afternoon. I'd been given the option of remaining in San Diego that weekend at the company's expense, but I woke up inexplicably at 3:00 A.M. with a primal longing for home. A moon the size of a dinner plate was propped up on the balcony outside my window, and the light falling across my face was almost bright enough to read by. I lay there, staring at the swaying shadow of palm fronds on the wall, and I knew that what I wanted most was to be in my own bed. I was tired of hotel rooms and meals on the road. I was tired of spending time with people I didn't know well or expect to see again. I got out of bed, pulled my clothes on, and threw everything I had in my duffel bag. By 3:30 A.M. I'd checked out, and ten minutes later I was on the 405 northbound, heading for Santa Teresa in my new (used) VW bug, a 1974 sedan, pale blue, with only one wee small ding in the left rear fender. Classy stuff.

At that hour, the Los Angeles freeway system is just beginning to hum. Traffic was light, but every on ramp seemed to donate a vehicle or two, people pouring north to work. It was still dark, with a delicious chill in the air, a ground fog curling along the berm like puffs of smoke. To my right, the foothills rose up and away from the road, the tracts of houses tucked into the landscape showing no signs of life. The lights along the highway contributed a nearly ghostly illumination, and what was visible of the city in the distance seemed stately and serene. I always feel an affinity for others traveling at such an hour, as if we are all engaged in some form of clandestine activity. Many of the other drivers had oversize Styrofoam cups of coffee. Some were actually managing to wolf down fast food as they drove. With the occasional car window rolled down, I was treated to bursts of booming music that faded away as the cars passed me, changing lanes. A glance in my rearview mirror showed a woman in the convertible behind me emoting with vigor, belting out a lip-sync solo as the wind whipped through her hair. I felt a jolt of pure joy. It was one of those occasions when I suddenly realized how happy I was. Life was good. I was female, single, with money in my pocket and enough gas to get home. I had nobody to answer to and no ties to speak of. I was healthy, physically fit, filled with energy. I flipped on the radio and chimed in on a chorus of "Amazing Grace," which didn't quite suit the occasion but was the only station I could find. An early morning evangelist began to make his pitch, and by the time I reached Ventura, I was nearly redeemed. As usual, I'd forgotten how often surges of goodwill merely presage bad news.

The usual five-hour drive from San Diego was condensed to four and a half, which put me back in Santa Teresa at a little after eight. I was still feeling wired. I decided to hit the office first, dropping off my typewriter and the briefcase full of notes before I headed home. I'd stop at a supermarket somewhere along the way and pick up just enough to get me through the next two days. Once I unloaded my duffel at home, I intended to grab a quick shower and then sleep for ten hours straight, getting up just in time for a bite of supper at Rosie's down the street from me. There's nothing quite as decadent as a day in the sack alone. I'd turn my phone off, let the machine pick up, and tape a note to the front door saying "Do Not Bother Me." I could hardly wait.

I expected the parking lot behind my office building to be deserted. It was Saturday morning and the stores downtown wouldn't open until ten. It was puzzling, therefore, to realize that the area was swarming with people, some of whom were cops. My first thought was that maybe a movie was being shot, the area cordoned off so the cameras could roll without interruption. There was a smattering of onlookers standing out on the street and the same general air of orchestrated boredom that seems to accompany a shoot. Then I spotted the crime scene tape and my senses went on red alert. Since the lot was inaccessible, I found a parking place out at the curb. I removed my handgun from my purse and tucked it into my briefcase in the backseat, locked the car doors, and moved toward the uniformed officer who was standing near the parking kiosk. He turned a speculative eye on me as I approached, trying to decide if I had any business at the scene. He was a nice-looking man in his thirties with a long, narrow face, hazel eyes, closely trimmed auburn hair, and a small mustache. His smile was polite and exposed a chip in one of his front teeth. He'd either been in a fight or used his central incisors in a manner his mother had warned him about as a child. "May I help you?"

I stared up at the three-story stucco building, which was mostly retail shops on the ground floor, businesses above. I tried to look like an especially law-abiding citizen instead of a free-lance private investigator with a tendency to fib. "Hi. What's going on? I work in that building and I was hoping to get in."

"We'll be wrapping this up in another twenty minutes. You have an office up there?"

"I'm part of the second-floor insurance complex. What was it, a burglary?"

The hazel eyes did a full survey and I could see the caution kick in. He didn't intend to disseminate information without knowing who I was. "May I see some identification?"

"Sure. I'll just get my wallet," I said. I didn't want him to think I was whipping out a weapon. Cops at a crime scene can be edgy little buggers and probably don't appreciate sudden moves. I handed him my billfold flipped open to my California driver's license with the photostat of my P.I. license visible in the slot below. "I've been out of town and I wanted to drop off some stuff before I headed home." I'd been a cop myself once, but I still tend to volunteer tidbits that are none of their business.

His scrutiny was brief. "Well, I doubt they'll let you in, but you can always ask," he said, gesturing toward a plain-clothes detective with a clipboard. "Check with Sergeant Hollingshead."

I still didn't have a clue what was going on, so I tried again. "Did someone break into the jewelry store?"

"Homicide."

"Really?" Scanning the parking lot, I could see the cluster of police personnel working in an area where the body probably lay. Nothing was actually visible at that remove, but most of the activity was concentrated in the vicinity. "Who's been assigned to the case, Lieutenant Dolan, by any chance?"

"That's right. You might try the mobile crime lab if you

want to talk to him. I saw him head in that direction a few minutes ago."

"Thanks." I crossed the parking lot, my gaze flickering to the paramedics, who were just packing up. The police photographer and a guy with a notebook doing a crime scene sketch were measuring the distance from a small ornamental shrub to the victim, whom I could see now, lying facedown on the pavement. The shoes were man-size. Someone had covered the body with a tarp, but I could still see the soles of his Nikes, toes touching, heels angled out in the form of a V.

Lieutenant Dolan appeared, heading in my direction. When our paths intersected, we shook hands automatically, exchanging benign pleasantries. With him, there's no point in barging right in with all the obvious questions. Dolan would tell me as much or as little as suited him in his own sweet time. Curiosity only makes him stubborn, and persistence touches off an inbred crankiness. Lieutenant Dolan's in his late fifties, not that far from retirement from what I'd heard, balding, baggy-faced, wearing a rumpled gray suit. He's a man I admire, though our relationship has had its antagonistic moments over the years. He's not fond of private detectives. He considers us a useless, though tolerable, breed and then only as long as we keep off his turf. As a cop, he's smart, meticulous, tireless, and very shrewd. In the company of civilians, his manner is usually remote, but in a squad room with his fellow officers, I've caught glimpses of the warmth and generosity that elicit much loyalty in his subordinates, qualities he never felt much need to trot out for me. This morning he seemed reasonably friendly, which is always worrisome.

"Who's the guy?" I said finally.

"Don't know. We haven't ID'd him yet. You want to take a look?" He jerked his head, indicating that I was to follow as he crossed to the body. I could feel my heart start to pump in my throat, the blood rushing to my face. In one of those tingling intimations of truth, I suddenly knew who the victim was. Maybe it was the familiar tire-tread soles of the running shoes, the elasticized rim of bright pink sweat pants, a glimpse of bare ankle showing dark skin. I focused on the sight with a curious sense of déjà vu. "What happened to him?"

"He was shot at close range, probably sometime after midnight. A jogger spotted the body at six-fifteen and called us. So far we don't have the weapon or any witnesses. His wallet's been lifted, his watch, and his keys."

He leaned down and picked up the edge of the tarp, pulling it back to reveal a young black man, wearing sweats. As I glanced at the face in side view, I pulled a mental plug, disconnecting my emotions from the rest of my interior processes. "His name is Parnell Perkins. He's a California Fidelity claims adjuster, hired about three months ago. Before that, he worked as a rep for an insurance company in Los Angeles." The turnover among adjusters is constant and no one thinks anything about it.

"He have family here in town?"

"Not that I ever heard. Vera Lipton, the CF claims manager, was his immediate supervisor. She'd have his personnel file."

"What about you?"

I shrugged. "Well, I haven't known him long, but I consider him a good friend." I corrected myself into past tense with a small jolt of pain. "He was really a nice guy . . . pleasant and capable. Generous to a fault. He wasn't very open about his personal life, but then, neither am I. We'd have drinks together after work a couple of times a week. Sometimes the 'happy hour' stretched into dinner if both of us happened to be free. I don't think he'd really had time to form many close friendships. He was a funny guy. I mean, literally. The man made me laugh."

Lieutenant Dolan was making penciled notes. He asked me some apparently unrelated questions about Parnell's workload, employment history, hobbies, girlfriends. Aside from a few superficial observations, I didn't have much to contribute, which seemed strange to me somehow, given the sense of distress I was feeling. I couldn't take my eyes off of Parnell. The back of his head was round, the hair cut almost to the scalp. The skin of the back of his neck looked soft. His eyes were open, staring blankly at the asphalt. What is life that it can vanish so absolutely in such a short period of time? Looking at Parnell, I was struck by the loss of animation, warmth, energy, all of it gone in an instant, never to return. His job was done. Now the rest of us were caught up in the clerical work that accompanies any death, the impersonal busywork generated by our transfer from aboveground to below.

I checked the slot where Parnell usually parked his car. "I wonder where his car went. He has to drive in from Colgate, so it should be here someplace. It's American made, a Chevrolet, I think, eighty or eighty-one, dark blue."

"Might have been stolen. We'll see if we can locate the vehicle. I don't suppose you know the license number offhand."

"Actually, I do. It's a vanity plate—PARNELL—a present to himself on his birthday last month. The big three-oh."

"You have his home address?"

I gave Dolan the directions. I didn't know the house number, but I'd driven him home on a couple of occasions, once when his car was being serviced and once when he got way too tipsy to get behind the wheel. I also gave Dolan Vera's home number, which he jotted beside her name. "I've got a key to the office if you want to see his desk."

"Let's do that."

For the next week, the killing was all anybody talked about. There's something profoundly unsettling when murder comes that close to home. Parnell's death was chilling because it seemed so inexplicable. There was nothing about him to suggest that he was marked for homicide. He seemed a perfectly ordinary human being just like the rest of us. As far as anyone could tell there was nothing in his current circumstances, nothing in his background, nothing in his nature, that would invite violence. Since there were never any suspects, we were made uncomfortably aware of our own vulnerability, haunted by the notion that perhaps we knew more than we realized. We discussed the subject endlessly, trying to dispel the cloud of anxiety that billowed up in the wake of his death.

I was no better prepared than anyone else. In my line of work, I'm not a stranger to homicide. For the most part, I don't react, but with Parnell's death, because of our friendship, my usual defenses—action, anger, a tendency to gallows humor—did little to protect me from the same apprehensiveness that gripped everyone else. While I find myself sometimes unwittingly involved in homicide investigations, it's nothing I set out to do, and usually nothing I'd take on without being paid. Since no one had hired me to look into this one, I kept my distance and minded my own business. This was strictly a police matter and I figured they had enough on their hands without any "help" from me. The fact that I'm a licensed private investigator gives me no more rights or privileges than the average citizen, and no more liberty to intrude.

I was unsettled by the lack of media coverage. After the first splash in the papers, all reference to the homicide seemed to vanish from sight. None of the television news shows carried any follow-up. I had to assume there were no leads and no new information coming in, but it did seem odd. And depressing, to say the least. When someone you care about is murdered like that, you want other people to feel the impact. You want to see the community fired up and some kind of action being taken. Without fuel, even the talk among the CF employees began to peter out. Speculation flared and died, leaving melancholy in its place. The cops swept in and packed up everything in his desk. His active caseload was distributed among the other agents. Some relative of his flew out from the East Coast and closed his apartment, disposing of his belongings. Business went on as usual. Where Parnell Perkins had once been, there was now empty space, and none of us understood quite how to cope with that. Eventually, I would realize how all the pieces fit together, but at that point the puzzle hadn't even been dumped out of the box. Within weeks, the homicide was superseded by the reality of Gordon Titus—Mr. Tight-Ass, as we soon referred to him—the VP from Palm Springs, whose transfer to the home office was scheduled for November 15. As it turned out, even Titus played an unwitting part in the course of events

2

CF had been buzzing about Gordon Titus since June when the quarterly report showed unusual claim activity. In an insurance office, any time the loss ratio exceeds the profit ratio by ten percent, the board begins to scrutinize the entire operation, trying to decide where the trouble lies. The fact that ours was the California Fidelity home office didn't exempt us from corporate abuse, and the general feeling was that we were headed for a shake-up. Word had it that Gordon Titus had been hired by the Palm Springs branch originally to revise their office procedures and boost their premium volume commitment. While he'd apparently done an admirable job (from the board's point of view), he'd created a lot of misery. In a world presided over by Agatha Christie, Gordon Titus might have ended up on the conference room floor with a paper spindle through his heart. In the real world, such matters seldom have such a satisfactory ending. Gordon

Titus was simply being transferred to Santa Teresa, where he was destined to create the same kind of misery.

In theory, this had little or nothing to do with me. My office space is provided by CF, in exchange for which I do routine investigations for them three or four times a month, checking out arson and wrongful death claims, among other things. On a quarterly basis, I put together documentation on any suspect claim being forwarded to the Insurance Crime Prevention Institute for investigation. I was currently pursuing fourteen such claims. Insurance fraud is big business, amounting to millions of dollars a year in losses that are passed on to honest policyholders, assuming there are still a few of us left out here. It's been my observation, after years in the business, that a certain percent of the population simply can't resist the urge to cheat. This inclination seems to cut across all class and economic lines, uniting racial and ethnic groups who otherwise might have little to say to one another. Insurance is regarded as equivalent to the state lottery. In return for a couple of months' premiums, people expect to hit the jackpot. Some are even willing to tamper with the odds to assure themselves of a payoff. I've seen people falsify losses on burglary claims, indicating goods stolen that were never, in fact, in their possession. I've seen buildings burned down, medical claims inflated, wounds self-inflicted, workmen's compensation claims extended far beyond any actual disability. I've seen declarations of property damage, lost earnings, accidents, and personal injuries that occurred only in the inflamed imaginations of the claimants. Happily, insurance companies have been wising up fast and have now instituted measures for sniffing out deceit. Part of my job entails laying the foundation for prosecution of these fraudulent claims. With Gordon Titus due to arrive any day, there'd been a sudden flurry of cases thrown in my direction and I was under pressure to produce quick results.

Vera passed along the latest of these questionable claims on a Sunday afternoon in late October. I had stopped by the office to pick up some estimated income tax files that had to go to my accountant first thing Monday morning. I parked my VW in the back lot as usual, entering the building by way of the rear stairs. I passed the darkened CF offices, let myself into my office, where I checked my answering machine for messages, did a quick sorting of Saturday's mail, and tucked the tax forms in the outside pouch of my leather shoulder bag. As I passed the CF offices on my way out again, I noticed there were lights on. I paused to peer through the glass doors, wondering if a thief was making off with all the office equipment. Vera crossed my line of vision, papers in hand, apparently on her way to the copy machine. She caught sight of me and waved, veering in my direction. She's thirty-eight, single, and the closest thing to a "best" friend I'm likely to have. The cluster of office keys was still in the lock and they jingled and clanked as she opened the door. "Hey, babe. I was looking for you Friday afternoon, but you'd already left. Must be nice knocking off at two," she said as she let me in.

"Where did you come from? The place was dark when I passed by a minute ago."

She relocked the door and continued toward the copier with me trailing along behind. She was talking over her shoulder, her manner relaxed. "I just popped by to use the Xerox machine. Don't tell anyone. This is personal business. A list of guests for the reception." She raised the lid on the Xerox machine and placed a paper on the glass, punching in instructions. She pressed the "print" button and the machine fired up. She was wearing black tights and knee-high boots with an oversize sweat shirt that hit her just below the crotch. She caught my look. "I know. It looks like I forgot to put on my pants. I'm on my way to Neil's, but I wanted to grab this while I could. What are you up to? You want to join us for a drink?"

"Thanks, but I better not. I have some work to do."

"Well, you missed the big excitement. The legendary Mr. Titus showed up Friday afternoon with three of his own hand-picked lieutenants. Two reps and a claims adjuster got canned to make room for them."

"You're kidding! Who?"

"Tony Marsden, Jack Cantheas, and Letty Bing."

"Letty? She'll sue!"

"I sincerely hope so."

"I thought he wasn't due here for another three weeks."

"Surprise, surprise. I'll probably be fired next."

"Oh, come on. You're doing a great job."

"Yeah, right. That's why claims posted six hundred thousand in losses."

"That was Andy Motycka's fault, not yours."

"Oh, who cares? I'm getting married. I can do something else. I never liked the job that much anyway. How's goes the shopping so far?"

"The shopping?" I said blankly. I was still trying to cope with the disaster at CF.

"For the wedding. A dress."

"Oooh. For the wedding. I've got a dress."

"Bullshit. You only own one dress and it's black. You're the maid of honor, not a pallbearer." Vera and her beloved were getting married in eight days, on Halloween. Everyone had given her infinite grief over her choice of dates, but Vera was adamant, claiming her natural cynicism was at war with sentiment. She'd never thought to marry. She'd been dating (she said) since she was twelve years old and had gone through countless men. Despite the fact that she was absolutely nuts about her fiancé, she was determined to turn tradition on its ear. I thought a black dress would be perfect for Halloween nuptials. Once the reception was over we could go trick-or-treating together and maybe pool the take. I wanted dibs on the Hershey's Kisses and Tootsie Rolls.

"Besides, you've had that damn dress for five years," she went on.

"Six."

"And last time you wore it you said it still smelled like a swamp."

"I washed it!"

"Kinsey, you cannot wear a six-year-old smelly black dress in my wedding. You swore you'd get a new one."

"I *will*."

She gave me a flat look, filled with skepticism. "Where will you go to shop? Not K Mart."

"I wouldn't go to *K Mart*. I can't believe you said that."

"Well, where?"

I looked at her uneasily, trying to come up with an answer that would satisfy. I knew the hesitation was just an invitation for her to step in and boss me around, but to tell you the truth, I hadn't the faintest idea what kind of dress to buy. I've never been a maid of honor. I don't have a clue what such maidens wear. Something useless, I'm sure, with big flounces everywhere.

She stepped in. "I will help you," she said, as though to a half-wit.

"You will? That's great."

Vera rolled her eyes, but I could tell she was thrilled that I was yielding control. People like to take charge of my personal life. Many seem to feel I don't do things right. "Friday. After work," she said.

"Thanks. We can have dinner afterward. My treat."

"I don't *want* a Quarter Pounder with cheese," she said.

I waved at her dismissively and headed toward the door. "See you in the morning. You want to let me out?"

"Hang on a minute and I'll go, too. Why don't you go ahead and pick up the case I tried to give you Friday. It's in the file in my out box. The woman's name is Bibianna Diaz. If you can nail her, maybe all of us will end up looking good."

I detoured into the glass cubicle she now occupied as claims manager, spotting the Diaz file, which was right on top. "Got it," I called.

"You can talk to Mary Bellflower once you've had a chance to review it. It was Parnell's to begin with, but she's the one who flagged it."

"I thought the cops took all his files."

"This wasn't in with the files on his desk. He'd given it to Mary the month before, so the cops never saw it." She emerged with her photocopies clamped between her teeth while she fished out her car keys.

"I'll see if there's a way to check the woman out before I talk to Mary. At least I can get the lay of the land that way first," I said.

"Suit yourself. You can work it out any way you want." Vera flipped the lights off and let us out of the office, locking the doors behind her. "If you have any questions, I'll be home by ten."

We left the building together, chatting idly as we trotted down the stairs. Ours were the only two cars in the lot, parked side by side. "One more thing," she said as she unlocked her car door. "Titus has asked to see you first thing tomorrow morning."

I stared at her across the top of her car. "Why me? I don't work for him."

"Who knows? Maybe he sees you as an 'important part of the team,' He talks like that. All this rah-rah horsepuckey. It's obnoxious." She opened the door and slid into the driver's seat, rolling the window down on the passenger side. "Take care."

"You too."

I let myself into my car, my stomach already churning. I didn't want to see Gordon Titus at all, let alone tomorrow morning. What a way to start the week. . . .

The parking lot was empty and the downtown was quiet. We pulled out at the same time, turning in opposite directions. All the stores were closed, but the lights along State Street and the smattering of pedestrians gave the illusion of activity in the otherwise deserted business district. Santa Teresa is a town where you can still window-shop after hours without (too much) fear of attack. During tourist season the streets swarm with people, and even in the off months there's a benign air about the place. I was tempted to grab some supper in one of the little restaurants in the area, but I could hear a peanut-butter-and-pickle sandwich calling me from home.

The neighborhood was fully dark by the time I parked the car and entered my gate. Henry's kitchen light was on, but I resisted the temptation to pop in to see him. He'd want to feed me dinner, ply me with decent chardonnay, and catch me up on all the latest gossip. At the age of eighty-two, he's a retired commercial baker, involved now in catering tea parties for little old ladies on our block. As a sideline, he writes those little crossword puzzle booklets you see in supermarket checkout lines, filled with puns, bons mots, and spoonerisms. When he's not doing that, he's usually chiding me about my personal life, which he thinks is not only dangerous, but much too uncivilized.

I let myself into my apartment and flipped on one of the table lamps. I dropped my handbag on the counter that separates my kitchenette from the designated living room. The place had been completely redone after a bomb blast had flattened it. I'd stayed with Henry until the construction was finished, moving back into the apartment on my birthday the previous May. And what a gift it was, like a pirate ship, all teak and brass fittings, a porthole in the door, a spiral staircase leading up to a loft where I could sleep now beneath a skylight salted with stars. My bed was a platform with drawers built into the base. Downstairs, I had a galley for a kitchen, an alcove for a stacking washer/dryer, a living room with a sofa that doubled for company, and a small guest bath. Upstairs, a second bathroom had a sunken tub with a jungle of houseplants on the windowsill and a glimpse of the ocean through the tree-tops.

The entire apartment was fitted with little nooks and crannies of storage space, cupboards, and hidey-holes, pegs for my clothes. The design was all Henry's, and he'd taken a devilish satisfaction out of shaping my surroundings. The carpet was royal blue, the furnishings simple. Even after six months, I walked around the place as if blind, touching everything, marveling at the feel of it, the scent of the wood. After my parents died, I'd been raised by a maiden aunt, a woman whose relationship with me entailed more theory than affection. Without ever actually saying so, she conveyed the impression that I was there on approval, like a mattress, subject to return if the lumps didn't smooth out. To give her credit, her notions of child raising, if eccentric, were sound, and what she taught me in the way of worldly truths has served me well. Still, for most of my life, I've felt like an intruder and a transient, merely marking time until I was asked to move on. Now my interior world had undergone a shift. This was home and I belonged here. While the apartment was rented, I was a tenant for life. The sensation was strange and I still didn't quite trust it.

I turned on my little black-and-white TV, letting the sound keep me company while I puttered around, making supper. I sat at the counter, perched on a barstool, munching on my sandwich as I leafed through the file Vera'd given me. There were copies of the initial claim—a single-car accident with personal injuries—a sheaf of medical bills, some correspondence, and an attached summary of the salient points. The adjuster, Mary Bellflower, had flagged the claim for a variety of reasons; the injury itself was "soft tissue" and subjective, impossible to verify. Ms. Diaz was complaining of whiplash, headaches, dizziness, lower back pain, and muscle spasms, among other things. The repairs to the car were estimated at fifteen hundred dollars, with additional medical bills (all third-generation photocopies, which would permit a bit of tampering with the figures) totaling twenty-five hundred dollars. She was also claiming twelve hundred dollars in lost wages, for a total of fifty-two hundred dollars. There was no police report from the accident scene, and the adjuster was astute enough to pick up on the fact that the collision had occurred shortly after Ms. Diaz's vehicle had been registered and insured. Also questionable was the fact that the claimant was using a post office box as an address. Mary had ferreted out an actual street address, which she'd included in her notes. I noticed she'd been careful to retain copies of the envelopes (showing date stamps) in which the claim forms had been returned. If charges were filed, these would provide evidence that the U.S. mails had been used, thus opening the matter to federal investigation under mail fraud statutes. In fraudulent cases, the claimant will often hire an attorney whose job it is to stick the screws to the claims representative, pressuring for a quick settlement. Ms. Diaz hadn't (yet) engaged the services of an attorney, but she was being pushy about reimbursement. I couldn't imagine why Parnell had turned the case over to Mary Bellflower. On a case this size the temptation is to approve payment fairly quickly to avoid any suggestion of "bad faith" on the part of the insurance company. However, because California Fidelity had recently chalked up such big losses, Maclin Voorhies, the company vice president, was taking a dim view of rubber stamping. Thus, the matter had been referred to me for follow-up. With Titus on the scene, it might turn out to be too little too late, but that's where matters stood.

It was ten when I finally turned the lights out and went up to bed. I opened one of the windows and leaned my head against the frame, letting the cold air wash across my face. The moon was up. The night sky was clear and the stars were as piercing as pinpricks. A weak storm front was moving in, and a chance of showers was being predicted sometime in the next couple of days. So far, there was no sign of rain. I could hear the muffled tumble of the surf a block away. I crawled under the covers and flipped on the clock radio, staring up at the skylight. A country song began to play, Willie Nelson in a wistful account of pain and suffering. Where is Robert Dietz tonight? I asked myself. I'd hired myself a private investigator the previous May when my name showed up as one of the four finalists on somebody's hit list. I'd needed a bodyguard and Dietz turned out to be it. Once the situation was defused, he'd stayed on for three months. He'd been gone now for two. We were neither of us letter writers and too cheap to call each other very often since he'd left for Germany. His departure was wrenching, the banal and the bittersweet mingling in about equal parts.

"I'm not good at good-byes," I'd said the night before he left.

"I'm not good at anything else," he'd replied with that crooked smile of his. I didn't think his pain was any match for mine. I might have been wrong, of course. Dietz was not the sort of man given to unrestrained expressions of anguish or distress, which is not to say such feelings didn't exist for him.

The hard part about love is the hole it leaves when it's gone . . . which is the substance of every country-and-western song you ever heard. . . .

The next thing I knew, it was 6:00 A.M. and my alarm was peeping like a little bird. I rolled out of bed and grabbed my running clothes, pulling on sweatpants, sweatshirt, crew socks, and Adidas. I paused to brush my teeth and then headed down the spiral stairs to my front door. The sun hadn't risen yet, but the darkness had eased up to a charcoal haze. The morning air was damp and smelled of eucalyptus. I clung to the front gate and did a couple of stretches—more form than content—using the walk over to Cabana Boulevard as a way of warming up to some extent. Sometimes I wonder why I continue to exercise with such diligence. Paranoia, perhaps . . . the recollection of the times when I've had to run for my life.

When I reached the bike path I broke into an awkward trot. My legs felt like wood and my breathing was choppy. The first mile always hurts; anything after that is a snap by comparison. I shut my mind off and tuned in to my surroundings. To the right of me, the ocean was pounding at the beach, a muted thunder as restful as the sound of rain. Seagulls were screeching as they wheeled above the surf. The Pacific was the color of liquid steel, the waves a foamy mass of aluminum and chrome. The sand became a mirror where the water receded, reflecting the softness of the morning sky. The horizon turned a salmon pink as the sun crept into view. Long arms of coral light stretched out along the horizon, where clouds were beginning to mass from the promised storm front. The air was cold and richly scented with salt spray and seaweed. Within minutes, my stride began to lengthen and I could feel a mindless rhythm orchestrate all the moving parts. As it turned out, this was the last time I'd have a chance to jog for weeks. Had I but known, I might have enjoyed it a lot more than I did.

3

Somehow I sensed, long before I actually laid eyes on the man, that my relationship with Gordon Titus was not going to be a source of joy and comfort to either one of us. Since he'd proposed the meeting, I figured my choices were obvious. I could avoid the office, thus postponing our first encounter, or I could comply with his request and get it over with. Of the two, the latter seemed the wiser on the face of it. After all, it was possible the meeting was a mere formality. I didn't want my lack of enthusiasm to be misinterpreted. Better, I thought, to appear to be cooperative. As my aunt used to say: "Always keep yourself on the side of the angels." It was only after she died that I began to wonder what that meant.

When I got to the office at nine, I put a call through to Darcy Pascoe, the receptionist in the California Fidelity offices next door to mine. "Hi, Darcy. This is Kinsey. I hear Gordon Titus wants to meet with me. From what Vera says, the guy's a real prick."

"Good morning, Miss Millhone. Nice to hear from you," she said in a pleasant singsong voice.

"Why are you talking like that? Is he standing right there?"

"That's correct."

"Oh. Well, would you ask him what time he wants me over there? I've got a few minutes now if it works for him."

"Just one moment, please."

She put me on hold long enough to convey the question and elicit a response. She clicked back in. "Right now would be fine."

"I'm so thrilled."

I hung up the phone. I can handle this, I thought. All of us are subjected to somebody else's power at some point. So once in a while you kiss ass. So what? Either you make your peace with that early, or you end up living your life as a crank and a misfit. As I headed for the door, I passed the wall-hung mirror and paused to check my reflection. I looked fine to me. Jeans, turtleneck, no dirt on my face, nothing green between my teeth. I don't wear makeup, so I never have to worry about caking or smears. I used to cut my hair myself, but I'd been growing it out of late, so it was now shoulder length, just the teeniest bit uneven. Fortunately, all I had to do was cock my head at a slight angle and it straightened right up.

It was with my head thus tilted that I entered the glass cubicle Gordon Titus was apparently using for his little get-acquainted meetings with the staff. Vera's office was located right next to his and I could see her at her desk, shooting me a profoundly cross-eyed look. She was wearing a subdued gray business suit with a plain white blouse, her hair tucked back in a bun. Mr. Titus stood up to meet me and we shook hands across the desk. "Miss Millhone."

"Hi. How are you? Nice to meet you," I said.

His grip was appropriately macho, firm and hearty, but not crushing, the contact maintained just long enough to show that his purpose was sincere. At first glance, I have to say he was a pleasant surprise. I pictured dry and gray, someone all tucked in and proper. He was younger than I expected, forty-two at most. He was smooth-faced, clean-shaven, his eyes blue, his hair prematurely gray and stylishly cut. Instead of a suit, he wore chinos and a blue Izod shirt. He didn't seem all that taken with me. I could tell from his glance that my professional attire was a bit of a shock. He covered it well, perhaps imagining that I'd come in to assist the charwoman with the floors before work.

"Have a seat," he said. No smile, no small talk, no social niceties.

I sat.

He sat. "We've been taking a look at the reports you submitted over the past six months. Nice work," he said. I could already sense the "but" hanging in the air above our heads. His eye traveled down the page in front of him. He leafed rapidly through the sheaf of notes clipped to the front of a manila file folder. The implication was that he had data on me going back to the first time I threw up in elementary school. There was a yellow legal pad in front of him on which he'd scribbled additional notes in ink. His handwriting was precise, the letters angular, with an emphasis on downward strokes. Occasionally, there were pits where the pen point had torn through the paper. I could picture his thoughts speeding across the page while his cursive stumped along behind, gouging out unsightly holes. He'd never forgotten how to do a formal outline. Topics were laid out with Roman numerals, subclauses neatly indented. His mind probably worked that way, too, with all the categories assigned up front and all the subordinate subjects carefully relegated to the lines below. He closed the folder and set it aside. He turned his attention to me fully.

I thought it was time to jump right in and make quick work of it. "I'm not sure if you're aware of it, but I'm not actually a California Fidelity employee," I said. "I work for the company as an independent contractor."

His smile was thin. "I understand that. However, there are several small issues we'll need to clarify for corporate purposes. I'm sure you can appreciate the fact that in a review of this sort, we need to see the whole picture."

"Of course."

He studied the first and second pages of his legal pad.

I glanced surreptitiously at my watch, under the guise of adjusting the band.

Without looking up, he said, "Have you another appointment?"

"I have a claim to investigate. I should be out in the field."

He looked up at me. His body was motionless. His blue eyes bored into mine without blinking. He was handsome, but blank, so expressionless that I wondered if he'd had a stroke or an accident that had severed all the muscles in his face.

I tried to keep my mien as dead as his. I'm a bottom-line kind of person myself. I like to cut straight to the chase.

He picked up his pen, checking item one, line one on his list. "I'm not clear whom you report to. Perhaps you can fill me in."

Oh, Jesus. "It varies," I said pleasantly. "I'm accountable to Mac Voorhies, but the cases are usually referred by individual claims adjusters." The minute I started speaking, he began to write. I'm an expert (she said modestly) at reading upside down, but he was using a shorthand code of his own. I stopped speaking. He stopped taking notes. I said nothing.

He looked up at me again. "Excuse me. I missed that. Can you describe the procedure on this? The file doesn't seem to indicate."

"Usually, I get a call. Or one of the adjusters might bring a case to my attention. I stop in the office two or three times a week." He managed to write at exactly the rate I spoke. I stopped. His pen came to a halt.

"In addition to meetings?" he asked.

"Meetings?"

"I'm assuming you attend the regularly scheduled office meetings. Budgets. Sales . . ."

"I've never done that."

He checked his notes, flipping back a page or two. A frown formed, but I could have sworn his confusion was pure theatrics. "I can't seem to find your 206's."

"Really," I said. "That surprises me." I hadn't the faintest idea what a 206 was, but I thought it should be his responsibility since he brought it up.

He passed a form across the desk to me. "Just to refresh your memory," he said.

There were lots of slots to be filled in. Dates, times, corporate numbers, odometer readings; clearly a formal report in which I was supposed to detail every burp and hiccup on the job. I passed the form back to him without comment. I wasn't going to play this game. Screw him.

He'd begun to make notes again, head bent. "I'll have to ask you to supply the carbons from your files so we can bring our files up to date. Drop them off with Miss Pascoe by noon, if you would. We'll set up an appointment to go over them later."

"What for?"

"We'll need documentation of your hours so we can calculate your rate of pay," he said as if it were obvious.

"I can tell you that. Thirty bucks an hour plus expenses."

He managed to convey astonishment without even raising a brow. "Less rental monies for the office space, of course," he said.

"In *lieu* of rental monies for the office space."

Dead silence.

Finally, he said, "That can't be the case."

"That's been my arrangement with CF from the first."

"That's absolutely out of the question."

"It's been this way for the past six years and no one's complained of it yet."

He lifted his pen from the page. "Well. We'll have to see if we can straighten this out."

"Straighten what out? That's the agreement. It suits me. It suits them."

"Miss Millhone, do you have a problem?"

"No, not at all. What makes you ask?"

"I'm not sure I understand your attitude," he said.

"My attitude is simple. I don't see why I have to put up with this bureaucratic bullshit. I don't work for you. I'm an independent contractor. You don't like what I do, hire somebody else."

"I see." He replaced the cap on the pen. He began to gather his papers, his movements crisp, his manner abrupt. "Perhaps we can meet some other time. When you're calmer."

I said, "Great. You too. I have a job to do, anyway."

He left the cubicle before I did and headed straight for Mac's office. All the CF employees within range were hard at work, their expressions studiously attentive to the job at hand.

I put the entire exchange in a mental box and filed it away. There'd be hell to pay, but at the moment I didn't care.

The address I'd been given for Bibianna Diaz turned out to be a vacant lot. I sat in my car and stared blankly at the parcel of raw dirt, crudely landscaped with weeds, palms, boulders, and broken bottles twinkling in the sunlight. A condom dangled limply from a fallen palm frond, looking like a skin shed by some anemic snake. I double-checked the information listed in the file and then scanned the house numbers on either side. No match. I flipped open the glove compartment and pulled out a city map, which I spread across the steering wheel, squinting at the street names indexed alphabetically on the back. There was no other road, drive, avenue, or lane listed with the same name or one that even came close. I'd dropped the Diaz file off at the CF offices before my meeting with Titus, so all I had with me were a few penciled notes. I figured it was time to check back with Mary Bellflower to see what else she might have in the way of a contact. I started the car and headed toward town, feeling strangely gratified. The nonexistent street address added fuel to the notion that Ms. Diaz was telling fibs, a prospect that excited the latent felon in me. In California jargon, I can "resonate" with crooks. Investigating honest people isn't half the fun.

I spotted a pay phone on the far side of a gas station. I pulled in and had my tank topped off while I called Mary at the CF offices and told her what was going on. "You have any other address for this woman?" I asked.

"Oh, Kinsey, poor thing. I heard about your meeting with Gordon Titus. I can't believe you gave him such a hard time. He was screaming at Mac so loud I could hear it back here."

"I couldn't help myself," I said. "I really meant to behave and it just popped out."

"Oh, you poor dear."

"I don't think it's that bad," I said. "Do you?"

"I don't know. I saw him go off with the corporate vice president and he seemed pretty upset. He told Darcy to take his calls. The minute he walked out the door, the tension level dropped by half."

"How can you guys put up with that stuff? He's a jerk. Has he talked to you yet?"

"No, but Kinsey, I can't afford to lose this job. I just qualified for benefits. I'm hoping to get pregnant, and Peter's group plan doesn't cover maternity."

"Well, I wouldn't take any guff," I said. "Of course, I'll be fired, but what the hell. I'll live."

Mary laughed. "If you can pull this one off, it might help."

"Let's hope so. Do you have any other address in the file?"

"I doubt it, but I can look. Hang on a sec." I listened to Mary breathe in my ear while she leafed through the file. Reluctantly, she said, "No, I don't see anything. You know, we never got a copy of the police report. Maybe she gave them the correct address."

"Good thought," I said. "I can stop by the station as long as I'm out. What about the telephone number? Can we check the crisscross?" I had the latest Polk directory in my office, detailing addresses sequentially by street and house number, a second section listing telephone numbers sequentially. Often, if you have one good piece of information, you get a line on a subject by cross-referencing.

She said, "Won't help. It's unlisted."

"Oh, good. A crook with an unlisted number. I love that. How about the license plate on the car? DMV might have something."

"Well, that I can help you with." Mary scouted out the plate number of Bibianna's Mazda and recited it to me. "And Kinsey, if you get the address, let me know right away. I have some forms I want to send her and Mac's having a fit. You can't send registered mail to a post office box."

"Right," I said. "By the way, how come Parnell didn't handle this one himself?"

"Beats me. I assumed he was just too busy with his other cases."

"Maybe so," I said with a shrug. "Anyway, I'll call as soon as I know anything. I'm planning to pop by the office later with an update for the files."

"Good luck."

I scribbled a few hasty notes to myself after we hung up. I fished out another couple of dimes and tried Bibianna's work number, a dry cleaning establishment on Vaquero.

The man who answered the telephone was terse and impatient, probably his chronic state. The excess stomach acid was audible in his voice and I pictured him tossing Tums in his mouth like after-dinner mints. When I asked for Bibianna Diaz, he said she was out. Period.

When there was no other information forthcoming, I gave him a prompt. "Do you expect her back soon?"

"I don't expect nothin'," he shot back. "She said she'd be out all week. Back problems, she says. I'm not gonna argue anybody has a bad back. First thing you know I get slapped with a goddamn workmen's comp claim and I'm out big bucks. Nuts to that. Who's this?"

"This is her cousin, Ruth. I'm passing through town on my way to Los Angeles and I promised I'd stop and see her. Is there any way you could give me her home address? She gave it to me last week when we chatted on the phone, but I walked off without my address book so I don't have it with me."

"Nope. Sorry. No dice. And you wanna know why?

Because I don't know you. You could be anyone. Nothing personal, but how do I know you don't go around slashin' young girls with a butcher knife? You see what I mean? I give out an employee's address and I'm liable for anything happens after that. Burglary, harassment, rape. Unh-hunh. No way. That's my policy." He sounded like he was in his sixties, a man besieged with lawsuits.

I started to say something else, but he plunked the phone down in my ear. I made a face at the receiver, a mature and effectual way of handling my irritation, I thought. I paid for the gasoline, got back in the VW, and drove over to the police station, where I paid eleven bucks for a copy of the accident report. The address listed was the same nonexistent street address I'd started with. The clerk working at the desk wasn't one I knew and I couldn't get her to run a check on Bibianna for me.

I left my car parked out front and walked the half block to the courthouse, where I tried the superior court clerk's office, scanning the dockets for some sign of Ms. Diaz. Not there. Too bad. It would have cheered me up enormously to learn she had a felony conviction lurking in her background. By now, without ever having laid eyes on the woman, I was operating on the assumption that she was up to no good. I wanted her address and I couldn't believe there wasn't a paper trail somewhere. I pulled up negative results from municipal court records, nothing from voter registration. I checked with the DA's office, where a pal of mine assured me Bibianna wasn't passing bad paper or late with any child support payments. Well, shoot. I'd just about exhausted the sources I could think of.

I picked up my car and hit the freeway, heading for the

county sheriff's department. I parked in the small lot out front and pushed through the glass doors into a small reception area, where I signed my name in the logbook. I walked down the hall a short distance to a cubbyhole marked "Records and Warrants." The civilian clerk on duty didn't seem like a promising source of confidential information. I judged her to be in her early thirties, roughly my age, with a frizzy pyramid of tightly kinked blond hair and way too much gum for the size of her teeth. She caught me surveying her dental misfortunes and pulled her lips together self-consciously. I checked for a name tag, but she wasn't wearing one.

"Can you run a computer check and see if this woman has ever been arrested in Santa Teresa?" I reached for the pad of scratch paper on the counter and jotted down Bibianna's name and her date of birth. I took out my wallet, laid the photostat of my P.I. license next to the note.

Her pale eyes came to rest on mine with the first real sign of recognition. "We're not allowed to divulge that information. The Department of Justice has very strict guidelines."

"Well, good for them," I said. "Why don't I tell you my situation and see if it helps. I'm investigating Bibianna Diaz for possible insurance fraud, and the company I work for, California Fidelity, needs to know if she's got a record."

She processed what I'd said and I watched her formulate a reply with care. She was not quick, this one. She operated with the sort of bureaucratic caution guaranteed to infuriate the honest citizen (also people like me). "If she's been tried and convicted, you can get that information from the court clerk's office. It's a matter of public record."

"I'm aware of that. I've already checked their files. What I'm wondering is whether she's ever been arrested or booked without being formally charged."

"If she was never charged or convicted, then the fact that she was arrested would be immaterial. It's a matter of the individual's right to privacy."

"I appreciate that. I understand," I said. "But suppose she's been picked up for burglary or theft and the DA's decided he can't make a case. . . ."

"Then it's none of your business. If she was never formally charged with a crime—"

"I get the drift," I said. It never pays to deal with the fly-weights of the world. They take far too much pleasure in thwarting you at every turn. I was silent for a moment, trying to compose myself. Situations like this bring up an ancient and fundamental desire to bite. I could envision a half-moon of my teeth marks on the flesh on her forearm, which would swell and turn all colors of the rainbow. She'd have to have tetanus and rabies shots. Maybe her owner would elect to put her to sleep. I smiled politely. "Look. Why don't we simplify life to some extent. All I really need is a current address. Could you check that for me?"

"No."

"Why not?"

"Because we can't give out that information."

"What about the Freedom of Information Act?" I said.

"What about it?"

"Is there anyone else here I could talk to?"

She didn't like my persistence. She didn't like my tone. She didn't like anything else about me, either, and the feeling was mutual. Her and Gordon Titus. God. Some days it doesn't pay to get out of bed. She left the desk without another word and returned moments later with a female deputy who was pleasant but unyielding. I went through the same tiresome routine again and got nowhere.

"Well, thanks anyway. This has really been fun," I said.

I sat in my car out in the parking lot, trying to decide what to do next. This is what happens when I tell the truth, I thought righteously. No wonder I'm forced to lie, cheat, and steal. Honesty will get you nowhere, especially with these law-and-order types. I glanced down at the police report sitting on the passenger seat beside me. I waited for my flush of frustration to subside and then I picked it up.

According to the account she'd given to the officer at the scene, Bibianna had been proceeding south on Valdesto at 30 MPH when she'd been forced to slam on her brakes, swerving to avoid a cat that streaked across her path. Her car had skidded sideways and she'd plowed into a parked car. There were no witnesses, of course. Paramedics called to the scene had administered first aid for superficial contusions and abrasions and then transported her to St. Terry's emergency room for X-ray examination when she complained of neck and back pain. I wondered if the hospital billing department had a good address for her. There was probably a second insurance company, representing the owner of the vehicle she'd hit, and it was always possible that the other claims adjuster had something in his files. Bibianna lived *somewhere* and I was determined to get a line on her. I went back to the office and made the requisite phone calls, which netted me nothing. I gave Mary Bellflower a quick call next door and told her I was still working on it.

At two-fifteen, aggravated, I set the matter aside and spent the rest of the day on routine paperwork. I knew I could ill afford to get obsessed with Bibianna Diaz. Now that I had Gordon Titus breathing down my neck, I was going to have to cover some ground. I plowed on, but even while I was concentrating on other cases, finishing off the paperwork, I could feel the pull. Something was bothering me. It's not like passing a file along to another adjuster is any big deal, but Parnell was dead and that seemed to make all the difference.

4

The next morning, I showered and donned my generic uniform. I had this outfit done up for me years ago by an ex-con who learned to sew working the big machines in some federal penitentiary. The slacks were blue-gray and unflattering, with a pale stripe along the seam. The matching pale blue shirt had a circle of Velcro sewn on the sleeve, which usually sported a patch that read "Southern California Services." The shoes, left over from my days on the police force, were black and made my feet look like they'd be hard to lift. Once I added a clipboard and a self-important key ring, I could pass myself off as just about anything. Usually, I pretend I'm reading a water meter or checking for gas leaks, any officious task that necessitates crawling through somebody's bushes and tampering with their security systems. Today, I slapped on an FTD patch and headed for the nearest florist, where I laid out thirty-six dollars for a massive bouquet. I bought a syrupy get-well card, scribbled an illegible name, and put in a quick call to the dry cleaning establishment where Bibianna worked. A woman answered this time.

"Oh, hi," said I. "May I speak to the owner, please?"

"This' the plant. He just left on his way over to the other place," she said. "You want that number?"

"Sure."

She recited the number to me carefully and I recited it back as if I were writing it down. What did she know? She couldn't see what I was doing anyway.

"Thanks," I said. I hung up and hopped in my car, flowers on the seat beside me. I drove over to the plant. There was a nice green length of curb out in front, fifteen minutes of free parking. I locked the car and went in. I stood at the counter briefly, waiting for service. The place smelled of soap products, damp cotton, chemicals, and steam. The area behind the counter was a forest of clothing in clear plastic bags. On my left, an elaborate electronic tram moved hanging garments in a tortuous track that snaked up and around, returning to the point of origin so that any garment on board could be delivered to the station when the proper number was punched in.

To the right, a maze of overhead pipes supported garments in the process of being pressed. There were ten women within my visual range, most of them Hispanic, working machines whose function one could only guess. A radio had been tuned to a Spanish-language station that was blasting out an up-tempo cut from a Linda Ronstadt album. Two of the women sang as they worked, moving men's shirts expertly across the machines in front of them. With the syncopated rhythm of the irons, the shirt machines, the clouds of billowing steam, the place looked like the perfect setting for a musical number.

One of the two singing women finally noticed me. She left her machine and came over to the counter where I was waiting. She was short and compact, with a round face, eyes the color of chocolate M&M's, and coarse dark hair pulled into a snood. The loose gold satin blouse she wore was sprinkled with sequins. She glanced at the bouquet. "Those for me?"

I checked the attached florist's card. "Are you Bibianna Diaz?"

"Nah. She's off this week."

"She won't be in at all?"

The woman shook her head. "She hurt her back in this accident . . . mmm, about two months ago, and it's still botherin' her. The pain flares up, she says, real bad. She can't hardly walk. Boss told her, No way, don't come in. He don't want no kind of lawsuit. She got a boyfriend?"

I turned the card over, holding it up to the light. "Looks like a get-well card, actually. Shoot. Now what am I supposed to do?"

"Take 'em to her house," she said.

"I can't. This is the only address he gave. You don't happen to have her home address, do you?"

"Nah. I never been there myself," the woman said. She turned to one of the other women. "Hey, Lupe. Where's Bibianna live?"

The second woman shook her head, but a third piped up. "On Castano. I don't know the number, but it's this big brown house in front and her place in back. She's got this little bungalow. Real cute. Between Huerto and Arroyo."

The woman at the counter turned back to me. "You know the block she's talkin' about?"

"I'll find it," I said. "Thanks. You've been a big help."

"I'm Graciela. Tell the guy to look me up he gets tired of her. I got all the same equipment, just arranged different."

I smiled. "I'll do that."

The second address on Bibianna turned out to be a dank-looking brown cottage at the back of a dank brown house, located in a midtown neighborhood distinctly down at the heel. I spotted the house in passing, then circled the block and parked across the street. I sat and scanned the premises. The lot was long and narrow, sheltered by the overhanging branches of magnolia, juniper, and pine trees. There was not a shred of grass anywhere and what vegetation there was seemed in desperate need of a trim. A cracked concrete drive cut along the property to the right. In the larger house in front, someone had nailed sagging floral print bedsheets across the windows in lieu of drapes.

There were no cars in the drive. According to the claim form, her 1978 Mazda was still in the body shop, having the right side panel replaced (among other things). I waited twenty minutes, but there was no visible activity. I torqued myself around, reaching into the backseat for the locked briefcase where I keep assorted false ID's for occasions such as this. I pulled a set for "Hannah Moore," neatly tucked into a plastic accordion file: California driver's license with my stats and a photo of me, Social Security, and credit cards for Visa and Chevron gasoline. "Hannah Moore" even had a library card since I wanted her to appear literate. I shoved my shoulder bag under the front seat and tucked the ID in my trouser pocket. I got out, locked my car, crossed the street, and made my way down the driveway.

The tall trees on the property shaded it to an unpleasant chill, and I found myself wishing I'd brought a windbreaker or a sweatshirt. The exterior of Bibianna's vintage cottage was a shaggy brown shingle, the perfect little snack for a swarm of hungry termites. I climbed two wide creaking wooden steps to a tiny porch piled with junk. A casement window on the right side had a length of red cotton hung across the glass. I tried to peek in, but I really couldn't see much. The interior seemed quiet and there were no lights visible. I knocked on the front door, taking advantage of the moment to survey my immediate surroundings. A metal mailbox was nailed to the siding near the front door. Seven addressed and stamped envelopes were loosely tucked in the catch rack, awaiting pickup by the mailman. So far no one had answered my knock. The cottage had an unoccupied air, and I fancied I could already pick up the faintly musty scent generated by some dwellings with even the briefest of absences. I knocked again, waiting an interminable few minutes before concluding there was really no one home. Casually, I looked toward the big house, but there were no signs of life, no accusing faces peering out the windows at me. I reached over and let my fingers tippy-toe through the envelopes. When no alarms went off, I picked up the whole batch and sorted through them at my leisure. Four were bills. She was paying telephone, gas, electricity, and a department store. There were two number ten envelopes, one addressed to Aetna Insurance and one to Allstate, both with "Lola Flores" listed on the return address. Oh, gee, wonder what that could be, I thought. Cheaters never quit. It looked like the scam extended beyond the claim against California Fidelity. The seventh piece of mail was a personal letter addressed to someone in Los Angeles. I plucked it out of the stack, folded it, slipped it down the waistband of my trousers and into my panties. Shame on me. That's a federal crime—the stealing part, not the underpants. I returned the rest of the letters to the catch rack. Suppressing the impulse to run, I sauntered off the porch, ambled up the drive, and crossed the street to my waiting car.

I opened the car door on the passenger side, tossed the clipboard on the front seat, barely missing the bouquet, and locked up again. I could see a minimarket at the corner of Huerto and Arroyo, about ten houses down on the right. I headed in that direction in hope of finding a telephone. The market was a tiny mom-and-pop operation, the front windows papered over with hand-lettered advertisements for beer, cigarettes, and dog food. The interior was dimly lighted and there was sawdust on the uneven wooden floor that looked like it had been there since the place was built. The shelves were a jumble of canned goods in no particular order that I could discern. Freestanding shelves formed two narrow aisles crowded with everything from Pampers to Jell-O to lawn care products. Near the front, there was a refrigerated soft drink case and an ancient crypt-style freezer filled with frozen vegetables, fruit juices, and ice-cream bars. "Mom" was standing at the front counter in a white wraparound apron, a half-smoked cigarette in one hand. She was probably sixty-five with a stiffly sprayed flip of blond hair and a wide scab mustache where she'd had the wrinkles dermabraded off her upper lip. The skin on her face had been hiked up and tacked behind her ears, and her eyes had been stitched into an expression of permanent amazement.

"You have a pay telephone?"

"Back by the stockroom," she said, pointing with her cigarette. A half-inch of ash dropped off and tumbled down the front of her apron.

I dropped four nickels into the coin slot and called Mary Bellflower, giving her Bibianna Diaz's hard-won address.

"Thanks. This is great," she said. "I've got a packet of forms I can ship right out. Are you coming back to the office?"

"Yeah, I'll be there in a bit. I thought I'd hang around for a while and see if Bibianna shows."

"Well, stop in later and we'll figure out where we go from here."

"Has Gordon Titus come back?"

"Nope. Not yet. Maybe it was a rout."

"I doubt that," I said. When I hung up the receiver, a nickel tumbled down into the return coin slot. My lucky day. On my left, there was a meat counter with a slanted glass front. A sign above it advertised the lunch special: chili beans, coleslaw, and a tri-tip sandwich for $2.39. The smell was divine. Tri-tip is apparently a regional phenomenon, some cut of beef nobody else has ever heard of. Periodically, a local journalist will try to trace the origin of the term. The accompanying article will show a moo-cow in profile with all the steaks drawn in. Tri-tip is on the near end, opposite the heinie bumper. It's usually barbecued, sliced, and served with homemade salsa on a bun or wrapped in a tortilla with a sprig of cilantro.

"Pop" emerged from the walk-in freezer. A breath of winter wafted out. He was a big man in his sixties, with a benign face and mild eyes. "What can I get you?"

"How about the tri-tip to go."

He winked at me, smiling slightly, and prepared it without a word.

Sandwich in hand, I grabbed a Diet Pepsi from the cooler and paid at the front register. I returned to my car, where I dined in style, being careful not to spill salsa down the front of my uniform. The flowers, getting limper by the minute, filled the VW's interior with the smells of a funeral home. I kept an eye on Bibianna's driveway for two hours, perfecting my surveillance Zen. In many P.I. firms, surveillance work is charged off at a higher rate than any other service offered because it's such a yawn. There were no signs of activity, no visitors, no lights coming on. It occurred to me if I intended to watch the place for long, I'd better contact the beat officer and let him know what was going on. Also, it might be smart to borrow another vehicle and maybe cook up some reason to be loitering in the vicinity. The postman came by on foot and picked up the letters waiting in Bibianna's box, replacing them with a handful of mail. I would have given a lot to see who was writing to her, but I didn't want to press my luck. Where was the woman? If her back hurt so bad, how come she was out all day? Maybe she was at the chiropractor's getting all her vertebrae lined up or her head replaced. At three I started up the car and headed back toward town.

When I arrived at the California Fidelity offices, I gave the bouquet to Darcy at the front desk. She had the good taste not to mention my little run-in with Titus. Her gaze rested briefly on my uniform. "You join the air force?"

"I just like to dress like this."

"Those shoes look like they'd be lethal in a kick-boxing contest," she remarked. "If you're here for Mary, she's got some clients with her, but you can probably mosey on back."

Mary had been hired as a CF claims representative in May, when Jewel Cavaletto retired. She'd been assigned the desk Vera had occupied before her promotion to the glass-enclosed office up front. Mary was smart but inexperienced, a young twenty-four, with the kind of face just pretty enough to net her second runner-up in a regional beauty contest. I gave her credit for the fact that she had flagged the Diaz claim. She had a good eye and if she could hang in long enough, she'd be a real asset to the company. She'd been married for three months to a salesman for the local Nissan dealership and was taking an avid interest in Vera's wedding plans. One of Mary's own wedding invitations (gauzy pink background depicting daisies blowing in a field) had been framed in brass and propped up on her desk. Where Vera had always tucked the latest issue of *Cosmopolitan* magazine under the stacks of claim folders on her desk, Mary read *Brides,* whose influence apparently extended from the engagement through the first year of marriage. Mary had once appealed to me for my recipe for chicken divan until Vera set her straight. Now she tended to regard me with the pity of the newly married for those of us determined to stay single.

I chatted with Darcy for a few minutes more and then made my way back to Mary's work station, pausing to say "hi" to a couple of other claims adjusters en route. Word of my skirmish with Titus had apparently spread and I'd been accorded celebrity status, which I figured would last until I got fired, one day at best. Mary's clients, a man and a woman, were just leaving as I reached her cubicle. The woman was in her thirties with a shaggy mane of bleached hair, the styling faintly punk. Her eyes were lined with harsh black, her lashes clearly false. Her patterned black hose and the trashy sling-back pumps with spike heels seemed at odds with the severe cut of her business suit. She seemed far less aware of me than I was of her, barely glancing in my direction as she passed by in the narrow aisle between cubicles. Her companion followed at a lei-surely pace, an attitude of arrogance displayed in the very way he walked. He had his hands in his pockets as if he had all day, but I could have sworn he was keeping a tight rein on himself. His dark hair was combed away from his face. He had thick brows above big, dark eyes, high cheek-bones, and a mustache cut so that it seemed to trail down around his mouth. He was well over six feet tall, the heft of his broad shoulders exaggerated by the padding in his plaid sport coat. He looked like the bad guy's ominous sidekick in a prime-time television show. As he came abreast of me, he tried to sidestep but bumped me in the process. He caught my arm apologetically and murmured a "Hey, sorry" as he headed on down the corridor. I caught a whiff of the hair tonic he was using to subdue the wave in his dark pompadour. I found myself staring after them as I moved into Mary's cubicle.

She wasn't at her desk, but she appeared a half second later, eyes pinned on a Dixie cup filled with water to the brim. She wore a red cashmere sweater with the sleeves pushed up. Her complexion was fresh and clear, her skin shiny with good health. Her coloring was the stuff of magazine ads. "Here we are," she said, and then she glanced up at me with some surprise. "Oh. Did they leave? The pair that was here?"

"They went that-a-way. You missed them by a half a second."

She peered out into the corridor, but there was no sign of them. "Well, that's weird. She said she wasn't feeling good, so I went to get her this."

"She looked okay to me."

Mary's mouth pulled down with puzzlement and she set the cup of water on her desk. "I wish they'd hung around. I was hoping you could talk to them."

"About what?"

She shook her head. "They're investigators from the Insurance Crime Prevention Institute. She was, at any rate. He's a special agent with the California Department of Insurance." She handed me the woman's business card.

"*Him?* Are you sure?"

"He was hired last month. She's been showing him the ropes."

"He looked like a hood."

She laughed uncomfortably as if she were somehow responsible for his appearance now that I'd mentioned it. "He did, didn't he? It's that tacky coat, I'm sure. I'd never let Peter out in public in a thing like that. Have a seat. Did you talk to Bibianna Diaz? God, now where'd I stick her file?" She sat down and began to sort through a stack of fat manila folders on her desk.

"Nope. She's still out. I may take my camera with me next time I go over there. Maybe I can snap a picture of her doing backflips on the lawn." I passed on the information about "Lola Flores" and the two other insurance companies. "Bibianna has to be running a second scam as Lola Flores. There's no telling how many other claims she's filed concurrently."

Mary was properly incensed. "Oh, God, I don't believe this. I'll get on it right away and let 'em know what's going on."

"Just make sure they start documenting any dealings they have with her. When we send the files to ICPI, they can send theirs along, too. It should make quite a splash."

I was still half distracted by the couple who'd just left. I checked the woman's business card. The ICPI logo was legitimate, looking somehow like a place mat complete with cutlery. According to the card, she was Karen Hedgepath from an office in Los Angeles. The problem was she didn't look like any ICPI investigator I'd ever met. Most of them are real button-down types—ties, white shirts, dark conservative business suits. This woman looked like a rock star in civilian clothes. I couldn't believe the regional manager would tolerate the punk hairstyle, let alone the spike-heeled shoes.

"Here we go," Mary said, extracting a file from the middle of the stack. The folder was marked "Diaz," a piece of scratch paper with the new address clipped to the front. She reached for an invoice stapled to the envelope it had arrived in. "I just got a whole new sheaf of bills. I guess she saw a chiropractor."

"Probably a subluxation specialist," I said, using the only chiropractic term I'd ever heard.

She punched some holes in the invoice and pronged it in the file. "Actually, they were here about Bibianna. That's why I wanted them to talk to you. I guess ICPI got wind she'd moved up here. She ran a couple of scams in Santa Monica last year and they were hoping to track her down."

"Well, that's nice. Insurance scams?"

"They didn't spell it out, but it almost has to be insurance-related, don't you think?"

I considered the situation briefly, wondering why an ICPI employee would "show the ropes" to someone working for another agency. It's not as though the ICPI and the Department of Insurance don't cooperate, but the Insurance Crime Prevention Institute isn't a law enforcement agency. And why would investigators make the trip up here in the first place? Why not put a call through to CF instead of driving the hour and a half? It just made no sense. Unless they lied. "Did you give them this address?" I asked, indicating the penciled note.

"I didn't give 'em anything. That's why I was so surprised when you said they'd left. All I did was confirm we were checking on a claim here. Why?"

"They could have spotted this while you were off at the water cooler. All they had to do was rifle the stack of files on your desk."

"Oh, come on. You don't think they'd really do that."

"Who knows? Let's just hope they were legitimate."

She put her hand on her chest like she was about to re-cite the Pledge of Allegiance. "Oh, Lord. What's that sup-posed to mean?"

"Well, you know how it is. You can hand out a business card that says anything. I've done it myself."

Mary seemed affronted, suddenly shifting from anxiety into action mode. "Give me that," she said. She snatched the woman's business card and laid it on the desk with a snapping sound. I watched her pick up the phone and punch in the telephone number with its 213 area code. "I'm going to kill myself if she isn't who she said she was." She listened for a moment and then her expression changed. She held up the receiver, which was emitting a sound like a garbage disposal grinding up a live duck.

"Maybe you dialed it wrong," I said helpfully.

"God, I can't believe I'd fall for something so obvious, but it never *occurred* to me to question her identity. How could I be so dumb?"

"Well, you don't have to be so hard on yourself. After years in the business, I can still be conned. It's human na-ture to trust, especially if you're honest to begin with. Not that I'm that honest, but you know what I mean."

"What do you think they were up to?"

"Beats me," I said. "Obviously, they knew Bibianna and they were aware of her inclination to cheat. The real ques-tion is, how'd they get to us? There must be a hundred in-surance agencies in Santa Teresa. Why CF?"

"This is terrible. I'm just sick. What could they want with her?" Mary's cheeks had turned a bright, wholesome pink.

"Probably nothing pleasant or they would have played it straight."

"What should we do?"

"I don't see what we can do until we know what's going on. Why don't you track down the current phone number for ICPI and ask if they're investigating her." I held the note up. "In the meantime, I'll try to catch up with her and we'll fake it out from there."

5

I went home and stripped off the uniform. I transferred
the fake ID from the pocket of my uniform pants to my
blue jeans, which I pulled on with a navy turtleneck. I
slipped into gym socks and tenny bops and headed back to
Bibianna's.

I hoped Mary Bellflower's naïveté hadn't put Ms. Diaz
at risk. There were still no cars in the drive and no sign of
the couple I'd seen at the CF offices. Had they already
looked up the address and hightailed it over here? They
had maybe thirty minutes on me, so it was always possible
that they were in the cottage right now or had been and
gone. *If* they'd actually been quick enough to nick off her
address. A few cars passed on the street, but no familiar
faces peered out. For the second time that day, I left my car,
locked, on the street and moved down Bibianna's driveway.
It was now four thirty-five, and I could see lights on in the
cottage. As I approached, I caught a tantalizing whiff of
onions and garlic being sautéed in olive oil. I climbed the

wide wooden steps. From inside, this time, I could hear the jaunty theme song of a television sitcom, probably a cable station doing reruns.

I knocked on the front door, which was opened moments later by a Hispanic woman of perhaps twenty-five. She was barefoot, dressed in a red satin teddy with a short red satin robe pulled over it and tied at the waist. She was slim—nay, petite—with flawless olive skin and big dark eyes in a heart-shaped face. She had two tortoiseshell hairpins clamped in her teeth as if I'd caught her in the midst of redoing her hair. Dark hair trailed halfway down her back like a shawl, a few silken strands spilling across her right shoulder. As I watched, she gathered the length of it and made a complicated knot, which she secured with the two hairpins. "Yes?"

My true inclination was to stand on tiptoe so I could peer over her shoulder at the space beyond. The interior of the cottage was essentially one big room, divided into living areas by the use of brightly dyed cloth panels that swayed with the eddy of moving air from the open door. A vibrant green panel separated the living room from the kitchen, an electric blue shielded most of a brass bed frame from view. The windows were draped in the bolt ends of purple cotton twisted across brass hooks. I'd seen the same idea in a women's magazine in the dentist's office but had never seen it used to such effect. The furniture was a mismatched collection of wicker and castoffs, swathes of navy-and-purple cotton distinguishing the worn arms, lending continuity to the look of the place. The effect was striking and seemed to suggest boldness and confidence.

I realized, belatedly, that I hadn't come up with a cover story. Happily, I'm an old hand at lying, and I could feel one bubble up. "Sorry to disturb you," I said. "I'm, uhm, looking for an apartment in the area and someone said you might be giving notice."

Her look was cautious and her tone was blunt. "Who said?"

"Gee, I don't remember. A neighbor, I guess. I've been knocking on doors for days, it feels like."

"Why you want to live around here? It's depressing."

"It's close to where I work," I said, praying she wouldn't ask where that was. I'd probably pretend to be a waitress, but I couldn't, for the life of me, remember any restaurants close by.

She stared at me. "Actually, I'm hoping to move in a couple of weeks," she said. "I got some money coming in that I should hear about pretty soon."

"That's great. Do you mind if I keep in touch?"

She pulled her mouth down in a shrug. "Sure. I'd let you see the place, but it's kind of a mess. It's only one room, but it's fine if you're by yourself. You got furniture?"

"Well, some."

"The landlord's pretty good about stuff like that. Most of this I'll leave when I move out. You'd need a bed."

"I got that," I said. "You have a pen I could use? I'll make a note of your name and number and maybe give you a call in a couple of weeks."

"Just a minute," she said. She closed the door, returning moments later with a scrap of paper and a pen. I looked at her expectantly.

She tilted her head so she could watch me write. "Diaz. Bibianna with two *n*'s."

"Thanks."

I left Bibianna and went home, where I finally had a moment to examine the letter I'd stolen from Bibianna's mailbox. I made a note of the name and address of the recipient, a Gina Diaz in Culver City, California. Bibianna's mother or a sister, by my guess. From my desk drawer, I pulled out an aerosol can of some chemical concoction that turns opaque paper translucent for thirty to sixty seconds. Spray it on an envelope and you can read what's inside without going to the trouble of steaming it open. Clearly marked on the can, of course, is a stiffly worded warning, reminding the user that tampering with written communications while in United States Postal Service channels is punishable by up to five years in prison and/or a $2,000 fine. God, I should really open up a little savings account in case I get caught doing stuff like this.

I depressed the nozzle and dampened the surface of the envelope with a fine mist, then held it up to the light. The note said: "Hi, Ma. I'm fine so far. $$ should come threw any time. Please don't let Raymond know you've heard from me. Love, B."

I watched the envelope become opaque again without any visible mark, discoloration, or odor. I took it out to the street and tucked it in my mailbox for tomorrow's pickup. I returned to my apartment and put a quick call through to Mary Bellflower. I caught her just as she was getting ready to close up her desk for the day. "Have you heard anything from ICPI?"

"Not really. I'm still waiting for a call back."

"Keep me posted," I said.

"Right."

I put on a pot of coffee and went up the spiral stairs to the loft. I changed clothes again, this time pulling on a black tank top, tight ankle-high black pants, short white socks with an edging of lace, and scuffed low-heeled black pumps. I ratted my hair, securing one hunk of it in a rubber band so that it stuck straight up like a little hair spout. I applied (inexpertly, I'll admit) eyeliner, mascara, blushers, and gaudy red lipstick, then clipped on big dangle earrings replete with red stones that no one in their right mind would mistake for rubies. Then I sprayed my entire upper body with cheap scent. I stared at myself in the bathroom mirror. I half turned away from the mirror and looked back, pulled one shoulder up, and pursed my lips. What a vamp . . . what a tramp! I didn't know I had it in me.

I clomped down my spiral stairs to the kitchenette and made myself an olive–pimento cheese sandwich, which I packed in a metal lunch box with an apple, some graham crackers, a Thermos of hot coffee, and a Dick Francis paperback. I grabbed my black leather jacket, tucked the fake "Hannah Moore" ID in my pants pocket, and snagged my car keys. I drove back over to Bibianna's neighborhood and parked a few doors away. I got out of the car and hiked down to the minimarket to use the pay phone. The meat counter was locked up and the guy was stocking shelves. I didn't see "Mom."

I dropped in two dimes and dialed Bibianna's number. When she answered after two rings, I held my nose and asked for Mame. I sounded like a cold sufferer on a TV commercial for an antihistamine.

"Who?"

"Mame?"

"You got a wrong number."

"Sorry," I said. I returned to my car and settled in.

From my position, I could see the mouth of the drive-way, much of the big brown house, and a portion of the yard, but nothing of Bibianna's cottage, which was located in the rear. My assumption was that if she left the premises, she'd surface somewhere in front and I could follow by car or on foot, whichever seemed more appropriate. I had no idea if she intended to go out or where she might go if she did, but she struck me as the restless type, and I was hoping she'd find some reason to stir, even if her purpose was no more important than a run to the corner market for a six-pack. I turned on the car radio just in time for the five-thirty news. The talk of rain was beginning to sound like something more than mere rumor. I stuck my head out the car window and stared upward. A ceiling of darkening clouds was creating the illusion of sudden twilight. The wind was picking up, blowing a dried palm frond along the street. Secretly I wished I could go back to my place and lock myself in for the night instead of spying on Bibianna Diaz. I switched from station to station, listening to a rotating selection of popular songs that all seemed to sound the same. I kept one eye on the driveway and one on my book, but the dark came so quickly I wasn't able to read much. The streetlights popped on and I could see that the tree leaves had taken on a patent-leather sheen, a deep, glossy green that seemed to shimmer in the darkness. At suppertime, the neighborhood began to stir with life, people coming home from work, houselights coming on.

A single-car surveillance is usually considered the least productive technique in any private investigator's little bag of tricks. In order to be discreet, you have to keep so much distance between yourself and the subject that visual contact is tough to maintain without being "made." Then, too, if Bibianna was picked up by car, I had a fifty-fifty chance of being headed in the right direction. If I'd guessed wrong, I was sunk. A sudden U-turn in a residential neighborhood is a conspicuous move and one almost guaranteed to alert the driver of the car you're following. With a two-car surveillance you can at least trade off positions and the subject is less likely to become suspicious. Unfortunately, I hadn't been authorized to hire outside help on this. For all I knew, Gordon Titus had fired me in absentia. It certainly seemed like the wrong time to ask for a cash advance. I was operating on the cheap, trying to establish a relationship with the woman so I could find out what she was up to. A well-documented claim file is fundamental to successful prosecution under "theft by deception" statutes. Before handing over the files to the Insurance Crime Prevention Institute, CF would want to provide proof of a material false representation, proof of intent to defraud, evidence that the claims adjuster relied upon representations by the claimant in paying the claim, and evidence of payment. If Bibianna was scamming Aetna and Allstate along with California Fidelity, it would probably mean hiring a handwriting expert to establish the links, though there might well be matching fingerprints on all the claim forms she'd sent. With fraud, as with most crimes, the perpetrator's job was a lot easier than ours.

At seven twenty-five, to relieve the boredom, I ate my

sandwich and two graham crackers. It was now fully dark, and a pale mist filled the air, a rain so fine that it scarcely dampened the pavement. I turned the engine on twice, letting it run for brief periods until the car warmed up. A pizza was delivered to a nearby apartment complex. The passing scent of pepperoni and melted mozzarella nearly brought tears to my eyes. An old lady walked by in a robe and a shawl with her cocker spaniel on a leash. Cars passed, moving in both directions, but none slowed down and there was no sign of Bibianna. By nine, I found myself slouched down on my spine, knees propped up against the steering wheel, trying to keep from nodding off. The couple from the CF offices had never made an appearance and I was about to write them off. Either they had no idea where Bibianna Diaz now lived or they had no compelling interest in her in the first place. I couldn't imagine why they'd gone to the trouble of tracking her down if they didn't mean to pursue the point. Maybe something had scared them off. Idly, I wondered if they were in a parked car nearby, waiting for her themselves.

At nine forty-five, quite suddenly, Bibianna appeared in the driveway. She was wearing red again, a body-hugging chemise that hit her midthigh. Dark hose and red spike heels. For someone so petite, her legs looked incredibly long and shapely, giving an impression of height when she was probably barely five feet one. She had one hand tucked in the pocket of a cracked brown leather bomber jacket that she'd left unzipped. With the other hand, she held a section of newspaper above her head, shielding her hair from the drizzle. She had her face turned in my direction, scanning the street, but she didn't seem to register the fact that she was being observed. Five minutes later, a Yellow Cab passed and came to a stop in front of her. She got in. I started my VW while she slammed the taxi door and settled herself in the backseat. I eased out into the street, flipping my headlights on as the taxi pulled away, hoping my appearance behind it would seem part of the natural flow of traffic in the area.

We traveled sedately on surface streets, heading toward Cabana Boulevard, the wide avenue that parallels the beach. This was my turf and I had to imagine she was heading toward the big restaurant/bar out on the wharf, or perhaps to one of the bawdy bars at the lower end of State Street. It turned out to be the latter. The cab slowed in front of a lowlife bar called the Meat Locker. The ABC had shut the place down twice in the past for serving alcohol to minors, and the previous owner had consequently lost his liquor license. The bar had been sold and was open now under new management. I drove on past. Through my rearview mirror, I watched as Bibianna emerged from the cab, paid the driver, and headed toward the entrance. I hung a left, drove around the block, and returned to the parking lot, where I squeezed the VW into a quasi-legal parking spot against the wall. As I locked the car, ducking my head against the sprinkle of rain, I could feel the pavement vibrate with the music from the bar. I took my last breath of fresh air and walked into the place.

Just inside the door, I paid the five-dollar cover charge and had the back of my hand stamped in purple with a USDA designation of "choice." The Meat Locker looked like it had been designed originally for industrial purposes and converted to commercial use without much concession to aesthetics. The room was cavernous and drab, with a concrete floor and metal beams showing high up in the shadowy reaches of the ceiling. A nineteen-foot bar ran along the wall to the right, packed three deep with guys whose faces looked like they belonged on the post office wall. The place smelled of beer and cigarette smoke, corn tortillas fried in lard, with an occasional whiff of dope wafting through the side door from the alleyway. All the houselights were blue. There was a live band, five guys who looked like junior high school thugs and sounded like they should still be practicing in someone's garage. The music was a raunchy blend of thumping bass, pulsing synthesizers, relentlessly repeated chords, and lyrics that were vile if you managed to discern the words above the piercing electronic howls. The dance floor was a portable wooden pallet, maybe twenty feet on a side, jammed with bouncing bodies, faces lathered in sweat.

This was where the C-singles came to hunt. There were no yuppies, no preppies, no slumming execs, no middle-class, white-bread college types. This was a hard-core pickup place for bikers and hamburger hookers, who'd screw anyone for a meal. Bar fights and knifings were taken as a matter of course, uniformed beat cops strolling through so often they were assumed to be customers. The noise level was intolerable, punctuated by an intermittent *bam!* and bursts of raucous laughter. The bar was famous for a drink called a "slammer": tequila and 7-Up in an old-fashioned glass. When the drink was served, a cloth napkin was placed across the mouth of the glass, which was then slammed down on a wooden board the waitress carried. The blow forced the tequila and 7-Up together in a high-test infusion, which the patron was expected to toss down in one gulp. Usually the limit was two slammers per customer. After two, most women had to be helped, toes dragging, to the car. After three, men had the urge to break wooden chairs or bash a hand through glass.

As I inched my way across the bar, I murmured, "Pardon me," "Excuse me," and "Oops, sorry," as I progressed, sensing an occasional anonymous hand on my ass. I found an unoccupied spot and claimed temporary ownership, leaning against the wall like everybody else. I ordered a beer from a passing barmaid who was decked out in an orange Day-Glo leotard that was cut straight up her crack in the rear. Her buns were hanging out like water-filled balloons. There was no place to sit, so I stood where I was, wedged in against a beam, while I surveyed the crowd.

I spotted Bibianna on the dance floor, undulating with remarkable energy and grace to some grinding sex tune. Men's eyes seemed to follow every shimmy, every bump. The blue lights reacted with the olive tones of her skin to create an unearthly radiance that emphasized the smooth oval of her face above the bulging breasts in the low-cut chemise. The dress seemed to glow more purple than red, pulled taut across the flat belly, slim hips, and trim thighs. When the music ended, she gave her dark hair a toss and moved away from the dance floor without a backward glance. Her partner, visibly winded, looked after her with admiration.

She began to make the rounds. She was apparently well known, pausing to exchange laughing comments with a number of guys. I made myself conspicuous, pretending to be oblivious when, by my calculations, her path would soon be intersecting mine. Foiled. Before she reached me, she changed directions, and I could see her inching toward the short corridor where the restrooms were located. I headed in that direction, risking rude remarks as I pushed my way through.

By the time I reached the ladies' room, she had entered one of the stalls. I stood at the mirror, fussing with my top-knot until the toilet flushed and Bibianna emerged. She moved to the sink beside mine, glancing at me idly in the mirror. I sensed more than saw the little jolt of recognition. She said, "Hey."

I gave her a blank look.

"Didn't you stop by this afternoon to ask about my place?"

I looked over at her politely and then allowed myself the same double take. "Oh, hi! I didn't realize it was you. What a coincidence. That's amazing. How are you?"

"I'm fine. How'd the house hunting go? Did you find anything?"

I made a face. "Not really. I got a line on an apartment about a block away from yours, but it isn't half as nice."

Bibianna took out her lipstick. She applied an arc of red to her lower lip, rubbing it against the upper lip until the color had spread uniformly across her mouth. I made a few little gestures of my own, imitating hers.

She capped the lipstick. "You ever been here before?"

I shrugged. "Couple of times. Before this new manage-ment. It's kind of unnerving, isn't it? I don't appreciate guys grabbing my butt every time I make a move."

She studied me briefly. "Depends on what you're used to, I guess. Doesn't bother me." She turned her attention from my reflection to hers, leaning forward to adjust the wisps of hair around her face. She checked her eye makeup for flaws, staring at herself gravely before she glanced back at me. "I hope you don't mind my saying this, but that hair and the getup are completely wrong."

"They are?" I looked down at myself, a feeling of despair washing over me. What is it about me that invites this kind of comment? Here I think of myself as a kick-ass private eye when other people apparently see me as a waif in need of mothering.

"Mind if I make a suggestion?" she asked.

"Fine with me," I said.

The next thing I knew, she'd whipped the rubber band out of my hair. She reached in her purse and took out some kind of bottled hair snot which she rubbed between her palms and then massaged through my hair. I felt like a dog being groomed, but I liked the effect. My tresses looked faintly wet now with just the suggestion of curl. The two of us checked my reflection in the mirror.

Bibianna's mouth pulled down judiciously. "Better," she said. "You got a scarf on you anywhere?"

I shook my head.

"Let me see what I got." She began to root around in her handbag, pulling out a joint in the process. "You want a smoke?" she asked idly.

I shook my head. "I already toked up out in the parking lot before I came in."

She tucked the dope away without further comment, intent on her search through the various compartments of her voluminous bag. "Here we go. How's this?" She pulled up a square of lime green silk and then made a face. "Eh, no good. Color's not right for you. Dump the earrings. That'll help."

How do women know these things? More important, how come I don't? I removed the gaudy baubles from my ears and massaged my lobes with relief.

Meanwhile, she'd managed to unearth a second scarf, this one hot pink. She held it near my face, squinting at it critically. I thought she was going to make me dampen it with spit so she could wash my face, but she did some kind of tricky fold and tied the thing around my neck. Immediately, my color seemed to improve.

"That looks great. Now what?"

"You come on with me. I'll keep the worst of these shit-heads away from you."

I followed her into the crowd like a rookie soldier into battle. Male eyes surveyed us from head to toe, grading us according to the size of our tits, how much butt we had hanging out, and how available we seemed. Bibianna netted a lot of mouth noises, a hand gesture, and some disgusting propositions which she seemed to find amusing, tossing casual insults at the guys most vocal in their appreciation. She was easygoing, good-natured, with a quick, infectious laugh.

The music started up again and she began to dance as she walked, snapping her fingers, working her way through the crowd with an occasional crotch-activating bump and grind. She was scanning faces and I wondered who she was looking for. It didn't take long to find out. Her animation kicked up a notch, like the sudden surge in electric current preceding a blackout. Her body seemed to suffuse with a palpable heat.

"Stick around," she said. "I'll be back."

A blond guy separated himself from the pack of studs at the bar. He was curly haired, with wire-rimmed glasses, a mustache, strong chin, a slight smile turning up the corners of his mouth. I found myself making note of his physical characteristics like a beat cop on patrol at the sight of a suspect. I knew the guy. He was of medium height, broad shoulders, narrow hips, dressed in jeans and a tight-fitting black Polo shirt with short sleeves pushed up by well-developed biceps. Tate. Crazy Jimmy. How many years had it been since I'd seen him? He looked at Bibianna possessively, his thumbs tucked into his belt loops so that his hands seemed to bracket the bulge in the front of his pants. His manner was tempered with self-mocking, an irresistible blend of humor and awareness. I watched as he moved in her direction, already engaging her in some kind of wordless foreplay. No one else seemed to be aware of them. They approached the dance floor from adjacent sides, meeting somewhere in the middle as if every move were choreographed. This was mating behavior.

A table opened up and I snagged one of the empty chairs, putting my jacket across the back of the chair beside me to ward off any poachers. By the time I looked back at the dance floor, I'd lost sight of Bibianna, but I caught a flash of her red dress in the pulsating mass of dancers and occasional glimpses of her partner's face. I had known him in another context altogether, and I couldn't quite reconcile the incongruity of my past perception of him with the setting in which I now saw him. His hair had been shorter then and the mustache was new, but the aura was the same. Jimmy Tate was a cop—probably an ex-cop by now if the rumors were correct. Our paths had crossed the first time in elementary school—fifth grade, where for half a year we were soulmates, bound by a pact we'd sealed by touching tongues. Solemn stuff. Jimmy was into what they call "acting out." I'm not sure what had happened to his parents, but he'd lived in foster homes all his life, getting kicked out of first one, then another. He was a kid who'd been labeled "incorrigible" by the age of eight, rebellious, prone to fistfights and bloody noses. He was frequently truant, and since I was given to truancy myself back then, we formed an odd bond. In many ways I was a timid child, but I had a wild streak of my own born of grief at the loss of my parents when I was five. My mutiny originated in fear, Jimmy's in rage, but the net result was the same. I could see that under his defiance, there was such pain and such sweetness. I may even have loved him in my own innocent, prepubescent way. He was twelve years old to my eleven when I met him, a bewildered boy who had no concept of self-control. More than once he came to my defense, beating the snot out of some bullying fifth-grade boy who'd tried pushing me around. I could still recall the exhilaration I felt every time we raced away from the schoolyard, giddy with freedom, knowing how short-lived our liberation would be. He introduced me to cigarettes, tried getting me high on aspirin and Coke, showed me the difference between boys and girls. I can still remember the mix of mirth and pity I felt when I realized all boys were afflicted with a doo-dad that looked like an ill-placed thumb stuck between their legs. Eventually, Jimmy's foster mother declared him out of control and sent him back to wherever it was unwanted kids were sent in those days. Juvenile hall, I guess.

I didn't see him for eight years, and then I was astonished when he showed up my first day at the police academy. By then, his toughness had a manic edge. He was a pretty boy and a boozer, out until all hours. How he got accepted into the academy, I'll never know. Candidates are put through rigorous psychological evaluation, at which point the unsuitable and the unstable are quickly eliminated. He must have eluded the wily probing of his examiners, or maybe he was one of those rare individuals whose personality flaws don't show up under scrutiny. His academy grades were usually borderline, but he never missed a class and his competitive nature kept him in the game. He was savvy enough to turn the heat down when he had to, but he never kept himself in check for long. He did manage to graduate with the rest of us, but he was always skirting disaster in some form. I'd kept my distance, too invested in my own career at that point to risk the taint of his reputation.

He'd applied for a job with the Santa Teresa Police Department at the same time I did, but he'd been turned down. I lost track of him for a while and then I heard he'd joined the Los Angeles County Sheriff's Department. Word of his exploits started leaking back to us. In bars after hours, the talk would start, cops trading tales about the crazy things Jimmy Tate had done. He was the kind of officer you wanted next to you any time there was trouble. In a pinch, he was absolutely fearless, oblivious of danger. In a pissing contest with the "bad guys," he was right out in front. His aggression seemed to generate a force field around him, a protective shield. Other cops had told me that watching him under fire, you became aware that in his own way, he was as dangerous as "they" were—the bank robbers, the dopers, gang members, snipers, all the lunatics who had it in for us law-and-order types. Unfortunately, his ferocity pushed him across the line more than once. I gathered he did things you didn't talk about later— things you pretended you hadn't seen because he'd saved your life and you owed him. Eventually, he was tapped as part of a special investigating unit put together to monitor the activities of known criminals. Six months later, the section was disbanded after a series of questionable shootings. Twelve officers were suspended, Jimmy Tate among them. All were reinstated after review by the police commission, but it seemed clear it was only a matter of time before something blew in a big way.

Two years ago, I'd come across his name in the *L.A. Times*. He'd been reassigned to a narcotics unit and had just been indicted, along with six other deputies, in a money-skimming scandal that was rocking the department. The details were spelled out day after day during preliminary hearings. Five of the six were bound over for trial and one of those blew his brains out. I followed the court proceedings in occasional copies of the *L.A. Times,* though I never heard the outcome. It wouldn't have surprised me to learn he was guilty as charged. He was reckless and self-destructive, but as odd as it sounds, I knew if I'd had a brother, I'd have wanted him to be exactly like Jimmy Tate, not for his conduct and the dubious underlying morality, but because of his loyalty and his passionate commitment to survival. We live in a society piously concerned about the rights of criminals when their victims' lives have been trashed without any consideration of the price in pain and suffering. With Jimmy Tate in charge, believe me, justice was served. There simply wasn't much attention paid to the technicalities involved.

He and Bibianna came off the dance floor. The band was taking a break and the noise level dropped so fast it was almost like turning deaf. I focused on Jimmy's face, knowing any minute he'd spot me and the recognition would leap in his eyes. The two of them sat down at the table, and Bibianna pulled her hair up with one hand and fanned her bare neck with the other. She was winded, laughing, the color high in her cheeks, her hair damp at the temples where the dark strands had separated into little tendrils. "This's the woman I was telling you about, came to look at my place," she said to him, indicating me. "What'd you say your name was?"

Jimmy's smile was polite as his gaze traveled from her face to mine. I held a hand out.

"Hello, Jimmy. I'm Hannah Moore," I said. "You remember me?"

Clearly he did, and I knew from his look my real name was attached to the recollection. Whatever his current status, he was still too thoroughly trained as a cop to blow my cover. He smiled as he took my hand, dosing me with the same low-voltage sexuality he'd turned on Bibianna. He lifted my hand to his mouth, kissing my knuckle affectionately. "God, babe. How are you? It's been years," he said.

"You two know each other?" she asked.

He returned my hand to me reluctantly. "We were in grade school together," he said without pause, and I felt myself flush with pleasure since that was the connection I cared about. The academy and whatever happened after that was the stuff of our grown-up years. The other had a magical quality that would always take precedence in my book.

He pulled a crumpled bill out of his pants pocket with a glance at Bibianna before his eyes returned to my face. "I need some cigarettes, doll. Can you do me that?"

She hesitated just long enough to let him know her co-operation was a gift. Her smile was underlined with irony and the look she gave me was knowing. She tucked the bill between her breasts and walked away without a word. Jimmy's gaze traced a loving line up her legs to her hips. She was moving with the self-conscious thrust and sway of a model or a starlet, aware of her effect. She sent a slow smile back to him, puckering her mouth in a gesture that was half pout, half promise.

I felt a laugh bubble up. "I can't believe running into you this way," I said. "How do you know Bibianna?"

He smiled. "I met her in L.A. at a Halloween party a year ago. I saw her a couple times down there, then ran into her again up here."

"I had no idea you were back. What have you been up to?"

"Not much," he said. His eyes flicked across my face as he checked me out. "How about yourself? Last I heard you'd left the department and were working for some agency."

"I was. I got licensed. Now I work for myself. Are you still with the L.A. County Sheriff's?"

"Not exactly."

"What 'exactly' are you doing? Last I heard you were being tried for theft," I said.

"She's something, isn't she?" he said, avoiding my question.

"What's the story, Jimmy?"

He propped his chin on his fist, smiling at me with his eyes. "I'm retired. I sued the shit out of them—ten million bucks."

"You *sued* them?" I said. "What about the charges?"

My reaction seemed to amuse him and I watched him shrug. "I was acquitted. That's the way the system works. Sometimes you get the bear, sometimes the bear gets you. I'd been on medical leave, collecting disability for job-related pain and stress. Next thing I know, there's a bunch of us charged with conspiracy, money laundering, income tax evasion, God knows what else. They put us through hell and by the time I got from under that, all my benefits were cut and I was being asked to resign. Forget that. No way. I found a lawyer and filed suit."

"After you were cleared?"

"Shit, yes. I'm not going to let them get away with that. The way they see it, I got off on a technicality. I was the only one acquitted, but I still did the whole nine yards the same as the others, so why am I being penalized twice? A jury said I was innocent."

"Were you?"

"Of course not, but that's not the point," he said. "The prosecution had a shot at me and couldn't make it stick, so now I'm off the hook. Doesn't matter if I did it or not. Court says I'm clear, I'm clear. That's the law."

"So they fired you?"

"In effect. What they did was they axed my disability. They decided I was trouble and they wanted me outta there, which is why they cut my benefits. Said I had an attitude. No way I was going to put up with that, so I sued their asses off. We just settled last week. Seven hundred and fifty thou. Of course, when the check comes through, my attorney's going to take his cut off the top, but I'm still going to end up with three sixty-five. My retirement fund. Pretty good, yes?"

"That's great."

"Meantime, I'm flat broke, but what are you going to do?"

"What about Bibianna? Does she know you're a cop?"

"Does she know you're a P.I.?"

I shook my head to one side, his smile fading as he saw my expression shift. "You're not investigating *her*?"

I didn't answer, which was answer enough.

"What for?" he asked.

I figured I might as well level with him. He'd find a way to get it out of me eventually. "Insurance fraud," I said, watching for his reaction. If I'd hoped to surprise him, I was out of luck.

"Who are you working for?"

"California Fidelity."

"Can you make a case?"

"Probably. By the time I'm done, at any rate," I said.

He looked away from me then, eyes straying toward the jukebox. I followed the line of his gaze, catching sight of Bibianna. A rainbow of lights played across her face. There was something about her—a dusky beauty, a physical perfection, that must have been irresistible, judging by the way he watched her. I saw her throw her head back and laugh, though the sound didn't carry. She was flirting with the drummer, one hand resting lightly on his arm in a gesture both intimate and casual. The drummer was tall and skinny with a face like a collie, his eyes close together and glittering with chemical substances the human body doesn't manufacture naturally. He was staring at her breasts, probably emitting the high-pitched, hopeful whine of a pup hoping for a Milk-Bone. She wasn't looking at us, but every phrase in her body language conveyed her awareness of Jimmy. Tit for tat, as it were. She turned to the jukebox and dropped in some coins, making her selection carelessly. After a moment, the pounding began, some popular song that was all bass and percussion. Bibianna moved out onto the dance floor with the drummer in tow. He was practically wetting himself, he was so excited by her attention.

"I always hated undercover," Jimmy said, raising his voice to be heard. He was still watching Bibianna, who'd begun to move with the beat, pelvis rolling like she was doing aerobic exercises to develop her glutes.

I took a sip of my beer, making no response. I'd never actually done undercover work myself, but I'd heard plenty, none of it good.

His eyes came back to mine. "Tell her what you're up to," he said.

"And blow this? You're crazy. I'm not going to do that. And you better not tell her, either. This is my turf."

"I understand that."

"Then what's the hesitation, Jimmy? I know that look."

"I'm crazy about this lady and I don't want to see her

hurt. I've been telling her for months she's going to get caught. If she knows you're on to her, she'll clean up her act."

"That's not my concern. She filed a fraudulent claim with CF, and God knows how many phony claims she's filed with other carriers. I'm going to turn her ass in."

"She's getting out of the business."

"I'll bet."

"No, she really is. She filed that claim months ago, but I talked her out of it. She's going straight, I swear."

"Dream on, Tate. Why not drop the claim, then, if she wants out?"

"She did."

"Bullshit! She's got a request for payment pending right this minute. I saw the damn thing myself. She's sticking it to us, putting the pressure on for a quick settlement. That's why the case was passed to me in the first place."

"I don't believe it."

"Ask her."

His smile was pained. "I can't very well do that without telling her what's going on."

"Then you better find a way around it before I wrap this thing up."

"There's more here than meets the eye."

"There's always more than meets the eye. It's usually crooked," I replied.

Jimmy's troubled gaze strayed back to Bibianna. He watched her with absorption, rubbing his thumb across his lower lip. He didn't want to believe me. His infatuation with the girl (and that's what she was, a girl) had apparently clouded his perception. After years of dealing with scammers, he'd suddenly decided that this one could change her wicked ways like magic if it suited her. He'd forgotten just how addictive crime can be. Repeat offenders are motivated more by withdrawal symptoms than necessity.

I'd never seen him caught up like this. In the past, his relationships with women had been easy to track, light-hearted forays with no emotional strings attached. A few laughs, some quick sex, a couple of weeks of companionship. I'm not sure how it appeared from their perspective. The women he dated were often smart but self-deluding, announcing up front that all they were looking for was fun and games when in fact they bonded with him at the drop of a hat and quickly shifted into emotional bait and switch. The turnabout became apparent in the way they looked at him, in their determination to be understanding, nonpossessive, compliant, and considerate. I'd watched eight or ten of these women pass through his life in a period of ten months. All were slim, attractive, bright, and competent—professional women with careers in advertising, sales, graphic arts, TV production. Each would become fixated, hooked by his availability, his casual charm, the sexuality that hovered in the air around him. They'd begin to service him, cooking meals, ironing shirts, subtly demonstrating how much better his life could be if they were somewhere on the premises. They'd begin to quiz him about his past relationships, trying to figure out what the last woman did wrong, trying to delete from their own behavior the qualities that had generated their predecessor's demise. This phase was brief because Jimmy's behavior would remain exactly the same throughout. Personal sacrifice netted these women nothing except, perhaps, a case of house-maid's knee. He was irresponsible, as promiscuous as ever, though he tried to be polite. He never flaunted his in-discretions, but he made no secret of them, either, since nonexclusivity was the agreement he and this latest girl-friend had started out with. Their anger would begin to surface because there was no payoff to the subservience. Each woman, in turn, would start to feel victimized, and Jimmy was the obvious target of the discontent. This, of course, provided him with the perfect justification to pull away from them. Within a month, never much more than two, they'd make some demand, perhaps complain, voic-ing barely controlled expressions of disappointment and rebuke. The minute that happened, Jimmy Tate was out the door without so much as a "Thank you, ma'am." I'd never seen him look at one of them the way he looked at Bib-ianna Diaz.

She returned to the table, where she arranged herself provocatively on Jimmy's lap, straddling him, with her skirt hiked up to her crotch, her breasts so close to his face I thought he'd munch on them like cupcakes. I spent the next half hour having my hearing impaired by the music while Jimmy Tate and Bibianna Diaz exchanged steamy glances, (more or less) making love in an upright position with their clothes on, the resulting friction scorching all the layers of fabric between them. The air smelled of de-sire, like the sweet perfume of wet grass after a rainstorm. That or cat spray.

The band finished one number and began the next, the only slow song I'd heard all night. Bibianna went off to dance with someone else. Jimmy didn't seem to mind. The fact that other men in the bar were seeking out her company apparently lent him stature. It also gave me time to figure out where his head was and whether he represented a help or a hindrance in my attempt to get close to Bibianna. Jimmy held his hand out. "Dance with me," he said.

7

put my hand in his and followed. He was one of those men who can make you feel like Ginger Rogers on the dance floor, conveying an entire set of suggestions in the way he applied pressure to the small of my back. He moved automatically while he scanned the bar, his gaze shifting restlessly across the room. It was behavior I recognized. There's really no such thing as an "ex-cop" or a cop who's "off-duty" or "retired." Once trained, once indoctrinated, a cop is always alert, assessing reality in terms of its potential for illegal acts. Whatever Jimmy's failings as a police officer, corruption being foremost, I couldn't picture him doing anything else with his life. It was hard for me to believe he'd sabotaged himself so thoroughly, cutting himself off from the only work he'd ever cared about. It wasn't really out of character for him, but it wasn't smart. What was he going to do now? Retire to what?

He sensed my preoccupation and refocused his attention. "Why so quiet?"

"I was thinking about the trial, wondering how you got caught up in that stuff to begin with."

"I started out as a JD," he reminded me.

"You were twelve. You didn't have anything at stake back then. I know you've had problems, but I never thought you were dirty."

"Lighten up. What's that supposed to mean? I'm no dirtier than anybody else. Come on, Kinsey. You know how it is. I palmed cash sometimes. Hell, everybody does. I saw guys palming cash the first day I ever went to work. So it's not like this was anything new—it just wasn't organized. I didn't cheat little old ladies out of their Social Security checks. These were fuckin' coke dealers—human garbage. The worst. The money wasn't even legal, but there it sat. You have any idea what it's like to make a bust like that? You could have two hundred thousand—hell, half a million dollars—layin' on the table in these nice neat stacks, all tied up with rubber bands. It doesn't even seem real. It's like funny money. Props. So who's gonna point a finger if a stack of bills disappears? The launderers? Get real. Those guys repudiate cash on the spot because then you got no hard evidence. By the time it gets booked in, there's twenty thousand less. Who knows where it went? Who even gives a shit?"

"You were skimming off more than twenty thousand, from what the papers said. Didn't it ever occur to you that you were being set up?"

"Sergeant Renkes was rakin' off four times the money we were, so why would I think he was setting us up? On the face of it, he had more to lose than we did."

"But why all the conspicuous consumption?" I said.

"The newspapers talked about speedboats and condos . . . luxury cars. On a cop's salary? Didn't you think any- body'd notice?"

Jimmy laughed. "Nobody said we were smart. I wanted the perks. We all did, and why not? So it turns out the whole thing was a setup. Maybe we shoulda guessed. Any- way, that's why Bosco blew his brains out. Because we'd been stung and he couldn't see any other way out. Renkes headed up the unit we were working . . . he set the game up, invited us to play, and then he turned us in. It was all departmental housecleaning, and Danny Renkes was the janitor."

"Did you know the bust was coming?"

"In some ways, sure. There were rumors for months. Nobody really wanted to believe it. I was on disability by then, so I wasn't an active player when the bust went down. I'd done my share, of course, and Renkes knew that. First time I heard the scuttlebutt, I started asking around. Everybody said the same thing. Run for cover, dude. Bail out. Get a lawyer before the shit hits the coast like a hurricane. I hired the smartest motherfucker in the business. Had to hock everything I owned to pay the man's retainer, but it was worth every penny. Wilfred Brentnell. You ever heard of him?"

"Who hasn't? I was told the only case he ever lost was up here. Nikki Fife, remember her? I guess the Santa Teresa courts weren't that impressed with his expertise."

"That's the price you pay for living in the provinces. The man's a whiz. First rate. They call him 'Bent Willy' because he's got a finger crooked like that from some kind of accident."

"What about Renkes? Aren't you bitter about him?"

"I don't hold it against him. I mean, I understand why the man did it. I wouldn't have done it myself, but then I wasn't caught first like he was. I didn't have the DA breathin' down my neck, cuttin' deals."

"Deals?"

"Shit, yes. They got him on another rap. You knew that, didn't you?"

I shook my head. "I only caught the story in fragments."

"Oh, yeah. They had that dude cold. Thing about Renkes is he sold out cheap. He got burnt. He should have taken it on the chin instead of blowin' the whistle on the rest of us. But that's life, right?"

The music ended. We moved toward the table, passing Bibianna. Jimmy uttered a low growl and gripped her by the back of the neck, claiming her with his touch. She turned with a smile and he pulled her in against him in a hip-grinding embrace, probably meant to reassert his proprietary rights. Bibianna pushed him away, but she was laughing as she did it and the gesture had no force. He slung an arm across her shoulder in an affectionate hammerlock. They kissed again. I could feel my eyes roll heavenward. We sat down and ordered yet another round of beers.

The noise level was rising, alcohol unleashing a manic babble of laughter and loud talk, with quarrelsome undertones. The air was gray with cigarette smoke, the sharp report of slammers coming down one after another in steady succession, like a trio of carpenters with hammers. The music started up again, this time with lighting effects added, guaranteed to send you into seizures. Out on the dance floor, a drunk toppled backward, crashing into a table. A shriek went up, a chair broke, glasses flew in a spray of glass shards and tequila. Jimmy and Bibianna didn't seem to notice. They were doing a sit-down version of the dirty-boogey, imitating all those terrible movie scenes where couples tongue each other on the screen and chew each other's lips. Being with lovers can be such a trial to those of us who are celibate. The very air was charged, sparks leaped between them in a nearly imperceptible arc. Every time their eyes locked, I could sense their underwear getting damp.

I glanced at my watch: eleven-fifteen. Enough of this. I scraped my chair back. "That's it for me," I said. "Time to go. Good night. It's been great." It took a while to get their attention. Jimmy managed to pull out of a nosedive of a kiss. He looked up at me with heavy-lidded surprise, still breathing hard.

"Hope I didn't interrupt anything," I said.

Lust had slowed his responses and I could see him grope for his speaking voice. "Don't go," he croaked. "Stick around. We need to talk."

"About what?"

Bibianna had to lean forward in order to be heard, but she seemed pretty cool by comparison. "Too noisy here. We're going next door to grab a bite to eat. Why don't you come with us?"

I was torn, I confess. I'd spent much of the day setting up the contact and I knew I'd be smart to cement the relationship. There was a possibility, of course, that Jimmy Tate might reveal the truth about my identity, but I thought

I could trust him to keep his mouth shut. At the moment, he seemed more concerned about getting laid. They were teasing themselves, postponing the inevitable, while I was only marking time. Oh, hell, I thought, I'm going to end up alone in my bed anyway, so why rush? I zipped up my leather jacket while I waited for them to disentangle all the various body parts. As we moved through the crowd toward the front door, I got a couple of offers, but I didn't take them seriously. Both were addressed to "Hey, you . . . yeah, you . . ." accompanied by much display and posturing. One kid looked like he was sixteen. The other had a big gold tooth sticking out in front.

The three of us left the bar, stepping into a light rain. Jimmy grabbed Bibianna's hand and they began to run. I trotted behind them, catching up when they reached the little restaurant three doors down. After the high-decibel racket in the bar, the cafe we entered was as quiet as a deprivation tank. Bourbon Street was small, essentially one long, narrow room that resembled a mock New Orleans alleyway. The walls were brick, broken up by a series of false windows and doorways, backlighted to create the illusion of warm interiors. A series of balconies jutted out at the level of the second floor, suggesting a gallery of apartments surrounded by wrought-iron railings, the pseudo–French Quarter setting complete with wall-mounted lamps in which tapered lightbulbs flickered like windblown candles. Fake green ivy snaked its way up the wall, looking so real I could have sworn I smelled the breeze that seemed to rattle through the leaves.

The restaurant kitchen was hidden around one corner where a wall angled out. The scent of shrimp *étouffée* and blackened redfish hovered in the air as if you'd caught a whiff of someone else's Sunday dinner. There were seventeen tables in all, most of them empty, each covered with white butcher's paper. Hurricane lamps provided illumination that flattered the patrons, at the same time dispensing light sufficient to eat by.

Jimmy ordered Cajun popcorn—crawfish parts fried crisp with a spicy sauce—and then a pot of jambalaya for the three of us. Bibianna wanted oysters on the half shell first. I watched them negotiate the meal, feeling strangely passive myself. They argued the issue of wine versus beer and finally ordered both. They'd become nearly playful, while I felt myself disconnect. I picked at a cornbread muffin, trying to figure out what time it was in Dietz's life. Germany was what, eight hours ahead of us? I entertained a few wicked fantasies about Dietz, while observing Bibianna and Jimmy idly as if through a two-way mirror. It seemed clear to me that there was more going on here than a quick fling. Jimmy Tate was a good-looking guy with all the sunny charm of a California surfer, wire-rimmed glasses adding interest to a face that might otherwise have been too handsome to warrant serious consideration. Handsome men have never held a fascination for me, but he was an exception, probably because of our shared history. He'd played hard in his life—booze and drugs, late nights, bar fights—and at thirty-four was just beginning to show evidence of self-abuse. I could see fine lines near his eyes, deeper lines around his mouth. Bibianna's youth and her dark Latina beauty were a perfect counterpoint to his blond, blue-eyed attractiveness. They seemed suited for one another, a crooked cop and a con artist . . . both willing to cut corners, both manipulating the system, looking for a fast buck. Neither was malicious but they must have recognized the lawlessness in each other's natures. I wondered what had drawn them together in the first place, whether they had sensed the shared bonds of mutiny and trespass. The similarities certainly weren't apparent on the surface, but I suspect lovers have some unerring instinct for the qualities that both attract and condemn them in relationships.

When the food arrived, they fell on it with the same lusty appetites they exhibited for one another, killing a bottle of red wine between them. I wasn't interested in anything more to drink. I concentrated on the meal in front of me with the kind of gusto that can only be thought of as sexual sublimation. After the beers I'd had, it was nice to have the opportunity to clear my head for the drive home. The place was beginning to fill up with the late night crowd. The noise was on the rise, but it couldn't begin to compete with the bar we'd just left. Dimly, I was aware of the front door behind me, opening at intervals as the midnight rush began—people looking for hot coffee, a wedge of sweet potato pie. Nature called again in response to all the beers I'd drunk. "Where are the restrooms?"

Bibianna pointed toward the rear. She and Tate were both bombed and I began to wonder if I'd have to ferry them both back to her place in the interests of safety.

"Be right back," I said.

I wound my way through the tables, spotting the posted sign that indicated the location of the restrooms and the public telephones. I pushed through hurricane shutters and found myself in a short corridor, lighted by the same flickering bulbs. At the end of the hallway, there were two pay phones flanking an exit with a sign above it reading THIS DOOR MUST BE KEPT UNLOCKED DURING BUSINESS HOURS. To my right were two doors marked *M* and *W*. I pushed into the *W*. The light was better. There was a two-sink counter to my left with a mirror running above it, a paper towel rack above a metal trash bin, and two stalls, one of which was in use. I entered the other. Under the raised partition between the stalls, I could see the feet of the other's occupant, whose copious urination sounded like a quart of lemonade being poured from a great height. I glanced idly at her shoes: patterned stockings, sling-back pumps with spike heels. I squinted, bending for a closer look. I'd seen the same shoes or a pair just like them on the blonde at the CF offices earlier. I heard the toilet flush. I reassembled myself in haste while she washed her hands and snatched a towel from the dispenser. I heard the rustle of paper as she dried her hands. I flushed the toilet in my cubicle, stalling for time. I didn't dare leave the cubicle until I knew she was gone because she might well recognize my face. I heard the tip-tap of her heels crossing the tile floor. As soon as the door closed behind her, I emerged and moved swiftly to the door. I poked my head out into the corridor. I caught sight of her at one of the pay phones, inserting numerous coins into the slot. She turned away slightly as if to insure privacy. It was the woman who called herself Karen Hedgepath: spiky, punk blond hair, severely cut business suit. She kept herself in profile with her right hand pressed to her ear to block out noises from the restaurant. From the shift in her posture, I guessed that her call had been picked up. She began to speak rapidly, making gestures with her free hand. I did an about-face and returned to the main part of the restaurant while she was still occupied. A quick check revealed the presence of the big guy with the plaid sport coat. He was seated with his back to me at a two-top on the side wall, but I recognized his jacket and the set of his shoulders. He was smoking a cigarette, a bottle of red wine visible on the table in front of him.

At our table, the seats were arranged so that I was facing the restrooms, my back to the front door, with Bibianna on my right and Jimmy Tate across from me. I kept my voice down, one eye cocked in case the blonde returned unexpectedly. Bibianna looked at me with curiosity, sensing my alarm. I handed her the menu and said, "I would like for you, very discreetly, to check that doorway leading to the restrooms. A blonde is going to make an appearance in a moment. See if you know her, but don't let her know you're looking. You got that?"

"Why? What's going on?" Bibianna said to me.

"I heard her on the pay phone outside the john and she was talking about you."

"About me?"

Jimmy leaned forward. "What is this?"

The blonde appeared, coming through the shutters from the corridor. Her gaze settled lightly on our table and moved on. "Do not crank your head around," I sang under my breath.

Bibianna's eyes flicked to the woman. The reaction was subtle, but I could see the animation fade from her face. "Oh, hell. I gotta get out of here," she said.

I handed her an open menu, pointing to the first item in

the dessert list, which was the key lime pie. Conversation-ally, I said, "Take your handbag and go to the ladies' room. Go out through the door at the end of that hall and wait at the mouth of the alley. One of us will pick you up. Leave your jacket draped across the chair. We don't want it to look like you're really going anywhere, okay?"

Jimmy's gaze shifted from my face to Bibianna's. "What's going on?"

Bibianna got to her feet, groping blindly for her hand-bag. Too late. The couple converged on us. The blond woman placed a firm hand on my shoulder, effectively nailing me to the chair. The guy pressed a Browning .45 against Bibianna's spine as if he might be an orthopedist probing for a herniated disk. I saw Jimmy reach for his .38, but the guy shook his head. "I got the option to smoke her if there's any problem whatsoever. Your choice."

Jimmy put both hands flat on the table.

Bibianna picked up her jacket and her handbag. Jimmy and I watched helplessly as the three of them moved to-ward the back door. Jimmy had better instincts about these things than I did. The minute they were out of sight, he bolted for the front, attracting startled looks from all the patrons he bumped in passing. He didn't bother to be po-lite. The front door banged open and he was gone. I threw some money on the table and headed after him.

By the time I hit the street, he was already pounding toward the corner, elbows pumping, gun drawn. The streets were damp, the air filled with a fine mist. I ran af-ter him, plowing straight through a puddle on the walk. In the distance, I could hear tires squeal in the alleyway where the couple must have had a car parked. I reached the intersection moments after Jimmy did. A Ford sedan shot out of the mouth of the alley three doors down. Jimmy, as if moving in slow motion, took a stance and fired. The back window shattered. He fired again. The right rear tire blew and the Ford took a sudden fishtailing detour into a van parked at the curb. There was the gut-wrenching *wham!* of metal objects colliding. The Ford's front bumper clattered to the pavement, and glass fragments showered down with a delicate tinkling. The few pedestrians within range were running for cover, and I could hear a woman's protracted scream. The front doors of the Ford seemed to open simultaneously. The blond woman emerged from the passenger side, the big guy from the driver's side, taking cover behind the yawning car door as he turned and took aim. I hit the pavement and flattened myself in the shelter of a line of trash cans. The ensuing shots sounded like kernels of popcorn in a lidded saucepan. I hunched my shoulders, tasting grit, sucking up the mixed smell of garbage and rain-wet cement. I heard three more shots fired in succession, one of them plowing into the pavement near my head. I feared for Jimmy, felt a sick sense of dread for Bibianna, too. Someone was running. At least somebody was still alive—I just wasn't sure who. I heard the footsteps fade, then silence. I pulled myself up onto my hands and knees and scrambled toward a parked car, peering over the hood. Jimmy was standing across the street. Abruptly, he sank down on the curb and put his head on his knees. There was no sign of the blonde. Bibianna, apparently unhurt, clung to the Ford's rear fender and wept hysterically. I rose to my feet, puzzled by the sudden quiet. I approached her with care, wondering where the guy in the plaid sport coat had gone.

I could hear panting, a labored moan that suggested both anguish and extreme effort. On the far side of the Ford, I caught sight of him, dragging himself along the sidewalk. There was a wet patch of bright blood between his shoulder blades. There was blood streaming down the left side of his face from a head wound. He seemed completely focused on the journey, determined to escape, moving with the same haphazard coordination of a crawling baby, limbs occasionally working at cross-purposes. He began to weep with frustration at the clumsiness of his progress. He must have been a man who'd always counted on his physical strength to carry him through, who'd enjoyed a certain unquestioned supremacy by reason of his size. Now the sheer bulk of his body was an impediment, a burden he couldn't quite manage. He laid his head down, resting for a moment before he inched forward again. A crowd had collected, like the spectators at the finish line of a marathon. No one cheered. The faces were respectful, uncertain, perplexed. A woman moved toward the injured man and dropped beside him, reaching out tentatively. At her touch, a deep howl seemed to rise from him, guttural and pain-filled. There is no sound so terrible as a man's sorrow for his own death. The woman looked up, dazed, at the people standing nearby.

"Help," she called hoarsely. She couldn't get any volume in her voice. "Please help this man. Can't anybody help?"

No one moved.

Already, there were sirens. Jimmy Tate lifted his head.

8

I crossed to the Ford. The left rear door was open and Bibianna sat sideways in the backseat, leaning forward with her elbows on her knees. She was shaking so hard that she couldn't keep her feet flat on the pavement. Her spike heels seemed to do a little tap dance as she pressed her hands together and clamped them between her thighs. I thought she was humming, but it was a moan she was trying to suppress through tightly clamped teeth. Her face was starchy white. I hunkered beside her, placing one hand on the icy skin of her arm. "You okay?"

She shook her head, a hopeless gesture of terror and resignation. "I'm dead meat. I'm dead. This is my fault. There's going to be hell to pay." Her gaze strayed vaguely toward the street corner, where a crowd had gathered. Tears rose in her eyes, not from sorrow as much as from desperation.

I gave her arm a shake. "Who *is* that?"

"His name is Chago. He's the brother of this guy I was

living with before I came up here. He said Raymond sent him up here to bring me back."

"Bullshit, Bibianna. They weren't going to take you anyplace. They were going to kill you."

"I wish I could have gotten it over with. If anything happens to Chago, Raymond's going to kill me anyway. He'll have to. Like a blood debt. My life's not worth shit."

"I thought Jimmy was the one who shot him. Why is it your fault?"

"What difference does it make? Raymond doesn't care about that. It's my fault I left. It's my fault he had to send Chago up here. It's my fault the *car* got wrecked. That's how he sees things."

"I take it the blonde was Chago's girlfriend," I said.

"His wife. Her name's Dawna. D-a-w-n-a. Do you love that? Shit, she'll kill me herself if Raymond doesn't kill me first."

Jimmy Tate approached and put his hand on the back of Bibianna's neck. "Hey, babe. How are you?"

She took his hand and pressed it against her cheek. "Oh, God, oh, God . . . I was scared for you."

He pulled her to her feet and took her in his arms, enfolding her, murmuring against her hair.

"Jesus, what am I going to do?" she wailed.

An emergency vehicle came barreling around the corner, orange light flashing as the siren ground abruptly to a halt. Two paramedics got out, one of them toting a first-aid kit. I rose to my feet, watching over the hood of the Ford as the two of them crossed rapidly to the guy, who was lying facedown on the sidewalk. His lurching journey to the corner had come to a sudden halt. I noticed he'd left a long, smeared trail of blood in his wake like a snail. The woman who knelt beside him was crying uncontrollably. I was certain she was a stranger, only connected to him by the quirk of fate that had placed her at the scene. Her two companions tried to coax her away, but she refused to relinquish her hold.

One of the paramedics knelt and placed his fingers against the guy's carotid artery, trying to get a pulse. He and the other paramedic exchanged one of those looks that in a television episode replaces six lines of dialogue. Two squad cars swung into view, tires squealing, and pulled up behind the emergency vehicle. A uniformed patrolman got out of the first car and Jimmy Tate walked over to meet him. The beat officer in the second turned out to be a woman, tall, sturdily constructed, her pale hair skinned away from her face and secured in a small, neat knot at the back of her neck. She was hatless, in dark regulation pants and a dark jacket with Santa Teresa Police Department patches on the sleeves. She crossed to the paramedics and had a quick conversation. I noticed that none of them jumped into any emergency procedures, which suggested the guy in the sport coat had already departed this life. The beat officer moved back to her patrol car and radioed the dispatcher, asking for someone from the coroner's office, the CSI unit, and backup on a Code 2—no sirens. She was going to need help securing the crime scene. The rain had begun again, drizzle lending the night air a softening haze. The crowd was subdued and there was no suggestion of interference, but someone was going to have to begin interviewing witnesses, collecting names and addresses, before people got restless and started leaving the area.

Bibianna slumped back into the backseat of the car again. Long minutes passed. Bibianna had lapsed into silence, but when the first backup unit arrived, she stirred, shooting a dark look in the direction of the two officers emerging from the black-and-white. "I don't want to talk to any cops," she said. "I hate cops. I don't want to talk to them."

"Bibianna, you're going to have to talk to them. Those people tried to kill you. There's a dead man on the sidewalk. . . ."

Fury flashed across her face and her voice rose several notches. "Just leave me alone!"

Several people turned to look at us, including the beat officer, who began to walk in our direction. She put a hand on her left hip, touching her nightstick like a talisman. As she approached, I checked the name on her tag. Officer D. Janofsky. Probably Diane or Deborah. She didn't look like a Dorothy. Up close, I could see that she was in her late twenties, probably new to the department. I knew most of the officers who worked in this area, but she was not one I'd met. Her manner was cautious, her expression alert. Like many cops, she'd learned to disconnect her emotions. "Everything okay here?"

She scarcely had the words out when a third patrol car skidded around the corner. All three of us turned as the car came to a halt some distance away. Tuesday night in Santa Teresa is usually very quiet, so aside from the obvious desire to assist a fellow officer, the officer responding must have been thrilled to see some action. This was better than rousting the homeless down at the railroad tracks. Janofsky turned her attention to Bibianna, whose face had darkened. I was keeping tabs on Tate out of the corner of my eye, and I realized, as had Bibianna, that he had been taken into custody.

"Keep her away from me," Bibianna said.

"We're fine," I said, hoping to defuse the situation.

Janofsky ignored me, fixing Bibianna with a testy look. "I'd like to see your driver's license." She reached for her flashlight as if she meant to examine the license once Bibianna had produced it. I knew from experience a flashlight that size could serve as a powerful protective weapon. I watched apprehensively.

"What for?" Bibianna asked.

"Ma'am, could you show me some identification?"

"Fuck you," Bibianna said. She managed to infuse the two words with maximum boredom and maximum contempt. Why was she being so belligerent? I could feel my own temper climb and I knew the policewoman was close to blowing. This was no time to fool around. For all Janofsky knew, Bibianna had shot the man herself.

"Her name is Diaz," I interjected. "She's upset about the shooting. Can I answer any questions for you? My name's Hannah Moore." I was babbling like an idiot, trying to offset some of the tension in the air. The patrol car with Tate in it pulled away from the curb, easing through the crowd of curiosity seekers that was milling about.

Bibianna turned on me. "Keep out of this. Where are they taking Tate?"

"Probably to the station. He'll be fine. Don't worry about it. Just cool it. You've already got enough trouble on your hands."

"Could you get out of the car, please?" the officer said. She backed up half a step and planted her feet.

I said, "Goddamn it, Bibianna. Would you just do what the lady says? You've got your tit in a wringer. Don't you get that?"

Bibianna bolted from the car abruptly and gave me a shove that nearly knocked me over backward. I caught myself on the open car door, grabbing at the handle to retain my balance. Bibianna drove a shoulder into Officer Janofsky, catching her off guard. Janofsky barked out an expletive, startled by the assault. Bibianna punched her in the face, swung around, and punched at me, too, grazing my temple with a fist the size and shape of a broken rock. That sucker *hurt*. For someone so petite, she really managed to pack a wallop.

Officer Janofsky went into combat mode. Before the other two officers even understood what was going on, she slammed Bibianna up against the car, grabbing one wrist in the process. Cops know how to pinch little hurt places on the human body that'll drop you in your tracks. I saw Bibianna stiffen and her face twist with pain as a pertinent nerve was tweaked beyond endurance. Janofsky jerked Bibianna's arms back and snapped a set of cuffs on her. I felt my heart sink. They'd march her off to jail and keep her there for life. I could see, in a flash, that if I wanted to maintain our connection, I only had one choice here. I grabbed Officer Janofsky by the arm. "Hey, get offa her. You can't treat her that way!"

Janofsky leveled me with a look. She was trembling with rage, in no mood to take any sass from the likes of me. "Back up!" she snapped.

"You back up!" I snapped back. Out of the corner of my eye, I could see two male cops coming up on my right.

Here goes "assault on a police officer," I thought. I hauled off and socked Officer Janofsky in the face. The next thing I knew, I was flat on the pavement, my wrists handcuffed behind me, the right side of my face being ground into the concrete. Some cop had his knee in the middle of my back. I could hardly breathe, and for a moment I worried he'd crush my rib cage. It hurt like hell, but I couldn't even get out a "guff" of protest. I'd been effectively incapacitated, not in pain, but certainly penitent. Having made his point, the guy got up. I stayed where I was, reluctant to risk a crack in the head with a nightstick. As an addendum to my discomfort, the drizzle was suddenly upgraded to a dainty pitter-patter. I groaned involuntarily. I heard Bibianna shriek, a sound more related to outrage than pain. I inched up my head in time to see her kick Janofsky in the kneecap. The officer's adrenaline was already up and I was afraid she'd go after Bibianna with the flashlight. She grabbed her by the throat, trying to get a choke hold. One of Janofsky's fellow officers intervened at that point, which was fortunate. I laid my cheek down against the pavement, waiting for the melodrama to play itself out. The raindrops, as they hit the sidewalk, rebounded in my face. I stared at the tiny pebbles embedded in the concrete, using auditory cues to re-create the activities taking place around me. It was like listening to a sporting event on the radio. I grew weary trying to visualize the play as it progressed. Drops of water began to slide down the side of my face, collecting on the pavement in a shallow pool near my cheek. I felt like one of those protesters whose pictures you see in the paper. I craned my head around, resting my chin on the walk.

"Uh, excuse me," I said. "Hey!" It was a strain to try to hold my head in that position, so I laid it down again. Several pairs of regulation cop shoes appeared in my line of vision. I hoped none of them belonged to Lieutenant Dolan. Somebody gave an order. Suddenly, there was an officer on either side of me. I felt myself hooked under the armpits and I was lifted to my feet, levitating into an upright position effortlessly. After a quick pat-down, I was hustled off to a squad car and shoved into the backseat. The door was slammed shut.

An unmarked car came down the street from the opposite direction, sliding to a halt on the rain-lubricated asphalt. I saw Bill Blair, the coroner's deputy, get out on the driver's side, taking a moment to shrug himself into his raincoat. Head bowed against the rain, he moved over to the body without looking in my direction. All the various crime scene personnel had begun to assemble: two guys from the Public Works Department setting up barricades, running tape around the perimeter, the CSI unit, along with the supervisor in a separate vehicle. As in the early moments of a play, the actors were appearing onstage, each with the necessary props, each with a bit of business to perform. Little by little, the drama of homicide was being played out again.

I sat forward slightly, peering through the metal screen that separated the front of the squad car from the rear. It was 1:17 A.M. and my head had begun to ache. The rain now formed a hazy curtain that seemed to blow against the streetlights, sending up whiffs of steam. The sound was homely, like uncooked rice grains falling on a cookie sheet. Within minutes, the precipitation increased rapidly to a steady drumming on the roof of the black-and-white. Ordinarily, I like sitting in a parked car in a downpour. It seems cozy and safe and surprisingly intimate, depending on the circumstances, of course. The same smattering of people stood outside on the darkened street, avoiding the sight of me as if I were leprous. Anyone sitting in the rear of a cop car looks guilty somehow. The emergency vehicle had been moved to one side to allow the coroner's deputy access to the body. Chago had been covered with a length of yellow plastic to shield him from the rain. Blood had coagulated on the sidewalk like a sticky patch of motor oil, and I could still smell cordite. The police radio was squawking incomprehensibly. There was a time in my life—during my days in uniform—when I understood every word. Not so, tonight. I'd lost my ear for it, like a foreign language I no longer had a use for.

Bibianna was being questioned by the police inspector, who'd appeared at some point. She was being pelted by the rain, the red dress clinging to her stained to a dark bloody hue. She looked like she was complaining, though I couldn't hear a word she said. Judging from the inspector's expression and the set of Bibianna's shoulders, she was subdued, but uncooperative. The inspector waved a hand at her impatiently. The same officer who'd ushered me to the patrol car steered Bibianna in my direction. She was frisked for weapons, a ludicrous formality under the circumstances. In the little mini she was wearing, what kind of weapon could she possibly conceal? The rear door of the squad car was yanked open and the officer pushed her head down and shoved her into the backseat beside me. She'd recovered some of her energy, jaws snapping at the guy's hand like a rabid dog. "Get your fuckin' hands offa me, you cocksucker!" she screamed.

Nice talk, huh? When you get arrested, these are the kind of people you're forced to associate with. Because of the handcuffs, her arms were pinioned awkwardly behind her, which meant she ended up lying halfway across my lap. Before the officer could close the door, she lashed a kick at him with one of her spike heels. He was lucky she missed. She'd have torn a hunk of flesh out of his thigh if she'd caught him right. He was amazingly polite— probably heartened by the fact that he could look up her dress—but I noticed he managed to get the door shut before she could kick at him again. She was a firecracker, absolutely fearless. For a minute, I thought she'd lie there and kick the windows out. She muttered something to herself and straightened up.

She flicked her hair away from her face with a shake of her head. A few drops of water flew off on me. "Did you see that? I could have been killed tonight! Those assholes tried to kill me!" She was referring to the cops, not Chago and the blonde.

"The cops didn't try to kill you," I said irritably. "What did you expect? You haul off and sock a cop, what'd you think was going to happen?"

"Look who's talking. You hit that bitch twice as hard as me." She turned a calculating look on me and I could see now that I had garnered a spark of admiration for my pugilistic skills. She began a staring contest with one of the cops standing near the car. "God, I hate pigs," she remarked.

"They don't seem all that fond of you," I said.

"I mean it! I could sue. That's police brutality."

"What's your problem?"

"Forget it. It's none of your business."

She peered out of the car window and I followed her gaze. Two cops were conferring, probably in preparation for removing us to the station. I wished they'd get on with it. I was cold. My tank top was soaked and my pants were soggy, clinging to my thighs like a lapful of wet sheets. I wasn't sure what had happened to my leather jacket. Somebody would steal it if I'd left it in the restaurant. Both my scruffy pumps and little white socks were mud-spattered and made squishing sounds every time I moved my feet. I could still smell the sooty cologne of second-hand cigarette smoke that permeated my hair. With my hands cuffed from behind, I had metal bracelets digging into the bruised flesh of my wrists.

Bibianna's mood underwent a shift. Her manner now seemed completely matter-of-fact, as if shoot-outs, death, and resisting arrest were an everyday occurrence. She held a foot up, inspecting her shoe. "Fuckin' shoes are ruined," she remarked. "That's the trouble with suede. One wet night and you're wearing slime. I wish I had a cigarette. You think they're going to bring my bag?"

"You better hope not. I thought you had a joint in there."

That warranted a half laugh. "Oh, yeah. I forgot. That's how my luck runs, you know? What's the point trying to straighten out your life if it's all going to turn to worms again?"

She peered out at the various law enforcement types milling around in the rain. "Hey! Let's pick up the pace, frog-lips. What's the delay?" It was pointless yelling with the windows rolled up. One of the beat cops turned and looked at her, but I was sure he hadn't heard a word she'd said. "Pig," she said to him pleasantly. "Yeah, you, dick-head. Get an eyeful." She stuck a leg up in the air. He looked away and Bibianna laughed.

9

Even with the harsh lights playing on her face, that fine dusky skin looked almost luminous. Thick lashes, dark eyes, a wide mouth still lush with flame-red lipstick. How'd she keep the stuff on like that? Anytime I tried lipstick, it ended up on the rim of the first glass I drank from. Hers looked fresh and wet, lending color to her face. Despite the foul talk, her dark eyes glinted with amusement. "I can't believe those guys get paid to stand around like that," she remarked with a glance at me. "How are you holding up?"

"I've been better. You have any idea where Dawna disappeared to?"

"She probably went to call Raymond. Oh, man, he's gonna have a fit when he finds out Chago's dead."

"Who are they?"

"Don't ask."

"What'd you do to piss 'em off so bad?"

"It's what I didn't do that counts."

"You owe 'em money?"

"No way, baby! They owe me. What I can't figure out is how they got a line on me in the first place. What'd you say your name was?"

For a minute, I couldn't remember which set of fake ID's I'd brought. "Hannah Moore."

There was a calculated silence. "What's the rest of it?"

"The rest?"

"You have a middle name?"

"Oh. Sure," I said. "Uhm, Lee."

Her tone of voice turned flat. "I don't believe it."

I felt my heart do a quick flip, but I managed a non-committal murmur.

"I never met anyone with three pairs of double letters in their name. Two *n*'s in Hannah. Two *e*'s in Lee and the two *o*'s in Moore. Plus, 'Hannah' is a palindrome, spelled the same way forward as it is backward. You ever had your numbers done?"

"Like numerology?"

She nodded. "It's a hobby of mine. I can do a chart for you later . . . all I need is your date of birth, but I can tell you right now, your soul number's six. Like you're big in domestic harmony, right? People like you, your mission is to spread the idea of the Golden Rule."

I laughed in spite of myself. "Oh, really. How'd you guess?"

A uniformed officer, toting Bibianna's handbag, moved over to the squad car and let himself in, locking eyes with me in the rearview mirror as he slammed the door shut. It was apparently his job to transport us out to the jail. He held the bag up. "This belong to one of you?"

"Me," Bibianna said, rolling her eyes in my direction. It was anybody's guess whether the joint in her bag would come to light or not. She was in deep doo-doo if it did.

He plunked the bag down on the seat beside him. "How you doin' back there?" He was in his late twenties, clean-shaven, his dark hair clipped close. The back of his neck looked vulnerable above the collar of his uniform.

None of this was lost on Bibianna. "We're great, sport. How're you?"

"I'm cool," he said.

"You have a name?"

"Kip Brainard," he said. "You're Diaz, right?"

"Right."

He seemed to smile to himself. He started the car and eased it away from the curb, radioing the dispatcher that he was on his way in with us. There was no more conversation. The rain had begun to sound like a pile of nails being dropped on the car roof, windshield wipers flopping back and forth without much effect, the monotonous calls from the car radio punctuating the silence. We reached the freeway and headed north. The windows were fogging over. In the warmth of the vehicle and the lulling drone of the engine, I nearly nodded off.

We took the off ramp at Espada and turned left onto the frontage road, proceeding about a half a mile. We turned right onto a road that cut around to the rear of the Santa Teresa County Correctional Facility, better known as the jail to those of us about to be incarcerated. On the far side of the property, the complex shared a parking lot with the Santa Teresa County Sheriff's Department. We pulled up at the gate. Kip pushed a button for the intercom. The master control regulation officer responded, a disembodied female voice surrounded by static.

"Police officer coming in with two," he said.

The gate swung open and we passed through. Once we were inside the fence, he honked the horn and the gate swung shut behind us. We pulled into a paved stretch enclosed by a chain-link fence. The whole area blazed with lights, the rain creating a misty aureole around each flood. A county sheriff's car had pulled in just ahead of us, and we waited in silence until the deputy was admitted with his prisoner, a vagrant who was visibly drunk and much in need of assistance.

Once they'd disappeared, Kip shut the engine off and got out. He opened the rear door on my side and helped me out, a clumsy procedure with my hands cuffed behind my back. "You gonna behave yourself?" he asked.

"No problem. I'm fine."

He must not have trusted me because he continued to hold on to my arm, walking me around to Bibianna's side of the car. He opened the door and helped her out of the backseat and then walked us toward the gate. A female jail officer came out to assist him. The rain was constant, unpleasant, a chill assault on my body, which was already trembling with accumulated tensions. Never had I so longed for a hot shower, dry clothes, my own bed. Bibianna's dark hair was plastered to her head in long dripping strands, but it didn't seem to bother her. All the earlier hostility had faded, replaced by a curious complaisance.

Reception at the county jail is approached through an exterior corridor of chain-link fencing that resembles a dog run. We were buzzed in, passing yet another check-point complete with electronic locks and cameras. Kip walked us along the passage, raindrops splashing up around us as our heels tapped across the wet pavement. "You know the routine?" he asked.

"Yeah, yeah, yeah. It's all the same, stud," Bibianna said.

"Let's make that 'Officer.' Can we do that?" he said dryly. "I take it you're an old hand at this."

"You got that right . . . Officer Stud," she said.

He decided to let it pass. I kept my mouth shut. I knew the drill from the old days in uniform. It was odd how differently I perceived the whole process now that I was the perp.

We reached a metal door. Kip pushed a button, announcing once more that he was bringing in two of us. We waited while the cameras inspected us. I've seen the big console where the MCR operator sits, surrounded by black-and-white monitors showing the equivalent of twelve totally boring Andy Warhol movies simultaneously. The operator buzzed us in. In silence, we walked down one corridor and then turned into a second, emerging eventually into the reception area where the male prisoners are booked in. I was hoping to see Tate, but he'd apparently been processed and taken to a cell. The vagrant, weaving on his feet, was emptying the pockets of his ragged sport coat. I knew him by sight, one of the town's perennial characters. Most afternoons he hung out around the courthouse having heated arguments with an unseen companion. His invisible chum was still giving him a hard time. The booking officer behind the desk waited with benign patience. I knew the deputy, too, though

I couldn't remember his name. Foley, maybe. Something like that. I wasn't close enough to read his name tag and I didn't want to call attention to myself by squinting at his chest.

I turned my head, staring off to the left to avoid any visual contact. It had been a good ten years since I'd last seen the guy, but I didn't want to chance his recognizing me, blowing the cover I'd set up. I probably flatter myself. I looked as respectable as the bum they were booking. I fancied I smelled better, but perhaps not. I've noticed that most of us don't have a clue what we smell like to other people. It's almost as though our noses blank us out in self-defense.

Kip buzzed at yet another locked door, and after a brief wait another female jail officer emerged from the women's side. Bibianna and I had our pictures taken in the kind of booth you see in Woolworth's, a sorry strip of poses appearing moments later in the outside slot. In mine, I looked like a suspect in a teen porno ring, the kind of woman who'd lure the young girls with glib promises of modeling gigs. We moved into the women's booking area, where we approached a row of holding cells. I went into the first and Bibianna the second. The officer with me did a quick pat-down and then removed the handcuffs.

"Lean up against the wall," she said. Her tone wasn't unfriendly, but it was devoid of real warmth. And why not? I was just one more in an endless stream of jailbirds as far as she knew.

I faced the wall, arms straight out in front of me, leaning my weight on my hands, which were spaced about four feet apart. She did a second, more thorough, pat-down, making sure I didn't have any tiny lethal weapons concealed in my hair. She allowed me to take a seat on a bench along the wall while the proper papers were assembled at the counter to my right. When the booking officer was ready, I emptied my pockets, passing my phony driver's license, my keys, my watch, my belt, and my scruffy shoes through the window slot. There was something pathetic about the sight of my personal possessions, which were not only meager, but cheap as well. We began to go through the catechism that accompanies the loss of freedom. Personal data. Medical. Employment. I said I was out of work, claiming "waitress" as my occupation. We went through the litany of facility and arrest data. I was being charged with assault, a misdemeanor, and battery on a police officer, which is a felony with a five-thousand-dollar bail attached. I assumed Bibianna was being booked on similar charges. I was offered the chance to post bail, but I declined, operating on the premise that Bibianna would do likewise. All I needed was to be stuck in jail while she found a way to get herself bailed out. I kept waiting for the booking officer to realize that my driver's license was a fake, but she didn't seem to notice. My few pieces of personal property were itemized and placed in a clear plastic boiling pouch, like a Seal-A-Meal. The whole procedure took about fifteen minutes and left me feeling unsettled. Oddly enough, I didn't feel humiliated so much as I felt misunderstood. I wanted to assert myself, wanted to assure them that I wasn't what I appeared to be, that I was really a decent, law-abiding citizen . . . on *their* team, in effect.

The booking officer completed her process. "You want to make any calls, there's a pay phone in the next cell."

"I can't think who I'd call anyway," I said, absurdly grateful that everyone was so polite. What had I expected, curses and abuse?

Padding along in my sock feet, I was taken down the corridor to the ID bureau to be fingerprinted. A second set of photographs were taken, front and profile this time. At this rate, I could put together a little album for Mother's Day. It was 2:13 A.M. by the time I was escorted to the drunk tank, a cell maybe fifteen by fifteen feet. A skinny white woman, with her back turned, slept on a mattress in the far corner of the room. There were no outside windows. The entire front wall was barred, with a lidless commode tucked into an alcove on the right. I've seen cells where the toilet seats are removed as well. I had to guess we were being trusted not to try to hang ourselves with this one. The floor was beige vinyl tile, the walls painted cinder block. There was a built-in bench running the width of the room with some one-inch mattresses rolled up and arranged haphazardly against the wall. I snagged one for myself and spread it out on the floor.

Bibianna arrived moments later, along with two other prisoners, a black woman and a weeping white girl in formal dress.

"Hey, Hannah," Bibianna said. "Old home week. This is Nettie." She turned to the second woman. "What's your name, babycakes?"

"Heather."

Bibianna said, "Heather, this is Hannah."

"Nice to meet you," I murmured dutifully. I didn't have a clue about jailhouse etiquette. The skinny woman in the far corner stirred restlessly in her sleep.

Bibianna pulled a mattress off the bench and dragged it over toward me. "Nettie and me did a little county time about a month ago, right?" No response.

Nettie, the black woman, looked to be in her late thirties. She was tall, with broad shoulders and breasts the size of torpedoes. Her hair was big and brushed over to the right, where the bulk of it stuck out stiffly as if blown by a hard wind. The black strands had a gray cast from all the split ends. She wore blue jeans, an oversize white T-shirt, and white crew socks. Bibianna arranged her mattress beside mine and took a seat, watching Nettie with respect. "She was charged with 'attempt to inflict bodily injury' and 'assault with a deadly weapon.' She attacked a wino with an uprooted palm tree. I guess it was a little one, but can you believe that?"

The other inmate, the white girl, was scarcely more than twenty, wearing an ankle-length organza dress and a corsage on one wrist. She was crying so hard it was impossible to figure out what her story was. She sank in a huddle and buried her face in her hands. She and Nettie both reeked of booze. The black woman paced restlessly, staring at Heather, who kept wiping her nose on the hem of her dress. Finally, Nettie stopped pacing and nudged her with a foot. "What's the matter with you, blubbering away like that? Hush up a minute and tell me what's wrong here."

The girl lifted a tear-streaked face, blotchy with embarrassment. Her nose was pink, her makeup smeared, her fine, pale hair coming loose from a complicated arrangement on top that looked like it had been done professionally. There were little sprigs of baby's breath tucked here and there like pale dried twigs. She paused to lick at a tear trickling toward her chin and then told a garbled tale of her boyfriend, a fight, being left penniless on the side of the freeway, too drunk to stand, picked up by a CHP cruiser and arrested on the spot. This was her twenty-first birthday and she was spending it in the county jail. She'd barfed on her dress, which she'd had on layaway for six months at Lerner's. Her daddy was on the city council and she didn't dare call home. By the time she got to this point, she burst into tears again.

The skinny woman on the mattress made a muffled response. "B.F.D. Big fuckin' deal."

Nettie, offended, turned on the woman, whom she apparently knew. She fired a dark look at the huddled form. "Mind your own business, bitch." She patted Heather awkwardly, unaccustomed to mothering but identifying with her plight. "Poor sweet baby. That's all right. That's just fine. Now don't you be upset. Everything's going to be all right. . . ."

I stretched out on my side, my head propped up on my hand. Bibianna had her back against the wall, her arms crossed for warmth. "What a crock of shit. People out there killing each other and they arrest someone like her. I don't get it. Call her old man and have him come get her out of here. He's going to call anyway once he figures out she's not home."

"How come you're so down on the police?" I asked.

Bibianna ran a hand through her hair, giving it a toss. "They killed my pop. My mom's Anglo. He was Latino. They met in high school and she was crazy about him. She gets knocked up and they got married, but it worked out okay."

"Why'd the cops kill him?"

"It was just something dumb. He was in a little market and lifted something minor—a package of meat and some chewing gum. The store manager caught him and they got into a tussle. Some off-duty cop pulled his gun out and fired. All for a pack of ground beef and some Chiclets for me. What a waste. My mother never got over it. God, it was awful to watch. She married some guy six months later and he turned out to be a real shit, knockin' her around. Talk about bad karma—the cops killed him, too. She'd kick him out. He'd disappear and then show up again, all contrite. Move in, take her money, beat the crap out of us. He's drunk half the time, doing 'ludes and coke, anything else he could get his hands on, I guess. If he wasn't pawing at her, he was pawing at me. I cut him once, right across the face—nearly took his eye out. One night, he got caught breaking into an apartment building two doors away from us. He barricaded himself in the place with a twelve-gauge. The cops swarmed all over the neighborhood. Television crews. SWAT teams and tear gas. Cops shot him down like a dog. I was eight. It's like how many times I gotta go through this, you know?"

"Sounds like they did you a service on that one," I said.

Her smile was bitter, but she made no response.

"Your mother still alive?"

"Down in Los Angeles," Bibianna said. "What about you? You got family somewhere?"

"Not anymore. I've been on my own for years. I thought you were going to do my numbers," I said.

"Oh, yeah. What's your birthday?"

The date I was using on the fake ID was a match for mine. "May fifth," I said, and gave her the year.

"And me without a pencil. Hey, Nettie? You got something to write with?"

Nettie shook her head. "Not unless you count Chap-Stick."

Bibianna shrugged. "What the hell. Look here." She licked her finger and drew a big tic-tac-toe grid on the floor. She wrote the number 5 in the center and raised it to the third power. The lights in the cell were dim, but the floor was so grimy I could read the spit graph without squinting. She said, "This is great. See that? Five is the number of change and movement. You got three of them. That's hot. You know, travel and like that. Growth. You're the kind of person has to be out there doing things, moving. The zero out here means you don't have any limits. You can do anything. Like whatever you tried, you'd be good at, you know? But it can scatter you. Especially with all these fives here. Makes it tough to pick the thing you want to do. You'd need to have the kind of job that would never be the same. Know what I mean? You have to be in the middle of the action. . . ."

She looked at me for confirmation.

"Weird," I said, for lack of anything better.

Nettie shot us a look. She had one arm around Heather, who had leaned against her for warmth. "We're trying to get some sleep here. Could you keep it down?"

"Sorry," Bibianna said. She abandoned the reading and stretched out on the mattress, making herself comfortable. The gridwork she'd drawn seemed to glow in the half-light.

The bulb in the cell remained bright, but we were reasonably warm. There was the sense of ongoing activity in the corridors beyond: a phone ringing, footsteps, the murmuring of voices, a cell door clanging shut. At intervals, the smell of cigarette smoke seemed to drift through the vents. Somewhere on the floor below us were the dormitory rooms that housed the fifty to sixty women doing county time in any given period. I could feel myself begin to drift. At least we were out of the rain and the bad guys couldn't get us. Unless "they" were somebody locked in the cell with us. Now, there was a thought.

"One good thing," Bibianna murmured drowsily.

"What's that?"

"They didn't find that joint. . . ."

"You are one lucky chick."

After that, there was quiet except for the occasional rustling of clothes as one of us turned on the mattress. The skinny white woman began to snore softly. I lay entertaining warm thoughts about Bibianna, realizing that from here on out, I'd remember her as the person I first got jailed with, a form of female bonding not commonly recognized. I'd have felt a lot better if Jimmy Tate had come to our rescue, but I really wasn't sure what he could have done to help. Right now, he was probably sitting in a cell over on the men's side in roughly the same fix. Crazy Jimmy Tate and Bibianna Diaz, what a pair they made. . . .

10

The next thing I knew, there was a jingling of keys. My eyes popped open. One of the female jail officers was unlocking the door. She was short and solid, built like she spent a lot of time at the gym. The other four women in the cell were still asleep. The jail officer pointed at me. Bleary-eyed, I propped myself up on one elbow, pushing the hair out of my face. I pointed at myself—did she want me? Impatiently, she motioned me over to the door. I curled forward, rising to my feet as quietly as I could. There was no way to judge what time it was or how long I'd been asleep. I felt groggy and disoriented. Without a word, she opened the door and I passed through. I followed her down the corridor in my sock feet, wishing with all my heart that I could brush my teeth.

I once dated a cop who had an eight-by-eleven-foot desk built for himself, boasting that the surface was the same size as the two-man cells in Folsom prison. The room I was ushered into was about that size, furnished with a plain wood table, three straight-backed wooden chairs, and a bulb covered with a milky globe. I would have bet money there was recording equipment in there somewhere. I peered under the table. No sign of a wire. I sat down on one of the chairs, wondering how best to comport myself. I knew I was a mess. My hair felt matted, probably sticking straight up in places. I was sure my mascara and eyeliner now circled my eyes in that raccoon effect women so admire in themselves. The trampy outfit I'd concocted was not only wrinkled, but still felt faintly damp. Ah, well. At least if I were subjected to police brutality, I wouldn't mind bleeding on myself.

The door opened and Lieutenant Dolan appeared in company with another (I was guessing) plainclothes detective. I felt a spurt of fear for the first time since this ghastly ordeal had begun. Dolan was the last man I wanted to have as a witness to my current state. I could feel a blush of embarrassment rise up my neck to my face. Dolan's companion was in his sixties, with a thick shock of silver hair brushed away from a square face, deep-set eyes, and a mouth that pulled down at the corners. He was taller than Dolan and in much better shape, substantially built with wide shoulders and heavy-looking thighs. He wore a three-piece suit in a muted glen plaid with a denim blue shirt and a wide maroon tie with a floral pattern more fitting for a couch cover. He wore a gold ring on his right hand, a watch with a heavy gold band on his left. He made no particular attempt to be polite. If he had an opinion of me, nothing registered on his face. Together, the two men seemed to fill the room.

Dolan leaned out into the hall and said something to

someone, then closed the door and pulled a chair up, straddling it. The other man sat down at the same time and crossed his legs at the knee with a slight adjustment of his trousers. He held his big hands loosely in his lap and made no eye contact.

Dolan seemed positively perky by comparison. "I'm having some coffee brought in. You look like you could use some."

"How'd you know I was here?"

"One of the deputies recognized you when you were booked in and called me," he said.

"Who's this?" I asked with a glance at the other man. I didn't think he should have the advantage of anonymity. He clearly knew who I was and enough about me to adopt an attitude of disinterest.

"Lieutenant Santos," Dolan said. Santos made no move. What was this, my week to meet hostile men?

I got up and leaned across the table with my hand held out. "Kinsey Millhone," I said. "Nice to meet you."

His reaction was slow and I wondered briefly just how rude he intended to be. We shook hands and his eyes met mine just long enough to register a stony neutrality. I had thought at first he disliked me, but I was forced to amend that assessment. He didn't have an opinion of me at all. I might be useful to him. He hadn't decided yet.

There was a rap at the door. Dolan leaned over and opened it. One of the deputies passed him a tray with three Styrofoam cups of coffee, a carton of milk, and a few loose packets of sugar. Dolan thanked him and closed the door again. He set the tray on the table and passed a cup to me. Santos reached forward and took his. I poured some milk in mine and added two packs of sugar, hoping to jump-start myself for the questions coming up. The coffee wasn't hot, but the flavor was exquisite, as soft and sweet as caramel.

"What happened to Jimmy Tate?" I asked.

"Right now, he's looking at homicide, murder two. A good attorney might get it knocked down to voluntary manslaughter, but I wouldn't count on it, given his history," Dolan said. "You want to fill us in on the shooting?"

"Sure," I said glibly, knowing I'd have to stretch the truth a bit. "California Fidelity asked me to investigate Bibianna Diaz for possible fraud in a claim she filed. I've been trying to get close enough to pick up concrete evidence, but so far all I've netted are some fashion tips. The dead man's name is Chago. He's the brother of Raymond Something-or-other, who's an old flame of Bibianna's. I gather Raymond sent Chago and his wife, Dawna, up here to abduct Bibianna for reasons unknown. I can't get Bibianna to tell me what's going on, but they're clearly pissed. . . ."

Santos spoke up. "She and Raymond Maldonado were supposed to get married. She backed out. He doesn't take kindly to that sort of thing."

"I believe it," I said. "He apparently gave Chago instructions to 'smoke' her if she didn't cooperate."

Santos shifted in his chair, his voice flat. "That's all bluff. Raymond wants her back."

I looked from one to the other. "If you already know all this stuff, why ask me?"

Both men ignored me. I could see there wasn't going to be any point in getting crabby about the situation.

Dolan consulted a small spiral-bound notebook, leafing back a page. "What's the story on Jimmy Tate? How'd he get involved?"

"I'm not sure," I said. "I gather he and Bibianna have been embroiled in some kind of heavy-duty sexual relationship for the past couple of months. It seems to be serious—for the moment, at any rate." I went on, detailing the day's work, filling in as much as I knew about the dead man, which wasn't much, and about Jimmy Tate, which was considerable. As fond as I was of Tate, I couldn't see any reason to shield him from police scrutiny when it came to the shooting. There were other witnesses at the scene, and for all I knew, Dolan had already talked to them.

When I finished, there was a silence. I looked down at my hands, realizing that I'd systematically destroyed my now empty cup in the course of my narrative. I placed fragments on the table.

"And Tate did the shooting," Dolan said at length.

"Well, I didn't actually see that, but it's a fair assumption. He fired twice at the car, and after I hit the pavement, there were several more shots fired. I don't think Bibianna was armed."

"What about the other woman, Dawna? She have a gun?"

"Not that I saw, at least not in the restaurant. She could have had one stashed in the car, I suppose. Hasn't she turned up?" I didn't think Dolan was going to answer, but I liked pretending we were equals. Just us law enforcement types having a friendly little tête-à-tête here at the county jail.

Dolan surprised me with a response. "She took a hit.

Nothing serious. Looks like a bullet ricocheted off something and grazed her collarbone. We picked her up in a phone booth a few blocks away. Probably interrupted a call to Raymond, though she wouldn't admit it."

"She's in the hospital?"

"For the time being. We'll hang on to her if we can, just to see what she has to tell us."

"About what?"

Dolan slid a look to Santos, like he was checking his hole card in a game of poker. I had the feeling Santos was making a decision. His expression didn't seem to change, but something must have been communicated between the two of them.

"I guess we better tell you what's happening," he said. His voice was rumbling and his delivery methodical. "You've stumbled into a bit of a sticky situation here."

"Oh, yeah, tell me about it."

Santos tipped his chair back against the wall and laced his hands across his head. "I head a task force made up of a number of agencies working to uncover what we believe is one of the biggest auto insurance fraud operations ever mounted in Southern California. You've worked in this business long enough to know what I'm talking about. Los Angeles County is the nation's automobile insurance fraud capital. Now it's spreading through Ventura and Santa Teresa counties. This particular ring is only one of dozens that generate an estimated five hundred million to a billion in phony claims every year. In this case, we're looking at fifteen lawyers, two dozen medical doctors, half a dozen chiropractors. On top of that, a rotating pool of some fifty to sixty individuals recruited to participate in the trumped-up incidents that comprise the claims." He pushed away from the wall, sitting upright, the front legs of the chair hitting the floor with a chirp. "You with me so far?"

"Oh, I'm here," I said.

He leaned forward, resting one arm on the table. I noticed his manner toward me was warming somewhat. He was a man animated by his work. I had no idea where he was going with the explanation, but it was clear he hadn't driven all the way up from Los Angeles in the dead of night just to deliver this deadpan rendition of his professional concerns. "We've put this case together bit by bit, piece by piece, over the last two years, and we're still not in a position to shut them down."

"I don't see the connection," I said. "Bibianna isn't part of the ring, is she?"

"She was. Raymond Maldonado started out as a 'capper.' At this point, we believe he's one of the kingpins, but we can't prove it yet. You know how these rings operate?"

"Not really," I said. "The people I'm used to dealing with are strictly amateurs."

"Well, the methods probably overlap to some extent," he said. "These days, the pros tend to avoid the big kill in favor of submitting fairly innocuous small claims that can be converted into large sums of money. They collect compensation for hard-to-disprove injuries like whiplash and lower back pain . . . you know the MO on that." He didn't really seem to require a response. "It's the capper's job to recruit the owner of a vehicle, usually someone unemployed who's hard up for cash. They take out an assigned-risk insurance policy on the car through the ring's agent. The capper then gives the car owner the names of two 'passengers'—totally fictitious—who 'ride' with the owner. He also comes up with names of people allegedly in the second car. We're talking about six or seven claims per incident. There's a variation on that one called 'bulls and cows,' where both cars are part of the scam. The 'bull'— the car with insurance—rams into the 'cow,' which is the uninsured car filled with passengers, all of whom suffer fictitious injuries. Most of the time the insured vehicle is some junker that's been insured without being examined."

"I've handled some claims where it's all faked—where there's not even a staged accident," I said.

"Oh, we got those, too. In Maldonado's case, some are paper accidents and some are staged. We got a line on this ring in the first place because the same set of names kept cropping up on supposedly unrelated claims. Same insurance agent, same attorney. The investigator finally had the names run through the computer and found links to twenty-five previous cases. Most of those were fictitious. One claimant's address turned out to be the La Brea Tar Pits. Another was an abandoned bus depot."

"What's their setup?" I asked.

"The ploy is called a 'swoop and squat,' which requires the use of two cars. They pull this maneuver out on one of the surface roads, probably five or six times a week. . . ."

"I'm surprised they don't try the freeways," I remarked.

He shook his head. "Too dangerous. These guys aren't interested in getting killed. What they do is choose a 'mark'—usually someone in an expensive vehicle or a commercial van—anything with a likelihood of being well insured. A vehicle they call the 'squat' car positions itself in front of the mark. These drivers are tooling down the road at thirty-five miles an hour, everybody minding his own business. At a signal, a second car, called a 'swoop,' cuts in front of the squat car, which brakes sharply, forcing the mark to rear-end it. The swoop car takes off. The squat and the mark pull over to the side like good citizens and exchange license numbers. At this point, the mark is usually pretty upset. Here, he's rear-ended another vehicle and he knows the responsibility is his. The driver in the squat car is full of sympathy—hell, he can afford to be—confirming just what the mark wants to believe, that it wasn't his fault."

"But his insurance company pays anyway," I said.

"Has to. You rear-end somebody, you're liable in this state. Turns out the squat's got all these 'problems' resulting from the accident. He sees a lawyer, who tells him he better see a doctor. Or he might be referred to a chiropractor. . . ."

"All of them in cahoots. . . ."

"All in cahoots," Lieutenant Santos said.

"And Bibianna got involved in the ring through Raymond?"

"It looks that way. From the information we've pieced together, Raymond recruited her two years ago, though he's known her much longer. They were all set to get married about a year ago, but for some reason she pulled out. March, she did a disappearing act and a short time later surfaced in Santa Teresa. It looks, on the face of it, like she meant to go straight, but she had a hell of a time finding work. She finally picked up a job with a dry cleaning establishment, but it doesn't pay much, and in the end, I guess she couldn't resist trying a little scam or two of her own."

I was beginning to see how it all fit together. "And now my investigation has jeopardized yours."

"Not yet, but it looks like you're getting close. We can't afford to have you blundering in unawares, which is not the only problem we face. It looks like we've got a leak somewhere, critical information spilling through the pipeline into Raymond's ear. On at least three occasions, we've had raids set up . . . most recently on an auto body shop he owns in El Segundo. We have arrest and search warrants up the yin-yang. By the time we get there, the whole operation's been shut down and we walk into an empty facility—nothing left on the premises but a tire iron and a Pepsi can."

"I don't get it. What are you looking for?"

Lieutenant Santos paused to clear his throat. "Files, records. You follow the paper and it leads right to Raymond. We can pick him up, but by then the evidence has either been moved or destroyed and the DA throws the case out."

"So it was all for nothing, this raid you talked about?"

"Not quite. We took out the guy at the top, plus half a dozen other players—couple of attorneys and some MD's, two chiropractors. Raymond just turned around and expanded his piece of the operation. He used the bust to move himself up into the slot we cleared for him. We're going after him again, of course, but we have to track down this snitch first or it's the same story all over. In the meantime, we're trying another angle we think might work. The problem is, since we don't know where the leak is, it's hard to know who we can trust."

Dolan stirred restlessly, speaking up for the first time

since Santos had started filling me in. "As much as I hate to say this, the breach might originate in one of the departments up here. We think that's how Raymond found out Bibianna was in Santa Teresa. She got arrested here a month ago and somebody dimed her out."

I could feel a quick spark of recollection. "Oh, yeah. I remember now she mentioned that. She's worried sick about Raymond finding her."

"She's got reason to worry. The man's got serious problems," Santos remarked. "I've seen the results of some of his handiwork."

"I still don't quite understand why you're telling me this stuff."

There was a brief silence and then Dolan spoke up. "If we can move you into position with these people, we might have another shot at them."

I stared at him blankly. "Oh, come on. You're not serious."

I looked from one to the other, but neither of them said a word. "How do you propose to do that?"

Dolan smiled with no particular mirth. "You've already done the hard part. You've established a relationship with Bibianna, which is something we can't do."

"What good is that? I thought you said she was finished with Raymond."

Dolan shrugged. "But he's not done with her. If Dawna managed to get word through to him, he's probably on his way up. Just stick with Bibianna, especially if he wants to take her back to L.A. with him. We want you on the inside."

"Wait a minute. I ran into Dawna over at the CF offices. What if she remembers me?"

"Don't worry about Dawna. We'll keep her out of circulation."

I ran a hand through my hair, which was so tricked out with hairspray, it felt like a wig. "Oh, man, you guys are really nuts," I said. "I don't know beans about undercover work."

"We're not asking you to go in there cold. . . ."

"Oh, that really sets my mind at rest."

He ignored that. "You'd be thoroughly briefed. We'd have backup in place, somebody who'd know where you were at all times."

I found myself looking from one to the other. I didn't trust them. I kept thinking there was a missing piece in here somewhere, something they were holding back. "Somehow I'm assuming you've tried it before."

"Without much luck," Santos said. "In this situation, we think a female could be effective. These guys don't credit women with much intelligence. You'd have some protective coloring despite the fact that you're not Hispanic yourself. Are you interested?"

"No."

Dolan put a hand behind his ear as if he hadn't heard right.

"I'm not going to do it, Lieutenant Dolan. It's been ten years since I was a police officer, and even then, I never did undercover work. Forget it. I'm not trained for that stuff and it's too damn dangerous."

"Sometimes it's the only option," Santos said.

"It might be your only option, but it's not mine."

Santos broke off eye contact. "You're looking at a year

of county jail time on this battery. Assaulting a police officer is a felony. We can have your license pulled."

I stared at him. "So now you're going to threaten me? Oh, great. I love that. Well, guess what? I'm not going to do your dirty work. I don't give a shit about Raymond Maldonado." I could feel the heat flash through my frame. "I hate to be bullied and I don't relish being beaten with a stick as the motivation for my behavior. You want a performance out of me, you better start someplace else."

Santos apparently intended to pursue the point, but Dolan made an impatient gesture, silencing him. "Let's just discuss it before you say anything."

"The answer's no."

Again, the two men exchanged a look I couldn't quite read. It seemed clear they were working every angle in the book, which was laughable in my view because I wasn't going to yield.

Dolan sat forward in his chair and his voice dropped a notch. "One more thing you should know and then you can do anything you want. Your friend Parnell Perkins was one of Raymond's employees. We think Raymond killed him, but we don't have any proof."

"I don't believe it."

"Perkins's real name was Darryl Weaver. He was working for an insurance company down in Compton. Raymond was running all his claims through Weaver until the two had a falling-out. Weaver left Los Angeles and moved up here, changed his name, and went to work for California Fidelity."

Suddenly I understood why he'd passed Bibianna's file

on to Mary Bellflower. He probably assumed that Raymond and Bibianna were back together, that Raymond would be on his trail if he didn't do something quick. The sight of Bibianna's name must have made his heart stop. . . .

Santos came to life again, taking up the thread. "He came to us about a month ago and offered to cooperate. After he was killed, Santa Teresa Police Department ran the prints and notified us, which is why I'm here."

"That's why you buried the homicide investigation," I said, "to protect the larger one."

"That's right," Dolan replied. "We can't afford to have Raymond find out what we're up to. We haven't dropped the investigation, we're just pursuing it quietly."

The room was suddenly still. They let the silence accumulate. I took my time, stalling long enough to consider the implications. A little voice inside sang, Don't do it. Don't do it. "What's the timetable?" I said cautiously. I was hooked and they knew it.

Dolan looked at Santos. "Tight. Half a day at best."

"What are you really asking me to do?"

"Three things. Find the leak. Find out where the files are, and find us proof that Raymond killed your buddy."

Santos chimed in again, the two of them working me like sheepdogs. "You just tell us what you need. We'll give you anything you want."

Dolan said, "The object is to get yourself recruited. You can take it from there, with or without Bibianna's cooperation."

I thought it over briefly, all the time wondering at the wisdom of my consenting. I could feel my mental processes kick in despite the lingering misgivings. "If you're talking about staged accidents . . . it seems like it'd be smart to have a dummy policy in the name of Hannah Moore."

"Could you arrange that through CF?" Dolan asked.

"I could, but it'd be better if it came from you. You'd have to clear it with Mac Voorhies and it'd probably still have to go through channels."

"The fewer people who know the better, and we have to work fast," Dolan said.

"Is that going to present a problem?" Santos asked me.

I said, "I think CF would be willing to cooperate."

"We'll ask you to wear a wire," Santos said. "We can get a tech here by nine this morning and get a unit on you then."

"Won't Raymond and his cronies search me?"

Santos said, "I doubt it, but if they do, we'll be in earshot, don't forget."

Dolan seemed to sense I wasn't comforted. "If you're wired, we can have a car full of plainclothes parked half a block away. We want you to have all the protection you can get. This may be the best opportunity we have to get at these folks and we don't want to blow it. Any questions?"

"I'm sure I'll think of some."

Santos said, "We'll have another chance to brief you. Right now, we're going to put you back in with Bibianna. Morning comes, we'll get the two of you bailed out. Take the credit yourself. It's good to have the woman in your debt. We'll delay your release until the wire tech comes in."

"Won't she be suspicious if she's out and I'm not?"

"I'm sure you'll find a way to cover," Dolan said dryly. "In the meantime, make arrangements to connect with her later in the day."

"What if Raymond shows up before then?"

"We'll think of something else. Oh, and while we're on the subject . . ." Dolan jotted down a special telephone number where he could be reached at any hour. I tucked the slip of paper in my sock. He glanced at his watch and then got up as a signal to end the meeting.

I got to my feet. Santos and I shook hands. "What time is it?" I asked.

"Two minutes after four."

"I'm too old to be up at this hour," I said, and then glanced at Dolan. "Can you do me a favor? I left my black leather jacket in the restaurant and my VW's still parked in the Meat Locker side lot. I probably can't get over there until this afternoon. Could you ask about the jacket and warn the meter maid? I don't want to get towed or ticketed."

"Will do. You don't want to screw around with those meter gals," Dolan said. He flashed a smile and then held out his hand to me. "Thanks."

"I haven't done anything yet."

The female corrections officer took me back to the drunk tank and locked me in. I felt nearly sick with fatigue, my brain buzzing from the coffee, body dragging from the lack of sleep. I moved over to my mattress and sank down gratefully, curling up on my side with my face turned toward the others. Bibianna was awake, her eyes pinned on me suspiciously. "Where have you been?"

"The homicide detective had some questions about the shooting."

"Has Dawna been picked up?"

"She's in the hospital at the moment with superficial injuries. Tate's here on the men's side. They're talking about charging him with murder, but I don't see how they can. Manslaughter's more like it."

"Bastards."

"He'll survive."

"Yeah, I suppose." Bibianna seemed on the verge of drifting back to sleep.

I hesitated briefly, then held my nose and plunged right in. "By the way, while I was out there I put a call through to my bail bondsman, who's posting bail for both of us. He'll be over here at eight."

Her eyes flew open. "You're bailing me out, too? Why would you do that? I don't have no kind of money like that. You're talkin' five hundred bucks!"

"So you can owe me. Don't sweat it."

Her look was puzzled. "But why now? How come you didn't do that in the first place?"

"I just remembered I had money in a savings account. My car's in the shop. I was saving to get the tranny fixed. What the hell. Let it sit. It's not doing me any good here."

She hadn't bought my story yet. "I can't believe you'd do that."

The skinny woman piped up from the mattress in an aggravated tone of voice. "What's the matter with you, crazy? Take the money and shut your mouth."

Bibianna flicked a look at the woman and smiled in spite of herself. She studied me for a moment and then murmured a "Thank you." Her eyes closed again. She turned over on her stomach and tucked her arms under her for warmth. Within minutes, she'd dozed off.

The air in the cell was permeated with the scent of sleeping bodies: damp socks, stale breath, unwashed hair.

I had thought my cellmates might waken with my return, but no one else stirred. The light in the corridor shone dimly. The quiet became absolute. On the floor, I could still see the numerology grid Bibianna'd drawn for me with spit. Movement and change. Well, now wasn't that the truth?

11

What happened next was the result of a bureaucratic error for which responsibility was never assigned. The paperwork came down at six and Bibianna and I were mustered out. Just like that. There was no word from Dolan and Santos, no sign of the tech who was supposed to fit me with a wire. I kept waiting for the jail officer to call me back, take me aside under some pretext or other for the promised briefing. What was the deal here? Had there been a change of plans? For the life of me, I couldn't think of a reason to delay my release. I'd just have to play the situation as it came to me. I was carrying my personal property, still sealed in the clear plastic pouch. They'd returned our shoes, belts, and other potentially death dealing items, like tampons. I was feeling vile, but the first breath of fresh air restored my good spirits to some extent. After a mere four hours in the slammer, the freedom had a giddiness attached to it.

The morning was cold and foggy, the ground still saturated from the rain the night before. The scruffy hills around the jail looked serene. Little birdies sang. The passing traffic out on the freeway seemed to ebb and surge, rhythmic white noise, very restful, like the ocean at high tide. I longed for a shower, for breakfast, for privacy. I'd have to conjure up an excuse to separate from Bibianna, contact Dolan, and find out what the hell was going on. In the meantime, I was going to have to stick to her like glue.

The first order of business, of course, was to find a ride home. I checked my plastic pouch, feeling like a mental patient just released from the institution. I had ten bucks in cash, which I decided to blow on a taxi. I'm too cheap for cabs as a rule, but I really felt I deserved this one. Bibianna and I clopped down the long drive that led away from the jail. I was a sight to behold, tank top and wrinkled black pants, my little white socks turning black where the dye on my wet pumps had rubbed off. Bibianna wasn't looking all that hot herself. The red of her dress was unflattering by day, a mismatch for the spike heels, which the rain had pulled out of shape. She was applying a fresh coat of lipstick, open compact held in front of her face as she walked. She'd stripped off her panty hose, which had been riddled with runs after our adventures of the night before. Her legs looked pale and scrawny in the harsh light of day, and her dress was as pleated across the lap as the bellows of an accordion. Oh, well. I suppose there are times when you rejoice just to find yourself on the move again. Behind us were the chain-link fences, incessant lights, the locks, the barred windows. In spite of our liberation, I couldn't think of a thing to say to her. "Thanks . . . it's been fun . . . we'll have to do this again sometime soon." The simple rules of etiquette didn't seem to apply.

Bibianna tucked her compact in her purse, her manner anxious.

"Did they ask you about the shooting?" I asked.

"Not yet. Some homicide cop is supposed to come around to my place later today."

"What are you going to tell them?"

"Who cares about that? I gotta find a way to get outta here before Raymond shows up. . . ."

I felt an anxiety of my own. What the hell was going on here? Where was Dolan? What was I supposed to do?

Suddenly, Bibianna clutched my arm, digging her nails into my flesh. "Sweet Jesus," she whispered, staring dead ahead.

I followed her gaze, realizing belatedly that her attention was riveted on a dark green Ford that was parked down the road, its rear end lowered until the pan nearly scraped the ground. Her fear was so palpable that the hair rose up on the back of my neck.

"Who's that?"

"It's Raymond. Oh, God." Her voice broke. Tears leapt to her eyes and she made a peculiar squeaking sound in her throat. I assessed the situation rapidly, without knowing quite what to do. Of all the bad luck. Apparently, Dawna had managed to put a call through to him.

He'd been leaning on the front fender, watching cars pass on the frontage road. When he caught sight of us, he began to amble in our direction.

"Bibianna, cool it. Just calm down. Let's head back to the jail. . . ."

She shook her head. "Even if the cops took us home, he'd catch up eventually. Don't leave me. Swear you won't. Whatever happens, just go along with it. Don't set him off or he'll tear the place apart and you along with it."

"All right, all right. Come on now. Just be cool. I'm not going anywhere."

"Promise you won't leave me."

"I promise," I said.

At first, I didn't get it. At that distance, the guy looked like anybody else. He was tall and very slender, with wide shoulders and a narrow waist. From what I could see of him, he was dressed like a fashion plate: leather sport coat, pleated trousers, pointy black patent-leather shoes capped with silver at the toes, mirrored sunglasses. He could have been Latino or Italian, dark hair and olive skin. I placed him in his early thirties. He had his hands in his pockets and his manner seemed relaxed.

Bibianna's fingers were ice cold. She clung to my hand the way a friend might in the middle of a horror movie just before the guy with the butcher knife leaps out. I couldn't see anything in his appearance that would warrant her response.

When he reached us, he took his sunglasses off. He had dark thick lashes, a full mouth, a dimple in his chin. Once he was in close range, I realized there was something wrong. His eyes had rolled back in his head, leaving narrow slits of white along the lower rims. His face and body underwent a series of convulsive movements; he blinked his eyes, the corner of his mouth jumped involuntarily, his lips opened wide, then his head jerked back twice. The effect was weird—a sequence of behaviors that set his whole body in motion, culminating in a sound that was half shout, half cough. He moved his right arm, rolling it in its socket as if to loosen tension. In memory, a buzzer sounded dimly, and I recalled the existence of some medical condition that produced just this effect—tics and shouts. He made no reference to it, nor did Bibianna, who seemed more concerned about his reaction to Chago's death.

"I didn't do it. I swear to God. I didn't kill him. I'm sorry. It was an accident. Oh, please. Raymond, I didn't have anything to do with it. . . ."

His expression had softened, becoming nearly wistful as he took her by the shoulders and pulled her in close to him, rubbing his hands up and down her bare arms. "You don't know how happy I am to see you. . . ."

I could see her tense up, holding herself away from him slightly, though she couldn't do much without perhaps risking some kind of outburst. He began to nuzzle her hair. "Oh, baby. Angel. Sweet thing, I'm glad to see you," he murmured, his voice soft. "This is beautiful. I really missed you, you know that?" He drew back from her then, clamping his fingers around her jaw so that she was forced to look at him. "Hey, it's all right. Everything's okay. Don't worry." His gaze moved across to me. "Who is this?" His head jerked twice.

"Hannah Moore," I said.

She flicked a look at him. "This is Raymond Maldonado."

He held his hand out. "Nice to meet you. Sorry about all this. My brother was killed last night."

We shook hands. His were warm and soft, his grip firm.

"I'm sorry about your brother. That's terrible." The pleasantries created an air of unreality.

Raymond glanced at Bibianna. "You ready?"

"I'm not going. Raymond, I mean it. I'm done with all that. I don't want to go back to Los Angeles. I told you. I didn't have anything to do with . . ." He took her arm and began to walk her toward the car. I could see her mouth twist and his fingers dug into her elbow painfully. She babbled on. He raised a hand as if to silence her, warding off the spill of words. She pressed a hand to her lips. He turned his head to one side. He hunched a shoulder, did a neck roll, and took a deep breath, eyes sliding up in his head. His face jerked to the right, once, twice. His eyes came open, the irises sliding into view—large, dark brown, and clear. He continued toward the car.

I followed without invitation, calculating rapidly. Here was my quarry, Raymond Maldonado in the flesh. I knew I was being offered the perfect opportunity, but I'd had no prep time. If I went in without a briefing, I could blow the whole operation. I couldn't afford to start playing under-cover cop, but what choice did I have? He was walking so rapidly, I had to do a quickstep to keep up.

Bibianna was getting into passive resistance, slowing down, hanging back. "Listen, Raymond. Maybe I could go another time, okay? Hannah's been talking about going home with me," she said. "And we do have plans. . . ."

He turned and smiled at me. "We're getting married."

"Today?"

He shook his head. "Soon, though. It was all set up, but she said she wasn't ready. Next thing I know she takes off.

Just like that, she's gone. Doesn't even leave me a note. I wake up one morning and she's disappeared. . . ."

Bibianna's face was drawn and pale. "I'm sorry. I didn't mean to hurt you, Raymond, but what could I do? What was I going to say to you? I tried to tell you. . . ."

He raised a finger to his lips and then he pointed it at her reprovingly. "You don't leave a guy, Bibianna." He turned to me, one hand out, palm up, arguing his case. "I've been in love with this woman for how many years now? Six? Eight? What am I going to do with her, huh?"

Bibianna was silent, her eyes full of dread. I couldn't believe the change that had come over her. All the confidence was gone, the high energy, the sexiness. My own mouth was getting dry, and a whisper of fear tickled me in the small of the back.

We reached the car. Another fellow stepped out, a Latino with a dark knit watch cap pulled down to his ears. His eyes were black, as flat and dull as spots of old paint. He had acne scars on his cheeks and a mustache made up of about fourteen hairs, some of which looked like they were drawn on by hand. He was my size. He wore sharply pressed khaki pants with numerous pleats across the front and an immaculate white undershirt. Tufts of underarm hair were visible, straight and dark. His bare arms were muscular, tattoos extending from his shoulders to his wrists—a graphic rendition of Donald Duck on his right and Daffy Duck on his left.

"That's a copyright violation," I remarked, nearly giddy with anxiety.

"That's Luis," Raymond said.

He had a gun. He held the rear car door open, like a well-mannered chauffeur.

Bibianna balked, one arm braced against the car. "I'm not going without Hannah."

Raymond seemed taken aback. "Why not?"

"She's my friend and I want her with me," she said.

"I don't even know this girl," he said.

Bibianna's eyes flashed. "Goddamn it! This is just like you, Raymond. You say you love me. You say you'll do anything. First thing I ask for, all I get is an argument. Well, I'm sick of it!"

"Okay, okay. She can go if she wants. Anything you say."

Bibianna turned to me with a look filled with mute pleading. "Please. Just for a few days."

I felt myself shrug. "I got nothing else to do," I said.

Bibianna got in first, sliding across the backseat. Raymond slid in beside her. I hesitated briefly, wondering at the wisdom of it.

Luis turned the gun so that it was pointing at my chest. It clarified my thinking most emphatically.

I got into the backseat. The dashboard was covered in white terrycloth with "Raymond and Bibianna" machine-stitched in glossy green script across the face of it. A rosary hung from the rearview mirror along with a Sacred Heart of Jesus, bleeding. The interior of the car, including front and back seats, was upholstered in white acrylic teddy bear fur. There was a Radio Shack car phone on the front seat. All the car lacked was a collection of bobbleheads on the rear . . . or a four-inch Virgin Mary with little magnetized feet. The minute I got in, I knew I'd made a mistake.

Luis started the engine without a word. The mufflers sounded like distant jackhammers as he pulled out onto the road. He kept both hands on the steering wheel with his arms fully extended, his trunk and head inclined back. He made a U-turn and sped toward the freeway. Raymond's ticcing recurred at perhaps three-minute intervals, sometimes less. I found myself unnerved at first, especially in the absence of any explanation. The others seemed to take it for granted. At first, I would jump every time he did it, but I found myself adjusting, marveling that anybody had to live like that. Was there no help for him?

Bibianna now seemed to be in the mood for an argument, maybe to forestall any amorous intentions. "How'd you find out about last night?"

"Dawna called and told me some of it before the cops picked her up. Who's the guy?"

"What guy?"

"The guy last night shot Chago."

"How do I know who he was? Just somebody in the restaurant with a gun."

"Dawna said you were with him."

"I was there by myself."

"Not what she says."

"She said that? It's bullshit. What'd he look like? She tell you that?"

"She didn't have a chance. Squad car pulled up and she hung up. Said some chick was there, too."

"She's blowin' smoke up your skirt. What a bitch! I was there by myself when Chago showed up with a gun. Maybe the guy was an off-duty cop or just your average citizen with a gun."

Raymond's face darkened. "That would really piss me off. What's the matter with people? Too many fuckin' handguns around." He turned and looked at me. "Every day in the paper, somebody gets blown away. *L.A. Times*. You read Metro? Scares the shit out of me." He held a hand up, blocking words in. "You know that slogan says, 'Guns don't kill people. People kill people.'? What a crock that is."

"Luis has a gun," I remarked helpfully.

"That's different. He's a lieutenant. He's like a bodyguard to me. I can't believe some joker in a restaurant shoots my brother for no fuckin' reason."

All the little birdies had flown out of this man's tree. I sat with my eyes straight ahead and my mouth shut, remembering what Bibianna had told me about his temper.

Raymond turned to Bibianna and started kissing her, his hands moving across her breasts with an intimacy I found embarrassing. She was compliant, but she rolled an eye at me frantically across his shoulder. I looked out the window.

I leaned forward and tapped Luis on the shoulder, trying the only Spanish phrase I'm familiar with. "Uh, *habla usted inglés?*"

"Shit, lady. What do I look like, a retard?" he said. His English wasn't even spoken with an accent, and I had to wonder if the gangbanger outfit was an affectation.

"Oh. Well, could you pull over at this next corner and let me the fuck out? I gotta make a quick phone call."

This did not produce the desired results.

I kept my tone conversational as I turned to Raymond, placing my mouth up close to his ear. "Excuse me, Raymond. Could you have the guy let me out up here?"

Raymond had run his hand up under Bibianna's skirt,

pushing the fabric back, running a finger under the rim of her underpants. There was nothing remotely sexual about it. He was claiming his rights. I could hear her murmuring, "Fantastic . . . oh, baby, that's great," anything to appease and placate his neediness. The driver caught my eye in the rearview mirror and winked at me conspiratorially. He flipped on the car radio to mask the escalating sounds. Salsa music filled the car. This was repellent.

I was fully prepared to fling myself out, risking concussion and broken bones, just to escape from this brothel of faux fur and religious artifacts. I waited until the car slowed as we approached the on ramp to the freeway, then I slid my hand under the door handle and gave it a yank. Nothing happened. Both of the window cranks had been removed in the rear. I leaned my forehead against the tinted glass, staring out the window. Behind me, I could hear Raymond fumble with his belt buckle and the zipper to his pants. This was worse than an X-rated video. I turned and stared at them.

"God, *Bibianna*," I said loudly. "How *rude*! How do you think I *feel* sitting here while you *screw* some stud! Why don't you keep your hands to yourself, okay?"

Raymond turned a sex-groggy face toward me, his eyes at half-mast. His mouth seemed gorged, his chin laved in lipstick, his hair standing straight up. The whole car smelled like hormones, sex juice, and underpants. Luis, all asmirk, tried to peer into the backseat through the rearview mirror.

I turned on him savagely. "Hey, Jack. What are *you* lookin' at?" And then to Raymond. "I'm sorry, Raymond. I know it's not your fault how these people act."

Bibianna pushed herself into an upright position, doing what she could to pull her skirt back into place. She murmured, "Sorry." She had a big hickey on her neck where Raymond had been slurping away on her.

Raymond actually seemed embarrassed, tucking in his shirt. He went through a sequence of behaviors that included the head jerking and the neck rolls.

I plowed right on. "I told her I got a steady boyfriend in the slammer," I said to him. "The last thing I need is watching you two get it on. God. She's got no class." I sat back in the seat, brushing imaginary lint off my black pants.

Raymond pulled out a handkerchief and wiped some of Bibianna's lipstick off his chin. His smile was sheepish. "Take it easy. It's not her fault. She can't help it," he said.

"Well, I get sick of hearing her brag about you. Why can't she keep her opinions to herself?"

"She brags about me?"

"No, Raymond. I'm just saying that to hear myself talk," I said. "I don't suppose I could trouble anybody for some grub. We haven't had breakfast and I'm starving to death."

Raymond leaned forward and gave Luis a thump on the head. "What's the matter with you? Pull off here. Didn't you hear what the lady said?"

Raymond studied me with amusement, talking to Bibianna over his shoulder. "I like your friend, here. She's got some spunk."

"This isn't *spunk,* Raymond. This is irritation," I said. Bibianna eyed me uneasily, but I was really on a roll. I was making up Hannah's character as I went along, and it was liberating as hell. She was short-tempered, sarcastic, out-spoken, and crude. I could get used to this. License to misbehave.

Raymond smiled at me.

"This okay, boss?" Luis, of the handsomely tattooed arms, was slowing near the entrance to a McDonald's on upper State Street.

"This okay with you?" Raymond said to me. He seemed genuinely concerned that the restaurant meet with my approval.

"Raymond, this is perfect. Way to go."

I ate three Egg McMuffins. If it had been 10:00 A.M., I'd have had a couple of QP's with cheese instead. Bibianna couldn't eat. She sat and picked at an apple Danish while Luis and Raymond, with a flair for the Gallic, ordered French toast and French fries, with a side of maple syrup. I had spotted a telephone in the narrow corridor leading to the ladies' room, but the wall-mounted instrument was in plain view of the table where the four of us sat. Raymond kept his arm loosely draped around Bibianna's shoulders, rubbing her upper arm in a manner meant to be sexy. Guys learn to do that in high school and it's very irritating. She was back to being passive, obsequious, and subdued. I wanted to see her sass him. Resist. I wanted her to thumb her nose at him. It was not going to help her to act like a whipped dog. It was time she stood up for herself again. If she acted like a victim, the guy was going to treat her like one.

I got up from the table. "I gotta go to the can. Come with me, Bibianna. You can rat my hair."

"I'm fine."

"Well, I'm not. Could you pardon us, Raymond? We have to go do some girl stuff."

"Have at it," he said.

I kissed my fingertip and placed it on the tip of his nose. "You're a peach."

He slid out of the booth so Bibianna could get up.

12

In the ladies' room, she turned on the faucet and splashed some cold water in her eyes. I pulled out a paper towel and passed it to her. She buried the lower half of her face in the paper toweling, staring at herself in the mirror above the sink. She wiped her hands and threw the paper away. "Thanks for what you did in the car. God, I can't stand this. I really hate his guts."

"He's certainly crazy about you," I said.

She moved into one of the stalls, trying the window above the toilet. "Shit. This is nailed shut. Do you think there's another way out of here?"

"I don't know. I'll check," I said. I was in a bit of a bind with Bibianna, wanting to help her without actually giving up proximity to Raymond Maldonado. I went over to the door and opened it a crack, making a show of searching for a rear exit. All I caught sight of was Raymond doing one of his head jerks. The public pay phone on the wall was tantalizingly near, but Luis was bound to spot me if

I tried to use it. I closed the door again. "What's the matter with Raymond?"

"He's getting worse," she said morosely. "I never saw him so bad."

"Yeah, but what *causes* that?"

"It's called Tourette. TS, whatever that is. It's like something in his nervous system—neurological and like that. All I know is he does that stuff over and over and sometimes he gets into uncontrollable rages. He's got pills he won't take because he can't stand the side effects."

"He's had it all his life?"

"I guess so. He doesn't ever talk about it much."

"But he's not doing anything for it?"

"Smokin' dope helps, he says, and he sometimes shoots up."

"Is that why you left, because of the Tourette?"

"I left because he's a jerk! The other I could live with, but the guy's turning mean. It's got nothing to do with his condition," she said. "Jesus, we gotta figure out how to get out of here." She moved into the second stall and tried the window there. Also locked. "The hell with it. We're going to have to make a break for it some other way. I wish Tate were here."

I said, "You and me both, kid. You think Raymond knows you're involved with him?"

"God, I hope not. He's so jealous, he can't see straight."

"How'd you meet Tate?"

"He crashed a costume party last Halloween. Dressed as a cop. Everybody thought it was a joke, except me. I can smell a cop a mile off." She took a brush from her handbag and ran it through her hair. "It's really different with Jimmy."

"Well, that's obvious," I said. "I take it you're in love with him."

She smiled fleetingly for the first time since we'd left the jail. "I better be. We got married week before last. That's why my place is coming up for rent. I'm moving in with him."

The door flew open. I must have jumped a foot. It was Luis with his .45 and his little smirking mustache. "All right, ladies. Time to go. Speed it up. Raymond says you been in here long enough."

I waved at him dismissively. "Oh, come off it, Luis. What is it with you? Running around acting like an idiot. I still have to tee-tee and so does she."

He colored faintly. "Snap it up."

"Right," I said, moving over to the first stall. Out of the corner of my eye, I saw him shove the gun in his waistband and back out of the room.

Ten minutes later we were on the road.

So that's how I came to be speeding down 101 in a low-rider Wednesday morning, October 26. Vera's wedding was coming up on Monday and I was going to miss it, sure as shit. If Raymond killed Bibianna, he was going to have to kill me, too. By Halloween, I'd probably be in the long-term parking lot at LAX, crammed in the trunk of some stranger's vehicle. Even in the hot sun, it can sometimes take days before anybody picks up the scent.

Luis drove while Raymond sat in the front seat fiddling with the radio. At irregular intervals, he would go through his ticcing sequence. If he was talking to Luis, the tics would seem to subside, only to assail him with a vengeance as soon as his mouth was shut. Bibianna had curled up on the backseat in a troubled sleep. At least now she wouldn't have to worry about being quizzed by the Santa Teresa cops. I was feeling wired. In the past couple of hours, I'd passed through fatigue to exhaustion and out to the other side. God knows my work exposes me to an occasional unsavory character, but I really don't like violence or danger or threats to my health. My semiannual visit to the dentist is as masochistic as I care to get. Yet here I was in the company of these *vatos,* wondering how I could get to the telephone number Dolan had given me. I missed my beloved handbag, my jacket, and my gun. At the same time, I confess, I felt extraordinarily alive. Perhaps I was merely experiencing one of life's peak moments before the bottom dropped out.

At Oxnard, we left the freeway and continued south on Highway 1, winding our way through the southeastern section of town. We passed the Naval Construction Battalion Center at Port Hueneme (pronounced "Y-knee-me"). The road began to parallel the deep blue green of the ocean, which was far off to our right. The beaches were deserted except for an occasional fisherman casting his line out into the water. The sand had been packed down and darkened by the rain, but the sky was now cloudless, a clear azure blue. The morning sun had burned the fog away, and I could see straight out to the horizon. On the landward side, loose sand swept down to the highway from rosy beige cliffs creased into folds by erosion, hills flattening out to pale gray scrub, freckled with vegetation.

After we passed Point Dume, houses began to appear, filling the widening strip of land between the road and the ocean, properties piling up rapidly as the miles accrued. In the parking lane, RVs and pickups were lined end to end. Guys in shorts and wet suits unloaded surfboards and windsails. By the time we reached Malibu, apartments and condos and single-family dwellings were crowded cheek by jowl, the architectural mix ranging all the way from chateaus to beach shacks, Italian villas, Tudor mansions, Cape Cod, and concrete. The rich folk with taste had apparently been elsewhere the day the planning commission took a vote. (What planning commission?) As a consequence, the road was densely lined now with retail businesses, signs advertising Texaco, Malibu Lumber, Crown Books, Shoes, Fast Frame, Jack-in-the-Box, Motel, Malibu Inn, Liquor, Jimmy's Ribs at the Beach, Budget Cars, Palm and Card Reading, Shell Gas, Realty, Arco AM/PM, Malibu Travel, Motel, Liquor, Pizza, Real Estate, Locksmith, Shoe Repair, Malibu Fish Market . . . a vulgar hodgepodge of neon, billboards, and blinking lights. Traffic was piled up in a perpetual gridlock of Mercedeses, BMWs, and Jaguars.

We hit the light where Sunset Boulevard dead-ends at Pacific Coast Highway. The woman in the little sports car idling next to us turned an uneasy eye on Luis with his watch cap and his Walt Disney arms. He had a truly vile suggestion he was kind enough to share with her. Raymond gave his head a censoring thump. Maybe that's why he wore the watch cap, to keep the brain damage to a minimum.

Luis rubbed his head irritably. "Hey, man. Take it easy."

"You take it easy," Raymond shot back with an apologetic glance at me. It was clear he'd pegged me as the refined one in the crowd.

When the light changed, Luis pulled out with a series of jerks that left the rear suspension bucking. Within minutes we had passed from prosperity to privation.

Our destination was a beach town a few miles south of the airport in an area tainted with poverty. To the east, the ghetto communities of Compton, South Gate, and Lynwood were rigidly subdivided into gang turfs where some fifteen to twenty homicides marred the average weekend. Here, there were only endless drab buildings decorated with angular territorial declarations thrown up by the taggers with cans of black spray paint. Wait until future cryptographers resurrect those stone tablets. Even the passing city buses were defaced, mobile messengers bearing insults from one gang to the next. The streets were littered with trash and old tires. The winos had already plucked up all the bottles and cans, anything that could be recycled in exchange for Thunderbird revenues. A dilapidated sofa sat on the curb as if waiting for a bus. Listless ghetto warriors loitered near a corner market. On the island side of the four-lane boulevard, every third storefront had been boarded up. Those still doing business were protected by steel bars across plate-glass windows papered over with advertisements.

I saw a Burger King, a Sav-On drugstore, a corner record shop with a big sign reading CLOSED, a post office branch with a U.S. flag drooping from its pole. On the ocean side of the street, there was a tired mix of small frame houses and boxy apartment buildings. All the yards seemed to be raw dirt surrounded by chain-link fences. The poor sections of every city I've seen have the following elements in common: sagging porches, flaking paint, grass that's tenacious if it grows at all, vacant lots filled with rubble, Pepsi-Cola signs, idle children, cars with flat tires permanently parked at the curb, abandoned houses, lethargic men whose eyes turn vacuously as you pass. Violence is a form of theater that only the disenfranchised can afford. Admission is cheap. The bill of fare is an ever-changing drama of life and death, drugs and stick-ups, drive-bys, retaliations, the fearfulness of mothers who look on in anguish from the sidelines. As often as not, it's the bystanders who fall prey to the spray of random bullets.

We cut inland, driving past six square blocks of housing projects. I could feel anxiety stir like a boiling sickness.

By the time we reached Raymond's place, I had no idea what part of Los Angeles we were in. We parked the Ford out in front of a three-story apartment building, across the street from an automobile salvage yard. There were probably forty units in the apartment complex, arranged in tiers around a concrete courtyard. At first glance, it didn't seem all that shabby to me. The neighborhood itself wasn't nearly as impoverished as some we'd traversed.

It was midmorning, and even with a nip still in the air, most of the apartment doors stood open. The interiors I glimpsed were crowded, overfurnished, and dismal. The televisions all seemed to be tuned to the Anglo soaps, while the radios, sitting atop the sets, played Hispanic music, curiously at odds with the gringo images. There were Halloween decorations everywhere, but some had been up so long, the pumpkins were getting soft and the crepe-paper skeletons were powdered with dust.

The four of us clambered up a rear staircase to the second floor, where we turned left, proceeding to an apartment that overlooked the street. "Is this your place we're going to?" I asked Raymond. He was walking with Bibianna, the two of them just ahead of me. Luis was bringing up the rear in case I tried to bolt.

"This is for when we get married," Raymond said with a shy glance at her. He felt in his pocket in a sudden recollection. He pulled out a key on a metal ring with a big plastic M attached, probably for Maldonado. He handed it to Bibianna. My guess was he'd meant it to be a ceremonial moment, but she shoved it in her handbag, barely honoring it with a look. Her face was stony and he seemed embarrassed that she showed no enthusiasm for matters that obviously obsessed him.

The problem with real life is there's no musical score. In movies, you know you're in danger because there's an ominous chord underlining the scene, a dissonant melodic line that warns of sharks in the water and boogeymen behind the door. Real life is dead quiet, so you're never quite sure if there's trouble coming up. A possible exception is stepping into a strange apartment full of guys in hairnets. Personally, I've never understood how wearing a hairnet ever came to symbolize the baddest of the bad-asses on the street. There were five of them, all Hispanics in their late teens or early twenties, all wearing heavy wool Pendleton shirts buttoned up to their chins. Three were sitting around the kitchen table, one with his girlfriend on his lap. A second girl sat with her bare legs outstretched, tight skirt hiked up to midthigh. She was smoking a cigarette, practicing smoke rings through pouty lips painted bright red. Two guys lounging against the wall came to attention as Raymond came in the door. On the wall was a large handmade sign with "R.I.P." at the top and Chago's name in caps below, a pair of praying hands and a crucifix drawn in the space between. Someone had tacked several snapshots of Chago on the wall nearby, along with what looked like a testimonial of some kind. Among the piles of papers on the table was a stack of homemade flyers, reproductions of the same neatly hand-lettered prose. From the somber expressions and the number of beer bottles evident, I gathered these were Chago's homies and that we'd interrupted an impromptu wake. I checked for Raymond's reaction, but he had none. Did he feel no sorrow for his brother's death?

I willed myself to behave casually, assuming an air of nonchalance. What did I have to fear? After all, I wasn't a prisoner, I was Raymond's guest. I could pick up the information for Lieutenant Dolan and then head on home. Granted, I don't usually hang out on gang turf, but I try to be open-minded. There were cultural differences here that I couldn't even guess at, let alone define. That didn't make anybody bad, right? So why expect the worst? *Because you don't know what the hell you're doing,* a little voice inside me said.

The air was gray with smoke, some of it marijuana, a substance I haven't abused since I was in high school (except for that brief period when Daniel Wade was in my life). The decor, at a glance, consisted of royal blue shag carpeting and the kind of furniture sold on the roadsides across the border in Mexico. (Also in Orange County on

Euclid, south of the Garden Grove Freeway.) It looked like Raymond had made an attempt to upgrade the place, covering the entire large wall to my left with smoky gold mirrored tiles. Unfortunately, the tiles had recently been smashed with a kitchen chair, which had been tossed to one side, its chrome legs askew. Most of the glass had been swept up, but I could see signs of blood on the bare wall behind. It wasn't bright red or dripping, but it was clear something frightful had taken place here not long ago. No one referred to the destruction. Raymond showed no curiosity at the sight, which lent support to the notion that he was responsible. Bibianna took it in at a glance but said nothing. Maybe she knew better than to mention the fact. I tore my gaze away.

On the right, the L of a kitchen was visible, every surface in it piled high with used paper plates, beer bottles, ashtrays, empty cans of Rosarito refrieds. The air smelled of cilantro, corn tortillas, and hot lard. Five brown grocery sacks bulged with refuse, grease showing through in big dark polka dots. On one bag, a quicksilver something disappeared from view.

One of the guys at the metal-topped kitchen table labored over a form he was filling out in pencil. His face was dark with frustration. His handgun rested casually on a stack of completed forms, serving as a paperweight. Fleetingly, I wondered if he was an illegal alien filling out fake INS documents. Behind him, daylight poured through a big picture window that cast him in silhouette. In the event of a drive-by, he'd be picked off like a metal bear in a shooting gallery. I heard Raymond call him Tomas, but I couldn't catch the rest of the conversation.

Of the two fellows leaning against the wall, one was wearing a Sony Walkman, a handgun shoved down in his waistband. The other played a hollow note across the mouth of an empty Dos Equis beer bottle. Both bore a passing resemblance to Raymond, and I wondered if they were related—his brothers or cousins. Apparently they all knew Bibianna, but none made eye contact. The two women seemed uneasy at her arrival, exchanging a guarded look.

I wasn't introduced, but my presence generated a sly interest. I was surveyed by several pairs of male eyes, and somebody made a remark that amused those who heard it. Luis appeared again, a Dos Equis in hand. He took up a squatting position, hunkering against the wall, body thrust forward slightly, his head thrown back, staring down his nose at me. There was something arrogant in his bearing, suggesting the sexual superiority of renegades and outlaws. Whatever his purpose, its effect was to establish his claim on me. The other guys seemed to posture for one another but displayed no plumage.

At the table, an argument broke out among the three who seemed to be speaking some cholo mix of Spanish and fractured English. I couldn't understand a word, but the prevailing tone was quarrelsome. Raymond shouted something I was glad I couldn't translate. The guy with the pencil and paper went back to work with a sulkiness that didn't bode well.

Bibianna, unimpressed with the lot of them, flung her purse in a chair and slipped out of her high-heeled shoes. "I'm taking a shower," she said, and padded out of the room. Raymond moved to the telephone, where he punched in numbers with his back half-turned. "Alfredo, it's me. . . ." He dropped his voice into a range I couldn't hear. From the rear, as he talked, I saw him go through a series of rapid tics, almost like a pantomime or a game of charades.

I thought I'd make myself inconspicuous while I decided what to do next. I looked around for a seat and changed my mind abruptly. Just inside the door, about three feet away, there was a pit bull. I don't know how I'd missed the mutt, but there he was. The dog had a brindle coat with a white chest and white legs. His head was wide and thick, ears uncropped, but tucked in close like a bat's. There was a leather collar around his thick neck with metal spikes sticking out. Was the blood on the wall connected with the dog? A length of slack chain was attached to his collar, extending about three feet, the other end wrapped around the leg of the oversize royal blue couch. The dog emitted a low humming growl while it stared at my throat. Dogs and I don't get along that well in the best of circumstances. I'm hardly ever smitten with a beast that looks like it's prepared to rip out my carotid artery.

One of the guys snapped at the dog in Spanish, but the animal didn't seem to understand the language any better than I did. The guy jerked his head in my direction, the knot of his hairnet sitting in the middle of his forehead like a spider in a web. "Don't make no sudden moves and don't never touch his head. He'll tear your arm off."

"I'm sorry to hear that. What's his name?" I asked, praying it wasn't Cujo.

"Perro," he said. And then with a grin, "Means 'dog' in Spanish."

"You think that up all by yourself?" I said mildly.

Everybody laughed. Ah, they do speak English, I thought.

His smile was thin. "He hates gringas."

I glanced at the dog again and shifted my weight, trying to ease away. How could the dog know my nationality? He flattened his ears and exposed his teeth. His upper lip curled back so far, I could see up his nose.

"Hello, Perro," I sang. "Nice dog. Good doggie." Slowly, I allowed my gaze to drift, thinking the eye contact was perhaps too aggressive for the little fellow's taste. Wrong move. The dog lunged, erupting into a savage barking that shook his entire body. I shrieked involuntarily, which the guys seemed to think was hilarious. The couch humped about four inches in my direction, bringing him almost in range of me. I could actually feel the hot breath of his bark against my leg like little puffs of wind. "Uh, Raymond?"

Raymond, still talking on the phone, held a hand up, impatient at the interruption.

"Could somebody call the dog, please?" I repeated the request, this time audibly.

Raymond snapped his fingers and the dog sat down. The guy with the Sony Walkman smirked at my relief. Raymond put a hand across the mouth of the receiver and jerked his head in the guy's direction. "Juan. Take the dog out." And then to me, "You like a beer? Help yourself. Soon as Bibianna's done, you can shower if you want." He returned his attention to the phone. I didn't move.

Grudgingly, Juan removed the handgun from his waistband and laid it on the table. He picked up a chain leash from the arm of the couch and attached it to Perro's collar.

The dog made a quick snapping feint at his hand. Juan pulled his fist back and for a minute the two locked eyes. Juan must have been alpha male because Perro backed down, reinforcing my contention that dogs aren't that smart. A drop of sweat began a lazy trickle down the small of my back.

Once the dog had been removed, I helped myself to a beer and then took a seat in a wide-armed upholstered chair on the far side of the room. I pulled my feet up under me just in case there were vermin cruising at floor level. For now, there was nothing to do except sip my beer. I laid my head against the chair back. The false high I'd experienced in the car had now drained away, replaced by a thundering weariness. I felt heavy with fatigue, as if tension had generated a sudden weight gain.

13

I must have dozed off because the next thing I knew, someone had removed the half-empty beer bottle from my hand and was giving my arm a gentle shake. I woke with a start, turning to stare at the woman blankly, trying to reorient myself. Oh, yeah. Bibianna. I was still caught up in the aftermath of the shoot-out between Chago and Jimmy Tate. Luis and Raymond were still in the apartment, but the others had gone.

Bibianna was looking better, some of the old confidence in evidence. She was wearing a thick white terrycloth robe, her hair wrapped in a towel. She smelled of soap. Her face had been scrubbed, shining now with the wholesome look of youth. She went into the kitchen and fetched herself a beer. Raymond, still on the phone, followed her with his eyes. I felt a surge of pity. He was a good-looking man, but his longing was unabashed and gave him a hangdog appearance. Now that Bibianna's cockiness had resurfaced, his uncertainty had surfaced, too. He seemed needy and insecure, qualities most women don't find that appealing. The macho swagger I'd seen earlier had been undercut by pain. He must have known she didn't give a rat's ass about him. The power had shifted, lodging now with her where it had once lodged with him.

"Come on. I got some clothes you can borrow," she said.

"I'd kill for a toothbrush," I murmured as we moved toward the bedroom.

She stopped, glancing back at Luis, who was now perched up on the kitchen counter. "Run over to the Seven-Eleven and pick up a couple of toothbrushes."

He didn't respond to the request until Raymond snapped impatient fingers at him. Luis hopped down and crossed to Raymond, who shoved some crumpled bills at him. As soon as he'd left, Raymond turned on Bibianna. "Hey. You don't talk to him like that. Guy works for me, not you. You treat him with a little respect."

Bibianna rolled her eyes and motioned me into the bedroom with her.

The room had been furnished with more of Raymond's roadside taste. The bed was king-size with red satin sheets and a big puffy comforter. The bed tables and chest of drawers looked like wood veneer over particleboard, in a "Spanish style," which is to say lots of black wrought-iron hinges and pulls. Bibianna slid the closet door open. "He moved all of my clothes from my other place. He didn't even ask me," she said. "Look at this. He thinks he can buy me, like I'm up for sale."

The wooden rod was crammed with hanging clothes, the long shelf above stacked with sweaters, handbags, and shoes. She crossed to the bureau and started opening drawers full of underwear, most of it new. She found me a pair of red lace underpants with the store tags still attached. She offered me a bra, which I declined. No point in putting apples in a sack meant for cantaloupes. In addition to the underwear, she rounded up some sandals, a red miniskirt with a matching red leather belt, and a white cotton peasant blouse with puff sleeves and a drawstring at the neck.

As she handed me the garments, she murmured, "Get out if you have the chance."

"What about Raymond?"

"Don't worry about it. I can handle him."

"Everything okay?"

Raymond was standing in the doorway. He'd taken off his sport coat and his shoulders looked narrow without its bulk.

She turned on him in a flash. "Do you fuckin' mind? We're having a private conversation here *if* it's any of your business."

He flicked a look at me, embarrassed.

"I think I'll take a shower," I murmured.

He held out a package. "Here's your toothbrush."

"Thanks."

I took the bag and moved past him, eager to escape. There's nothing worse than being present when a couple gears up for battle. Both were making covert attempts to enlist my sympathy, and the nonverbal recruitment process was making my stomach churn.

I went into the guest bathroom and locked the door behind me. I hung my tank top over the doorknob to discourage anyone from peeping through the keyhole. My toes started curling at the state of the bathroom, which had all the charm one might picture in a military latrine. I've never been good at walking around barefoot in public locker rooms, where the floors always seem to be littered with hair, rusted bobby pins, and disintegrating clumps of spongy wet Kleenex. I won't describe the sink. The glass shower door had been cracked and mended with plumber's tape, and the metal track in which the door slid was crusty with soap scum. A long pointed stain extended from the shower head to the top of the tub itself. There was a plastic bottle of generic shampoo in the corner and I picked it up gingerly, my lips pursing with distaste.

I put paper on the rim of the toilet and availed myself of the facilities. While I was sitting there, I extracted Dolan's telephone number from my right sock. I committed it to memory, tore the slip of paper in tiny pieces, and tossed them in the bowl, flushing it afterward. The water wouldn't go down. The tiny pieces of paper, like confetti, whirled around and around with an agonizing laziness while the water level rose dangerously close to the rim. Oh, great. The toilet was going to overflow. I began to wave my hands, whispering, "Get back . . . get back." Finally, the water subsided, but I didn't care to try to flush again until the tank refilled. I cupped a hand to my ear without picking up any indication that this was happening. If Raymond burst in, would he fish out the pieces of the note and try to paste them all together? Surely not.

I opened the toilet tank. There were plastic packets taped along the sides of the tank . . . probably heroin or cocaine. Now there's a concept. If the cops ever raided the place, they'd sure be fooled by *that*. One of the pouches was jammed up against the ball cock mechanism. I pushed it aside and rattled the lever. The tank began to fill. Finally, the toilet flushed with gallumphing sounds—a triumph of personal ingenuity and low-grade plumbing skills. My Dick Tracy secret code was safely washed out to sea.

The shower water was tepid to begin with, but I managed to lather myself with a tiny bar of soap that said "Ramada Inn." I shampooed my hair and was just rinsing it when the hot water ran out. I finished in haste. The only towel in the bathroom was thin, stiff, and dingy from use. I patted myself dry with my tank top and got dressed.

When I emerged from the bathroom, dirty clothes in hand, the apartment was quiet. I peered into the living room. Luis had apparently gone home. Raymond and Bibianna were nowhere in sight. The door to the master bedroom was closed, and I could hear voices raised heatedly in Spanish. I leaned my head close, but I really couldn't understand a word of it. I returned to the living room. Perro had been secured to the couch again, and he was chewing happily on the leather portion of the chain leash that restrained him. The minute he saw me, he rose to his feet, the hair standing up along his back in a ridge. He lowered his head and began to hum down in his chest. To reach the front door, I'd have to pass within inches of him. Skip that, I thought.

The telephone, a touch tone, had been sitting on the coffee table. Now there was no sign of it. I scanned the room without result. Apparently, Raymond had unplugged the instrument at the jack and had taken it into the bedroom with him. That wasn't very trusting. I backed up, turning left into a short hallway. The other bedroom contained a dilapidated brown couch and a bare mattress with a couple of pillows minus the cases.

I went to the window overlooking the street. I flipped open the locking mechanism and pushed at the aluminum-framed sliding window, which I managed to hump back in its track with a minimum of squeaks. It's not that I was looking for an immediate avenue of escape. I just like to know where I am and what's possible in the event of an emergency. I leaned close and angled my head so I could see in all directions.

To my right, the face of the building was shabby and plain, a sheer drop of some twenty-plus feet to bare sidewalk. No balconies, no wood trim, and no trees within range. From what I could see, this was a neighborhood of *tacquerías* and strip joints, auto body shops and pool halls, all of it as torn and deserted as a war zone. I checked to my left and was heartened to see a zigzagging metal stairway. At least in a pinch, I'd have access to the world at large.

I surveyed the room behind me, so exhausted I could hardly stand. I opted for the lumpy couch, which was slightly too short to stretch out on fully. The cushions smelled of dust and stale cigarette smoke. I pulled my knees up and crossed my arms, hugging them in against me for solace. I didn't care what was happening, I had to get some sleep.

When I woke, I could tell from the slant of light in the room that it was close to four o'clock. The days had already begun to seem truncated, the premature darkness signaling the sudden onset of winter. At this point, annually, all the furnaces are turned on. The new cord of oak is delivered and stacked. This is the season when Californians, by agreement, begin to bring out their woolens, complaining loudly of the cold when it's only fifty degrees out—as close to freezing temperatures as we're likely to get.

The apartment was still quiet. I got up and tiptoed out to the living room. Perro was snoring, but I figured it was just a ruse. He was hoping I'd try to sneak past him so he could leap up and tear my ass off. I edged to my left, into the dining area, which formed a straight line with the galley-style kitchenette. I'd popped in there briefly when I helped myself to a beer, but I hadn't been able to check for exits. I was hoping for a back door, but the kitchen was a dead end and there didn't appear to be any other way out.

I glanced over at the kitchen table, which was still covered with stacks of papers. I picked up a sheaf and sorted through. What ho! Well, at least now I knew what had made the guy so cross. These vicious-looking *batos locos* had been licking their pencil points, trying to fill out insurance forms for a series of bogus injuries they couldn't even spell right. "Wiplash" and "bruces" and "panes in my looer and uper bake." One had written: "Were drivin north wen this car hit us from behine and nockt us into a telepone phole. I bump my hed on the winsheld, suffrin bruces. Ever sins the acident, I hadve wiplash and panes in my nek. Also, bad hedakes, dobull vishun and shoot-in panes in my bake."

The attending physician on most forms was a Dr. A. Vasquez, with a chiropractor named Fredrick Howard running a close second in popularity. Now that I looked closely, I realized that all the "victims" had given identical accounts of their "accidents." What Tomas had been doing was copying out the same information on form after form. Properly briefed or not, my investigative instincts began to stir and I could feel my excitement mount. This was part of what Dolan and Santos were looking for, grand theft in progress with the names of the players spelled out nice and neat. There was no sign of a file cabinet, from what I'd seen so far, but Raymond had to keep all the paperwork somewhere. I chose a completed claim form at random, folded it quickly, and shoved it down my blouse front, patting it into place. I left the remaining papers as I'd found them and returned to the spare room, crackling faintly as I walked. When I reached the doorway, I spotted Raymond standing near the window, going through the pouch of personal possessions I'd brought with me from the jail.

"Help yourself. All I got on me is ten bucks," I said from the doorway.

If he was embarrassed to be caught, he gave no indication of it. There was a brief pause while he went through a series of tics we both ignored. "Who's Hannah Moore?"

"Excuse me?"

"Hannah Moore's not your real name."

"It isn't? Well, that's news to me." I tried for a tone somewhere between facetious and perplexed.

"This driver's license is a fake." He tossed the license on the floor and turned his attention to the other items in the bag.

"If it's any of your business, my license was suspended about a month ago," I said snappishly. "A friend of mine put this one together for me. You have a problem with that?" I crossed the room and snatched it from the floor, plucking the plastic pouch from him in the same agitated movement.

"I don't have a problem," he said. He seemed amused by my display of temper. "How'd you get your license yanked?"

"I was picked up on a DUI. Two of 'em since June."

I could see him digest the information, undecided at this point whether he believed me or not. "What happens if you get stopped by a cop and he runs the fake?"

"I'll end up in jail again. What difference does it make?"

"So what's your real name?"

"What's yours?"

"Where's your car at?"

"Out of commission. I need some work done on the tranny, but I don't have the bucks."

We locked eyes. His were large and darker than I remembered. He needed a shave, his jaw shadowed by a day's growth of beard. He'd changed into casual slacks and a short-sleeved silk shirt in a teal shade that made his eyes look very warm. His taste in clothing was sure classier than his taste in household furnishings. I had to guess he was making money, especially if what Santos said was true. Raymond's neck jerked, after which he turned his head and yelled something with his hand against his mouth as if coughing.

I heard the door to the master bedroom open. A moment later, Bibianna padded into the room. She was barefoot, wearing a short white silk shift that made her skin seem dark by contrast. She stood in the doorway while she lit a cigarette, watching me with interest, her eyes unreadable.

She had her hair pulled up in a slatternly knot on the top of her head. Her gaze slid over to Raymond. "Where's the telephone?"

"It's broken."

"It's not broken. I saw you using it a little while ago."

"Now it is. You don't need it."

"I want to call my mother."

"Some other time," he said.

She pushed away from the doorframe and turned on her heel, disappearing down the hall toward the living room.

He stared after her. A nearly imperceptible tic had started near his mouth. He did a neck roll and moved his right arm in its socket to ease the tension. The man had to be exhausted at the end of a day. He shook his head. "I don't get it. I've done everything for her. Bought her clothes. I take her fancy places, get her anything she wants. She doesn't have to lift a finger. She doesn't even have to work. I took her on a big cruise. Did she tell you about that?"

I shook my head.

"You ask her. She'll tell you. All the food you could eat. They had a six-foot swan made of ice, this fountain pouring champagne. I get her this apartment. You know what she says to me? It's trash. She hates the place. What's the matter with her?" His bafflement was mixed with belligerence. "Tell me what I did wrong. Tell me what I have to do yet."

"I'm not exactly an expert on what makes a relationship work."

"You know the problem? I'm too nice. It's the truth. I'm too good to the woman, but I can't help myself. That's just how I am. We were all set to get married. Did she tell you about that?"

"You mentioned it, I think."

"She broke my heart and I can't figure out why she did it. . . ."

"I got news for you, Raymond. You can't hang on to someone who doesn't want to be here."

"Is that it?" He studied me so intently that for a moment I thought I might actually persuade him to let go of her. He shoved his hands in his pockets, his look brooding in the fading light.

"Raymond?" Bibianna called him from the living room. "What's this?"

"What."

A moment later, she reappeared. She had a knife in her hand, a narrow switchblade with a bone handle. The blade was dark with dried blood.

His eyes settled on the knife. "Where'd you get that?"

"It was on the kitchen counter. This is yours. I recognize it."

He held his hand out, ignoring the original question. I thought about the smashed mirror tiles and the broken chair leg, blood splattered on the wall. Hesitantly, Bibianna placed the knife in his hand, her expression troubled. Again, the power had shifted. He pressed a button on the handle, easing the blade into its slot. He tucked it in his pants pocket. He blinked. He jerked his head to the side and his mouth opened wide.

She watched him with caution. "Where'd all the blood come from?"

"Put your clothes on. I'll take you out to dinner. We can bring something back for her," he replied.

I felt a momentary stir of excitement, longing for a short period of unsupervised time.

"Why can't Hannah go? She's probably starving."

"She can have a bowl of chili until we get back. There's a big pot on the stove."

I spoke up casually. "Really, Bibianna. I'm fine. I'll just keep the dog company." Like me and Perro were old pals. I was dying to be alone, eager to get a call through to Dolan while I could.

The two of them went through a long debate—where to go, what to wear, whether they should wait for Luis and make a foursome out of it. I could feel my stomach shrivel from anxiety, but I didn't want to seem too impatient for their departure. Raymond was all in favor of waiting for Luis, but Bibianna said she didn't want to eat a meal with him and Raymond didn't press. I could feel myself mentally shifting from foot to foot.

14

They didn't leave until nearly seven, after an agony of argument and indecision. Perro remained in his usual place by the door, gnawing on his chain. He had the kind of teeth you might see on a dinosaur skeleton, perfect for grinding up alligators and other modest-size mammals. Once the door closed behind them, I headed for the spare bedroom, where I took a minute to fish the claim form out of my bodice and tuck it under one of the couch cushions for safekeeping. Then I began to search for the missing telephone. I started in the master bedroom, checking every drawer. I couldn't believe he'd have stashed the phone among her possessions, so I skipped her chest of drawers and concentrated on his. She'd probably gone through a brief search herself without luck.

His top drawer on the left was a mass of unmatched socks, clumsily folded handkerchiefs. The drawer on the right held the sorts of odds and ends you can't bear to throw out: matchbooks, cuff links, tie tacks, a roach clip, loose change, a wallet in good shape but emptied of credit cards. A flat brown bank book for a savings account showed a balance of forty-three thousand bucks. Down a drawer were folded shirts and under them the sweaters. In a box, near the back of the drawer, I found two handguns. One was a semiautomatic, a .30-caliber broomhandle Mauser in an imprinted case, with an extra magazine, cleaning brush, test target, and a box of bottleneck cartridges. I bent my head and sniffed the barrel, without touching it. It hadn't been cleaned, but it hadn't been fired recently, either. The second gun was a SIG-Sauer P220 .38 Super, which probably cost three hundred and fifty bucks. Did I dare steal one for my very own? Nah, not at this point. It wouldn't be smart. Under the box was a jumbled collection of California driver's licenses with assorted ID's. I made a mental note to go through them later if I could find an opportunity. I put the guns back on top of the documents.

I checked the closet, top and bottom, sorting through any pile of articles large enough to conceal an unplugged telephone. I peered under the bed, searched the drawers in the bed tables. I went into the master bathroom, which was larger than the other but not any cleaner. The medicine cabinet was too small to hide anything. I dug through the clothes hamper. The telephone was tucked down in the bottom. I emitted a little yelp and pulled it out from under a mound of dirty underwear. I knew there was a jack in the living room, but I was too nervous to plug in the phone out there. Luis was due any minute. I didn't want him to find me with my mouth against the receiver.

I scanned the baseboards in the bedroom for another

jack. There were none in the immediate vicinity. I got down on my hands and knees and crawled around the perimeter, toting the telephone along with me as I peered behind the chest of drawers and the bed table. I finally spotted a jack on the wall behind the king-size bed, just about dead center. By stretching out on my belly and extending my arm through the dust bunnies and the woofies, I contrived to press the little gizmo on the phone into the matching hole in the jack. I was lying on the floor between the bed and the closet when the dog began to bark. Luis. Shit! I snicked the line from the jack and jerked the length of it out from under the bed. Perro was barking so loud, I couldn't tell if Luis had let himself in or not. I made a beeline to the master bathroom, wrapping the cord and the phone as I went.

"Hey! Where is everybody?" He was in.

"Luis? Is that you? I'm in the bathroom," I called.

I shoved the phone to the bottom of the hamper and piled the dirty clothes on top. I checked my reflection in the mirror and picked a dog hair off my lip. I just had time to wrap a bath towel around my head, turban style, when Luis appeared in the bathroom doorway. He'd pulled a flannel shirt on. Long sleeves now concealed the handsome tattoos on his arms, but I could still see the two pairs of duck feet sticking out of his sleeves. He surveyed the room. His look flicked to me, his eyes chilly with suspicion.

"Where's Raymond?"

"He and Bibianna went out."

"What are you doing in here?"

"Bibianna said I could borrow her hair dryer," I said,

praying she really had one. I glanced at the hamper. A length of telephone cord was dangling down the side, coiled in a tiny noose. I shifted my weight, effectively blocking his view. "I'll be out in just a second."

He stared. His face was an oval with high cheekbones and a little pointed chin. His teeth were in good shape, but he had a thin, mean-looking mouth, accentuated by that pathetic mustache. His dark hair was straight, slicked back in a ponytail, previously concealed by his watch cap. He had to be in his late twenties. "What time did they say they'd be back?"

"Could we talk about this in a minute? I'd like to do my hair," I said. I moved to close the bathroom door, which forced him to back up a foot. I shut the door emphatically, waited half a second, and then jerked the door open again. He straightened up, embarrassed. He tucked his thumbs in his belt loops and ambled casually toward the living room.

"You are too considerate," I called after him, and slammed the door shut for emphasis. I found the hair dryer and turned it on, then laid it on the toilet lid and let it run while I wrapped the cord around the phone and placed it carefully down in the hamper where I'd found it. I rearranged the clothes on top. With the lid in place, I turned and checked my hair in the mirror. I picked up the wheezing dryer and bent over at the waist until my head was upside down. I blew a jet of hot air through my mop for about a minute. When I straightened up, it didn't look any better, but it did look different, like a sticker bush without leaves. I flipped the hair dryer off and went out into the living room.

The evening was spent peaceably. Luis didn't seem to

be plagued by intellect or curiosity, so there was little conversation. He sat on the nondoggie end of the couch while I sat in the chair. He turned on the television set. He had a limited attention span and very little patience for complexity. Once in a while, he'd do something that indicated a curious awareness of me, nothing overt, but palpable nevertheless. His sexuality was oppressive, like the smell of orange blossoms on a humid summer night. He watched several shows simultaneously, using the remote control to switch from channel to channel. The dog stared at me intently through the car chases and canned laughter, and if I chanced to glance at him, he seemed to squint his little eyes.

At ten-twenty, Raymond and Bibianna came back with a bucket of parts from some Kentucky Fried Chicken rip-off. I was so hungry by then that I devoured five pieces, along with a carton of mashed potatoes with brown sludge, a squat container of coleslaw, three misshapen biscuits, and a fried pie with hardly any filling. Luis ate right along with me and finished up any food that was left. At midnight, Bibianna found me a blanket and a nightie. I trundled off to what I now considered my bedroom. I shut the door, stripped my clothes off, slipped into the nightie, and settled down on the lumpy couch.

I awakened with a start. At first I had no idea where I was or what was happening. It was the dead of night. I strained against the gloom, doing a visual search of the room I was lying in, caught in a moment of sleep-induced amnesia. A pale wash from the streetlight cast a plank of yellow on the ceiling. A thin scent of lard-fried tortillas hung in the air. I remembered Raymond. Had I heard something? Whatever the noise, I must have incorporated it into a murky dream which had evaporated on waking. Only the feeling of the dream remained—heavy, anxious. I could sense a presence in the room. My eyes were becoming accustomed to the dark. I divided my visual field into sections, which I studied one by one. My heart lurched. The door to my room now appeared to be open a crack. Luis? I struggled, trying to see if I could distinguish a silhouette against the paler gray of the corridor. The door swung open, a widening gap filled the shadows. I whispered, "What do you want?"

Silence.

I heard a tapping, the sound of metal being trailed across the floor. Fear flared in me like a match. It was the dog. I remembered him chewing the leather strap that connected his leash with the chain securing him. God only knew how long he'd been free, roaming the apartment. I could see the glint of his dark eyes, his head low. I had no weapon in range, no way to protect myself. He seemed to be sifting the air for human scent. If I could remain absolutely still, he might lose interest and turn away, heading for the room where Raymond and Bibianna slept. I held my breath. The pit bull advanced toward the couch where I was lying rigidly, his toenails tap-tapping on the bare wooden floor. I was on my right side, my face almost level with his. I had my right arm tucked under me, but my left was hanging off the edge of the couch since there was no place else to put it. The dog extended his snout until the leather of his nose touched the fingers of my left hand. I could feel the coarse bristles on his muzzle brush against my wrist. I waited, unmoving. Finally, with infinitesimal care, I began to ease my hand away. I heard him growl low in his throat. I froze, not daring to retract my fingertips. He edged closer until he was resting his chin on the edge of the couch, his mouth level with mine. He made a whining sound. I felt my brain go blank. Within seconds, he had scrambled right up on the couch with me, crowding me against the back cushions, his bony front legs pinning me in position. Tentatively, I placed a hand on his head between his ears. He licked my palm.

"I thought you hated having your head touched," I said indignantly. Clearly not. I began to rub the silky flap of one ear. The dog panted happily. His body heat quickly enveloped me from chest to knee. I didn't dare complain, even though he did exude a rich cloud of doggie B.O. It was the first time I'd ever had a bed partner who smelled like hot pork. When I woke again, he was gone.

It's amazing how quickly one adjusts to strange surroundings and altered circumstances. By morning, the place seemed familiar in a cockroachy sort of way. Bibianna lent me a clean T-shirt to wear with my red miniskirt. For breakfast, Luis made some bean and cheese burritos, which we washed down with Pepsi-Colas. By then, the fastidious streak in my nature had emerged in earnest. I found a sponge and some Comet and attacked the surfaces in the bathroom, scouring the floor, the sink, the toilet, the tub, and the grubby tile around the shower. I prevailed upon Bibianna to get the bags of garbage removed from the kitchen, and then I scoured the sink, the stove top, and counters. Perro, the pit bull, was back in his position by the door, standing guard. Like a one-night stand, the surly ingrate was acting as if he didn't know me from a lamppost, and he growled ominously every time I made eye contact. It was not like I expected slobbering devotion, but a simple gesture of recognition might have soothed my punctured ego.

At 9:00 A.M., Raymond left the apartment without a word of explanation. Bibianna went back to bed. I wondered if she was going to keep herself zoned out—drugged, or stoned, asleep—anything to avoid dealing with Raymond's sexual demands.

Luis surprised me by taking over the kitchen. He'd apparently decided it was time to cook. Maybe I'd inspired him by wiping all the sludge from the top of the stove, scraping grunge from between the cracks in the tiles with the blade of a knife. Nobody seemed to have heard of real dishes. I'd tossed tilting piles of flimsy paper plates and twelve place settings of plastic flatware. The remaining cheapware—plastic glasses, kitchen utensils crusted with food barnacles—I'd left to soak in a sink full of water I'd boiled first on the stove. A short time later, Luis set to work. Briefly, I wondered if in private he, too, nearly levitated trying to keep his bare feet off the crud on the bathroom floor. For lack of anything better to do, I leaned against the kitchen counter, watching him.

Hitherto hidden aspects of his nature were made manifest. Every act was small, precise. He peeled an onion. He flattened cloves of garlic with the side of a cleaver, lifting the papery skins away like insect shells. He charred peppers under the broiler, seeded and peeled and chopped them. The smell was acrid, but it awakened hunger. He was completely self-absorbed, involved in the task like a woman applying makeup. I always find myself fascinated by expertise. He opened a large can of chopped tomatoes and dumped them in the pan I'd washed. He added the onions, garlic, and chilies. There was a certain style to the work, a fastidious ordering of events. It was clearly learned behavior, but who had taught him? The air began to smell wonderful.

"What is that?" I asked.

"Enchilada sauce."

"Smells great." I leaned against the counter, wondering how to frame the next question. "What's the story on Chago? Will they have a funeral for him?"

Luis concentrated on his saucepan to avoid eye contact. "Raymond talked to the cops. They won't release the body until the autopsy's done. Might be as early as tomorrow, they won't say."

"Does he have other brothers?"

"Juan and Ricardo. They were here yesterday."

"What about parents?"

"His father was sent to prison for child abuse. He was killed in prison when they heard what he did to Raymond."

"Which was what?"

Luis looked up at me. "He don't talk about that and I don't ask." He went back to his saucepan, stirring hypnotically. "His mother ran off and left when he was seven or eight."

"He's the oldest?"

"Of the boys. There's three older sisters hate his ass. They think it's his fault what happened to the parents."

"Another happy childhood," I said. "How long have you known him?"

"Six, eight months. I met him through a capper of his named Jesus."

Bibianna appeared in the doorway, a blanket across her shoulders like an Indian. "Raymond back yet?"

Luis shook his head.

She disappeared again, and a short time later I could hear shower water running. Luis left the sauce to simmer on the stove and prepared to take the dog for a walk. When he picked up the chain, he discovered the chewed leather section of the leash. Under his breath, I heard him murmur a worried "Shit." I kept my mouth shut, imagining I might engender a sense of loyalty in the mutt. Luis found another way to attach the leash to Perro's collar, and the two left the apartment.

Bibianna reappeared, fully dressed this time. She found a dog-eared deck of cards and sat on the floor next to the coffee table, where she laid out a game of solitaire. I considered hunting for the phone, but I didn't want to call Dolan with Bibianna close by. The less she knew about who I was, the better. I flipped on the television set. The day already had an odd feel to it—idle, unstructured, without purpose or appeal—like a forced vacation in a cut-rate resort.

Bibianna seemed preoccupied and I hated to cut into that, but we seldom had time alone and I needed information.

"How often does he get violent?" I asked.

She turned a dark look on me. "Not every day. Sometimes two or three times a week," she insisted. "I talked to Chago about it once and he told me it started when Raymond was just a little kid. He'd blink his eyes and then the twitches started and pretty soon he was barking and coughing. His father figured he was doing it on purpose, just to get attention, so he used to beat him up. He did some other stuff, too, which got him thrown into prison. Poor Raymond. He was hyperactive in school, in trouble all the time. It's probably why his mother left. . . ."

"And he's done it ever since? The whole time you've known him?"

"He got better for a while, but then it started up again, worse than before."

"Can't the doctors do anything?"

"What doctors? He doesn't see doctors. Sometimes sex calms him down. Booze or sleep, dope. Once he got the flu and had a fever a hundred and three? He was fine, no problem, never even had a twitch. He was great for two days. Flu went away, he was at it again, this time licking his lips, doing this weird thing with his hands. I don't want to talk about it anymore. It's depressing."

Raymond returned just before lunch with a folded newspaper and a bag of doughnuts. Luis and the dog came in right behind him. If Raymond was in mourning for his brother, I saw no signs of it. The ticcing seemed less evident today, but I couldn't be sure. He left the room at intervals and I began to suspect he was venting in the other room. That or shooting up. I was just getting into a really trashy soap, my bare legs thrown over the arm of the chair, sandal flapping on one foot, when he and Luis sat down at the kitchen table, talking softly in Spanish. During the next commercial, I went into the kitchen and got myself a glass of water. I paused, peering over Raymond's shoulder to see what they were up to. It was pure nosiness on my part, but he didn't seem to mind. What I'd thought was the daily paper turned out to be a throwaway rag filled with classifieds. Luis flipped to the automobile section and folded back the pages. I checked the dateline. Thursday, October 27. These were probably new listings for the weekend coming up. Luis skipped over the trucks, vans, and imports and concentrated on the domestic cars for sale.

"Here's one," Luis said. With a Magic Marker, he circled an ad for a 1979 Caddy. I leaned closer, reading, "Good condition. $999. OBO."

"What's OBO?" I asked. I knew, but I wanted to demonstrate some interest and I thought showing ignorance was the safest bet.

"Or best offer," Raymond said. "You want a Cadillac?"

"Who, me? Not especially."

"I like that Chrysler Cordoba," Raymond said to Luis, pointing to the next box. Luis drew a wobbly-sided egg around the ad for a "'77 white. runs/looks great. $895/obo." A telephone number was listed on both ads.

Raymond got up and left the room, returning with the telephone, which he plugged into the wall jack. I pulled up a chair and sat down. Luis continued to circle ads while Raymond placed call after call, inquiring about each car that interested them, making note of the address. When this exercise was complete and they'd culled out the ads of interest, Luis made a list on a separate piece of paper.

Raymond glanced at me. "You have car insurance?"

"Sure."

"What kind?"

I shrugged. "Whatever the state of California requires.

I've been thinking I should drop it since my car's dead. Why?"

"You have liability *and* collision?"

"How do I know? I don't walk around with the details of my car insurance memorized. The policy's up in Santa Teresa."

"Can't your insurance company give you the information?"

"Sure. If they looked it up."

"Might be worth it to get your car fixed if you got collision coverage." Raymond lifted the telephone receiver and held it out to me. "Call 'em."

"Right now?"

"Is that a problem?"

"Not at all," I said with an uneasy laugh. I could feel my heart start to bang in my chest. The thumping felt so conspicuous I checked to see if my T-shirt was pulsating in the front. For a moment my mind went blank. I couldn't remember California Fidelity's number, I couldn't remember the contact number Dolan had given me, and I couldn't decide which to try in any event. I took the receiver.

I punched in the 805 area code, hoping for the best. Automatically, my fingers moved across the face of the telephone, dialing CF in a medley of musical tones that sounded like "Mary Had a Little Lamb." I wondered if Dolan had been in touch with Mac Voorhies. Was I going to have my cover blown right here on the spot?

The number rang twice. Darcy answered. I hoped I didn't sound like myself when I said, "May I speak to Mr. Voorhies?"

"Just a moment, please. I'll ring his office."

She clicked off. Music played in the background, filling telephone limbo with an orchestrated rendition of "How High the Moon." Inexplicably, the lyrics popped into my head unbidden. I thought about Dawna, wondering how long the cops could hold her. Wounded or not, she was dangerous.

15

Mac came on the line. "Voorhies."

"Mr. Voorhies, my name is Hannah Moore. I have car insurance with your company and I wanted to check on my coverage."

There was dead silence. I knew he recognized my voice. Raymond leaned his head close to mine, angling the phone so he could listen to the conversation.

Mac hesitated. I could hear him grope with the request, trying to figure out what was going on and what he could say without jeopardizing my situation, whatever that might be. He knew me well enough to realize I wouldn't make such a call without a good reason. "Is this regarding an automobile accident?" he asked cautiously.

"Well, no. I, uhm, might be driving a friend's car and he doesn't like the idea unless he knows I'm covered." Raymond's face was six inches away from mine. I could smell his after-shave and feel the warm, slightly adenoidal character of his breath.

"I can understand that. Is your friend there now?" Mac asked.

"That's right."

"Do you have the policy number handy?"

"Uh, no. But the agent is Con Dolan."

Raymond drew back and reached for a piece of paper, scratching out a note. "Ask about collision." I hate it when people coach me when I'm on the phone. He pointed significantly. I waved at him with irritation.

"Uh, it's really the collision I need to know about," I amended.

Another awkward pause. I smiled at Raymond wanly while Mac cleared his throat. "I tell you what I'll do, Miss . . ."

"Moore."

"Yes, all right. Why don't I see if I can get in touch with Mr. Dolan. He's no longer with the company, but I'm sure he's still in town. I can check our files for the coverage and get back to you. Is there a number where you can be reached this afternoon?"

Raymond pulled his head back and put a finger to his lips.

I said, "Not really. I'm staying with this guy in Los Angeles, but I'm not sure how long I'll be here. I could call again later if you'll tell me what time."

"Try five this afternoon. I should have the information by then."

"Thanks. I'd appreciate it." I handed Raymond the receiver and he hung it up.

"What'd he say?"

"He's going to check. I'm supposed to call him back this afternoon at five."

"But as far as you know the insurance is in effect."

"I told you it was."

Raymond and Luis exchanged a look. Raymond looked over his shoulder at Bibianna, still intent on her game of solitaire. "Get your jacket. We're going out." And then to me. "You need a jacket? She'll give you one."

"What's happening?"

"We're going on a drive-down."

"Whatever *that* is," I said.

We took Sepulveda Boulevard up to Culver City, with Luis at the wheel. Bibianna was being sullen, sitting silently in the backseat with her arms crossed while Raymond either made calls on the car phone or rubbed, petted, and generally annoyed her, rambling on about all the money he meant to make, all the things he'd done, and all the big plans he had for the two of them. I had to give that guy some lessons. He was going about this all wrong. Aside from the fact that (unknown to him) she was already Mrs. Jimmy Tate, she was never going to tumble to all the smoke he was blowing. Women don't want to sit around listening to guys talk about themselves. Women like to have conversations about real things, like feelings— namely, theirs. Raymond seemed to think he just hadn't persuaded her yet of the depth of his affection. I wanted to scream, "She knows that, you dummy! She just doesn't give a shit."

We pulled up at the first address.

The '79 Caddy was parked at the curb, a black Seville,

being offered by a muscular black guy with a pink shower cap, a tattooed teardrop on his cheek, and a gold hoop through his left ear. Honestly, I'm not making this stuff up. He wore a T-shirt and low-slung jeans, with his Calvin Kleins sticking out above his belt. He was actually very cute with a mustache and goatee, a mischievous smile, and a little space between his teeth. Bibianna stayed in the car, but I got out and stood around with the guys, shifting from foot to foot while the three of them entered into a long and tedious negotiation. Raymond went through several sequences of ticcing, but the black guy didn't react except to stop making eye contact. I could see that in some circles, Raymond would be treated like a walking basket case. I wanted to speak up protectively and say, "Hey, the guy can't help it, okay?"

The OBO turned out to be a hundred dollars less than the $999 listed in the paper. Raymond turned his body slightly and took out a fat cylinder of bills with a rubber band wrapped around them. He slipped the rubber band over his wrist while he peeled off the right denominations. The pink slip was signed and changed hands, but I couldn't believe Raymond was actually going to take it down to the DMV. Habitual criminals never seem to be troubled about things like that. They do anything they please while the rest of us feel compelled to play by the rules.

The black guy strolled off as soon as the transaction was completed. Raymond and Luis made a study of the car, which seemed to be in reasonable shape. Chrome flakes were peeling off the bumper and the right rear taillight had been smashed. The tires were bald, but the body didn't show any major dents. The interior was gray, a rip in the passenger seat neatly sutured with black thread. The floor, front and back, was littered with fast-food containers, empty soft drink cans, crushed cigarette packs, newspapers. Luis took a few minutes to shove it all into the gutter, emptying the ashtray in a little mountain of cigarette butts.

"What do you think?" Raymond asked me.

I couldn't imagine why my opinion mattered. "Looks better than anything I ever drove."

He stuck a finger in the key ring and flipped the keys into his palm. "Hop in. Bibianna goes with him."

I glanced over at the dark green Ford where Bibianna sat. She was perched up on the backseat, using the rearview mirror to braid her dark, glossy hair. "Fine with me," I said.

I got into the Caddy.

Raymond got in on the driver's side and slipped his seat belt on. "Buckle up," he said. "We're going to have an accident."

"Is this car insured? We just bought the damn thing," I said with surprise.

"Don't worry about that stuff. I can call my agent later. He does anything I want."

I buckled up, trying to picture myself in a neck brace.

The transmission was automatic. The car had power locks and power brakes, power windows. Raymond started the engine, which thrummed to life. He adjusted the rearview mirror and waited while a silver Toyota passed at cruising speed before he pulled into the lane of traffic.

I tried the power windows, which went up with a quiet hum. "How do we do this?" I asked.

"You'll see."

We seemed to drive randomly, taking Venice Boulevard through Palms, turning right on Sepulveda into an area called Mar Vista. These were neighborhoods of small stucco bungalows with small yards and tired trees with leaves that were oxygen-starved from all the smog in the air. Raymond watched the streets like a cop looking for the telltale indications of a crime in progress.

"What makes this a drive-down?"

"That's just what we call it when we're out cruising for an accident. Car's called a bucket. I got a fleet of buckets, a whole crew of drivers doing just what we're doing. You're a ghost."

I smiled. "Why's that?"

"Because you don't get paid, therefore you don't exist."

"How come I don't get paid?"

"You're a trainee. You're just here to beef up the head count."

"Oh, thanks," I said. I turned and looked out the window on the passenger side. "So, what are we looking for?"

Raymond glanced at me sharply, suspicion etched in his face.

"I'm just trying to learn," I said.

"A victim. We call 'em vics," he replied in belated answer to my question. "Somebody running a stop sign, backing out of a drive into the right-of-way, pulling out of a parking space . . ."

"And then what?"

He smiled to himself. "We hit the guy. You want to catch the rear quarter panel because the damage shows up nice and nobody gets hurt."

We drove around for an hour, unable to conjure up a traffic offender for the life of us. I could see that Raymond was impatient, but oddly enough, there was no twitching whatever during the time in the car. Maybe work was soothing to his battered nervous system. "Let me try," I said.

"You serious?"

"If I score, I want the money. What's it pay?"

"A hundred bucks a day."

"You're full of shit. I bet you make a fortune and I want a fair shake."

"Pushy bitch," he said mildly.

We traded places. I took a moment to slide the front seat a little closer to the gas pedal and the brake. I eased the Caddy into traffic. By then, we'd worked our way up Lincoln Boulevard to the outskirts of Santa Monica. At Pico, I cut left, picking up Ocean Avenue at San Vicente. Raymond hadn't paid much attention, but when he saw the direction I was taking, he looked at me with surprise. "What's wrong with Venice?"

"Why not Beverly Hills?" I asked. At first the idea seemed to unsettle him, but he could see the possibilities. We worked our way up to Sunset Boulevard and headed east, passing the northern perimeter of the sprawling UCLA campus. Just past the Beverly Hills Hotel, I took a right onto Rexford. I found it soothing to cruise along the wide tree-lined streets. This was an area known as the "flats" of Beverly Hills. The houses were oversize and filled the lots from side to side. All the lawns were green, the shrubs trimmed, gardeners blowing errant leaves down the driveways. Shade trees were planted along the grassy stretch between sidewalk and street, sycamores interspersed with oaks. High fences shielded the backyard tennis courts from sight. Now and then, I caught a glimpse of a swimming pool and cabana. The stoplight at Santa Monica Boulevard was green. I drove the Caddy sedately into the heart of the Beverly Hills shopping district.

Technically, I knew I was skating on thin ice with this drive-down. The only thing I remembered about undercover work from police academy days is that it's against "public policy" for an officer of the law to participate in the commission of a crime or incite someone to do so. Happily, I wasn't actually an officer of the law, and if it ever came right down to it, it would be Raymond's word against mine. Helping Raymond stage a few fraudulent accidents seemed to me the quickest way to persuade him I was on the up-and-up.

Raymond stared out the window, his manner uneasy. "You're never going to find any business up here."

"Want to bet?" I had just spotted a late-model Mercedes pulling out of a parking lot in the middle of the block, left turn signal blinking. The car was a four-door sedan, a conservative black with a vanity plate that read BULL MKT. The woman driving was probably forty years old, with a cap of blond hair and big round sunglasses pulled down toward the tip of her nose. I slowed the Caddy, mentally apologizing for my sins in advance. I came to a full stop and politely waved her out. She gave me a quick wave and a smile, showing perfect caps.

"What are you *doing*?"

"Yielding the right-of-way," I said with innocence.

As soon as the Mercedes eased into my path, I gunned

the Caddy and rammed the left rear quadrant with a thump. It was just like bumper cars and I felt the same sick charge, half guilt, half thrill. The indentation was nicely placed. The woman shrieked and turned to look at me openmouthed with astonishment.

Raymond was out of the Caddy in a flash. "What the fuck are you doing? You pulled out right in front of us!"

I got out and moved to the front of the Caddy, where I checked the broken headlight and flaking bumper. Not bad. The damage to the other car was six grand at least. The blonde had recovered from her initial dismay. She got out of the Mercedes and slammed the car door. She was dressed for tennis, little white skirt, green-and-white-striped Polo shirt, long, tan legs, little socks with jaunty green pompoms sticking out above her spotless white tennis shoes. The Mercedes's left rear quadrant, recently a pristine shiny black, now sported a dent of substantial proportions, fender crumpled, chrome sticking out like a horizontal antenna. The rear door would have to be pried open with a crowbar. I could see the color rising in her face as she surveyed the damage. She turned and jabbed an angry finger in my face. "You fucking asshole! You sat there and motioned me out!"

"She did not!" Raymond said.

"She did, too!"

"Did not," I inserted to show where my loyalties lay.

Raymond said, "Look at my car! We just bought this car and now look what you've done!"

"*Your* car! Look at *mine*!"

I put a hand against my neck and Raymond turned to me with concern.

"Are you okay, hon?"

"I guess so," I said without conviction. The neck roll I did was accompanied by a wince.

Raymond dropped his irate manner and substituted an air of studied calm that was more effective in its way. "Lady, I hope you got good insurance coverage. . . ."

The afternoon was marked by Raymond's intermittent demolition derby, surreal in its fashion, depressing in its effect. We backtracked from Beverly Hills into Brentwood, through Westwood, and then south into Santa Monica again. We sought out areas congested with traffic, watched for minor violations, inattentiveness, and lapses in judgment. Raymond kept a meticulous record of each accident we staged—four in all—noting time and location, the other driver's name and insurance company.

The Caddy performed like a first-rate battering ram, sustaining very little damage for the losses we inflicted on other unsuspecting motorists. The victims seemed so gullible somehow, distressed, apologetic, sometimes irate, but usually worried they'd be slapped with ruinous lawsuits. I played my part—righteous and upset, pretending sudden shooting pains in my neck or back—but I couldn't bear to look at them. This was not a kind of cheating I did very well, and I could proceed only by employing the same mental detachment I adopt when I enter a morgue. Raymond, of course, was only interested in filing phony claims for vehicular damage and whatever injuries we could fake as a consequence. His skills at manipulation were honed by long practice.

At four, much to my relief, he decided we'd done enough. I'd been at the wheel for the first couple of accidents. Then Raymond had taken over. He found an on ramp for the 405 and headed south, toward the apartment. I felt like a traveling salesperson, on the road with my boss. My questions to Raymond had the same banal thrust you'd imagine from a Fuller Brush trainee. "What's your background for this?" said I, much as if I were inquiring about his qualifications for a career with *Encyclopaedia Britannica.*

"Some guy taught me the business when I was first starting out. He's in the slammer, so it's my operation."

"Like a promotion."

"Yeah, right. Exactly. I got a stable of doctors and attorneys who do the actual paperwork. I'm strictly supervision. Times are slow I do a little work like this. I like to keep a hand in."

"Your job is what, supplying the claimants?"

"Well, yeah. What do you think we been doing all afternoon? Right now, I got a crew of ten, but that goes up and down. It's hard to get good help."

I laughed. "I bet."

"I'll tell you a little secret. And this is the key to sound business management. Be careful of the guy right below you on the pyramid. You don't tell him jackshit."

"Because he might want to take over?"

"That's right. He's the dude wants to put a knife in your back. You take Luis. I love the guy like a brother, but certain things I don't tell him, people he doesn't see. That way I don't have to worry, know what I mean?"

"The money must be good."

Raymond shook his head. "Are you kidding? The money's great. I make maybe a thousand a case, depending on the nature of the 'injury.' The GP or the chiropractor probably clears another fifteen hundred."

"God, that's amazing. What do they do, pad the fees?"

"Sometimes they do. Or they charge for services never rendered. The insurance company doesn't know the difference, and either way, the doc makes out. Plus, you have the attorney on top of that," he said. He smiled wryly. "Of course, the biggest chunk goes to me."

"Because you take all the risks?"

"Because I put up all the dough. Bankroll the cars, pay all the cappers up front. I probably shell out five or six grand per crew to get 'em rolling. Multiply that by ten, twenty crews working seven days a week? It adds up."

"Sounds like it," I said, and let the subject drop.

A long silence followed. I still didn't have a fix on the mental arithmetic, but the money was clearly huge. I laid my head back against the seat. It wasn't hard to see the appeal. For a guy like Raymond, the money was a lot better than an honest day's work. Hell, I could make more money crashing cars than I did as a P.I. Of course, there was a downside. With all the bumps, smacks, and minor episodes of whiplash, my head was pounding and my neck was seizing up. I massaged the muscles along one shoulder, feeling tense.

"What's the matter?"

"My neck's stiff."

"You and me both," he said in a moment of self-mockery. He looked at me closely. "For real?"

"Raymond, we've just been in four auto accidents! That last one we had, I nearly slid off the seat. You could have warned me."

"You want to see a doctor? I can set it up. Heat treatments, ultrasound, anything you want. It's one of the perks."

"Let me see how I feel when we get back to the apartment. Where's Bibianna? I hope I'm not the only one out here risking my neck."

"Her and Luis are doing a drive-down same as us."

"Good. I'm glad to hear it."

He looked over at me, trying to gauge my mood. "You like it so far?"

"It sure beats working for a living."

He flashed a smile, eyes returning to the road. "Doesn't it?"

We stopped briefly at Buddy's Auto Body Shop across the street and two doors down from the apartment where Raymond lived. The garage itself sat in one corner of a property that extended from street to street. In the far corner, there was a corrugated metal shack surrounded by chassis, fenders, bumpers, engines, tires. A dilapidated chain-link fence enclosed maybe two full acres of wrecked cars and assorted parts. A sign read: BUDDY'S AUTO SALVAGE OPEN 6 DAYS TOP $$ FOR YOUR CAR OR TRUCK. ONE OF THE LARGEST SELECTIONS OF USED PARTS IN SOUTHERN CALIFORNIA. A big black rottweiler, with a head as craggy as a tree stump, was asleep in the dirt beside a pickup truck.

I said, "Does Buddy work for you?"

"*I'm* Buddy. Guy runs the place is Chopper. Back in a minute," he murmured as he got out. Raymond apparently operated his "repair" business in conjunction with an auto wrecking and salvage company, probably dismantling vehicles once he'd maximized the insurance potential.

I waited until he went into the garage and then I got out myself and ambled over to the Pepsi machine just inside the door. I took my time tucking coins in the slot, extracting a can of Diet Pepsi. I popped the top and downed it, idly taking in my surroundings. There was not another soul in sight and no indication of any work being done. The late afternoon sun slanted onto the cracked concrete floor in tawny yellow strips. The air smelled of oil, old tires, and hot metal. A pyramid of bright blue metal barrels had been laid on their sides and served now as storage bins for a jumble of rusted car parts. I could see Raymond through the open doorway of an area marked off as office space. The flat-roofed building appeared to be converted from a very small stucco house. Additional office space was provided by a single-wide trailer tucked between the fence and the building. The horizontal panes of a pair of dusty louvered windows were slanted open to let in some air. A wooden pallet was leaning up against the trailer. There was an alarm company sign affixed to the side of the trailer, but I didn't take it seriously. This didn't look like an establishment famous for its security.

Raymond finished his business and emerged from the garage with a guy at his side whom he introduced as Chopper. He was an Anglo in his forties, balding and squat. His breathing was labored and his face freckled with sweat.

I said, "Great dog," hoping to ingratiate myself with his owner.

"That's Brutus." Chopper gave a piercing whistle and Brutus awoke obligingly and lumbered to his feet. The poor dog was ancient, so crippled by arthritis that he walked with a rocking motion, approaching by degrees. Up close, I could see his black hair was dusted with white.

He paused beside me, his manner humble. I put my hand down near his nose and he licked me. I felt embarrassingly dewy-eyed about the damn beast.

Raymond and Chopper finished their business and we walked on back to the apartment building, leaving the car where it was.

16

Bibianna was already home, seated at the kitchen table, applying a coat of bright red polish to her nails. She was wearing red shorts and a halter top in a vivid jungle print, red, black, olive green, and white. Her hair was pulled up in a glossy coil on top. Luis was out somewhere walking the dog. I marveled that Bibianna hadn't escaped while she could. Raymond had forgotten to return the telephone to its hiding place. He didn't seem aware of it, but Bibianna sure was. She ignored the instrument so studiously I had to guess she'd used it. I caught her eye with a visual query, but she kept her expression blank. I wondered who she'd called. Her mother? Jimmy Tate? Could he be out of jail yet?

Raymond glanced at his watch. "Hey. It's nearly five. Time to call your insurance agent."

My conversation with Mac was brief. Raymond let me handle the transaction without his ear pressed to the phone along with mine. I identified myself as Hannah Moore and

Darcy put me through to Mac, who spelled out the particulars of my insurance coverage, making sure the message would sound benign to anybody listening. "Mr. Dolan assured me you were covered in case of accident. Do you still have his number?"

"Yes, I've got it. Thanks for the information. I appreciate your help."

"Anytime," he said. "And keep safe."

"I hope to."

Once I'd hung up, I finished jotting down notes: policy number, my deductible, liability, collision, major medical, and death benefits. I was assuming Mac had set up a special policy under the name "Hannah Moore," with a flag on the computer so he'd be alerted if a claim came in. I gave Raymond the policy number and the data Mac had relayed.

Shortly thereafter, I heard Perro tapping along the walkway outside, his breathing hoarse and wheezy as he strained against the leash. Luis opened the door and the dog bounded in. Somewhere, in a brain about the size of a BB, this beast had suddenly decided he remembered me. He charged at me joyfully, knocking into Bibianna as he vaulted across her lap. When he reached me he jumped up, propping his paws on my shoulders so we could stare into each other's eyes. I leaned sideways against the kitchen table while he slopped a tongue across my mouth. Bibianna had leapt away from him with a shriek, her fingers held aloft so he wouldn't screw up her nails. Raymond snapped his fingers, but the dog was too intent on true love to obey. Raymond yelled something, which he covered with a cough. I caught a glimpse of his face just as his eyes began to roll back. A tic was tugging at his mouth, his lower lip pulling down grotesquely. His head jerked twice to the left, mouth coming open. His temper seemed to snap and he went for the dog, landing an ill-aimed blow at Perro's meaty shoulder. The dog snarled and lunged. Raymond punched at the dog again, catching him in the nose. Perro yelped and scrambled away from him, cowering submissively. I moved into the path of Raymond's fist, blocking his next punch while Bibianna threw herself against him. Raymond shoved her out of the way. He knocked me aside and would have punched the dog again, but Luis hauled Perro by the choke chain and dragged him toward the door. Raymond stood and panted, eyelids fluttering, white slits visible along the rim. The rage and cruelty in his face were frightening, especially since his outburst was directed at the poor dog. Pit bull or no, Perro had a goofy innocence about him and all of us felt protective.

Bibianna pushed Raymond into a chair. "What's the matter with you!"

Raymond rubbed at his fist, his self-control returning by degrees. Luis and the dog disappeared. My heart began to pump belatedly. Raymond was breathing hard. I saw his head jerk. He eased his right arm in its socket and did a neck roll to relax. The tension drained from the room.

His gaze focused on Bibianna, who was pinning him to the chair, pressing down on his shoulders to prevent his getting up. She straddled his lap, the long, flawless legs anchoring him into place. It was the same move I'd seen her use with Tate the night before last. Hard to believe that less than forty-eight hours ago, she'd been with him.

Raymond stared up at her. "What's the matter? What's happening?"

"Nothing. Everything's fine," she said tersely. "Luis took the dog for a walk."

The moment passed. I was beginning to recognize the shifts in his moods. The spill of rage stirred sexuality. Before he could slide his hands up along her thighs, she removed herself from his lap as if she were getting off a horse. She smoothed her shorts and crossed to the television set, where she scooped up the deck of cards that was sitting on top. "Let's play gin rummy," she said. "A nickel a point."

Raymond smiled, indulging her, probably thinking he would nail her later.

When Luis came back with the dog, Bibianna lent me some jeans, a T-shirt, and some tennies so we could go out to dinner. The four of us left on foot and headed into the dismal commercial district that bordered the apartment complex. We crossed a vacant lot and went in through the rear entrance of a restaurant called El Pollo Norteño, which by my translation meant the North Chicken. The place was noisy, vinyl tile floor, the walls covered in panels of plastic laminate. The room felt close, nearly claustrophobic from the flame grills in the rear. Countless chickens were trussed on a rotating spit, brown and succulent, skins crisp and glistening with sputtering fat. The noise level was battering, mariachi music punctuated by a constant irregular banging of the cleavers whacking whole chickens into quarters and halves. The menu was listed on a board behind the register. We ordered at the counter, picked up four beers, and then canvassed, looking for a booth. The place was crowded, patrons spilling out onto a makeshift wooden deck that was actually an improvement. It was quieter out there and the chill California night air was a distinct relief. Moments later, a waitress appeared with our order on a tray, setting down paper plates and plastic flatware. We tore the chicken with our hands, piling shreds of grilled meat onto soft corn tortillas, spooning pinto beans and fresh salsa on top. It was a three-paper-napkin extravaganza of messy hands and dripping chins. Afterward, we adjourned to a bar two doors away. It was nine by then.

The Aztlan was smoky, cavernous, ill lighted, occupied almost exclusively by Hispanic men whose eyes, at that hour, were turning slippery from all the alcohol they'd consumed. The laughter came in constant, raucous bursts that were sly and assaultive, very worrisome. There was, on the surface, a thin veneer of control. Under it, and unpredictable, was the boiling violence of youth. The Spanish music was cranked up to a feverish pitch, forcing loud talk in aggressive tones that even merriment couldn't mask. I took my cue from Bibianna, who seemed watchful, her sexuality under wraps. Here, there was none of the familiar bantering I'd seen in the Meat Locker. Raymond was too easily set off and her intentions were too readily misunderstood. Luis seemed right at home, sauntering to the bar with his macho attitude. In his snowy white undershirt, his bare arms were a moving cartoon, Daffy Duck and Donald Duck in aggressive black and yellow.

While Luis fetched four more beers, we pushed through the crowd toward the back. In a second room about half the size of the first, there were three pool tables, two of them occupied. The felt surfaces looked as green as grassy islands under hot hanging lights. The dark of the ceiling was broken up by the blinking of multicolored Christmas tree lights that were probably strung up year-round. Raymond found an empty booth and Bibianna slid in. I was bringing up the rear, sidetracked by the jostling of the intervening mob. I felt a hand on my arm, impeding my progress.

"Hey, babe. You play pool?"

I knew the voice.

I turned and it was Tate.

I could feel my heart do a flip-flop, fearing Raymond's reaction. I glanced back at Bibianna automatically. She was squeezed into the booth, facing in my direction. She must have recognized Tate about the time I did because her face seemed to pale.

"Let's just mosey over to the pool table," Tate said under his breath. "Has Raymond figured out yet it was me killed Chago?"

"If he did, you'd be a dead man. Dawna got picked up before she could tell him everything. Why don't you get out while you can," I murmured.

Tate took my arm, moving me toward the pool table. "Aren't you happy to see me?"

I closed my eyes briefly. "Jesus, Tate. Get away from me. What are you *doing* here?"

He took my hand. I was forced to follow as we crossed to the rack of pool cues, where I watched Tate select one. "I had to see Bibianna. She tell you about us?"

"Of course. You could have told me yourself if you'd trusted me."

"Who had time? I'se busy shooting bad guys." He raised the cue to shoulder height and sighted down the length of it like a rifle. "Boom."

"How'd you know where we'd be?"

"Pick a cue stick," he said.

I chose one at random, too distracted to be particular, not that I have a clue about the qualities of a good cue.

"Not that one." He handed me another cue stick and then continued casually. "This is Raymond's hangout. You don't have to be Sherlock Holmes to figure out where he'll be. By the way, if Raymond comes over and wants to know what's going on, tell him the truth—we went to grade school together."

"How'd you get out of the slammer? I thought you were broke. What's bail on a murder charge, two hundred thousand bucks?"

"Two fifty. I got a friend in Montebello who put up his house. My attorney got bail knocked down to a hundred grand. I'm out on OR plus bail. . . ."

"And they let you leave the county?"

"Quit worryin'. It's legitimate. I talked my probation officer into an eight-hour turnaround. My wife's sick, I said. I'm due back in Santa Teresa by six A.M. or they'll throw me in the can again." Tate arranged the balls in the rack and broke. Balls scattered everywhere with a satisfying crack.

"What are we doing? I haven't played pool for years."

"Eight-ball. It's your shot."

"You're very cute," I said without much conviction. "Just tell me what to hit and let's get on with it."

"You think I can have time alone with her?"

"No."

"Would you give her a message? Would you tell her I'm doing everything I can to get her out of here?"

"Sure."

We played pool. Jimmy Tate pretended to tutor me and I took instruction, all in the interest of conducting a tense conversation overlaid with bright smiles. From a distance, I hoped we'd look like potential bedmates to someone who would kill us if he figured out what was actually happening. Tate loved it, of course. This was just the sort of situation he thrived on—out there on the front line, taking flak, taking risks in the name of I don't even know what. I was feeling that same sick sensation that prefaces a tetanus shot. Something bad was going to happen and I couldn't figure out how to escape it.

Tate said, "You taking good care of her for me?"

"I'm a real champ," I said. "This is the last time I'm ever doing shit like this for anyone."

He smiled. "That's because you'd rather kick butt."

"You got *that* right."

Tate cleaned up the table and we joined the other three, who were bunched into the booth. Luis got up and I slid in beside Tate, who remained carefully attentive to me in the process. Luis found an empty chair and pulled it over to the table. I think it was the first time I ever served as a "beard" in a dangerous liaison. Liar that I am under ordinary circumstances, I found it a tricky business to fake a flirtation. I felt awkward and false, reactions not lost on Raymond, whose radar was telling him enemy aircraft were somewhere in the area. I felt his eyes scan my face with a half-formed question. Maybe he'd write me off as a hopeless social oaf. Certainly the woodenness of my response to Tate was obvious.

Tate proceeded to tease me outrageously under Bibianna's watchful gaze. She was feigning indifference, but her interest was obvious. Aside from the fact the situation scared me silly, I was glad to have Tate on the scene. I hadn't realized, before he showed up, how isolated I was feeling. I was still vulnerable, of course—more so with him there—but at least I had a friend, and I knew, from my long experience, he'd lay down his life for me if it came to that.

Bibianna, in range of Jimmy Tate again, began to do the ritual dance. There was nothing overt in her behavior. She went out of her way to cater to Raymond, tucking her arm in his, leaning against him so that her breast brushed his arm enticingly. She and Tate avoided eye contact, ignoring one another so pointedly I'd have thought them rude if I hadn't known their true relationship. As it was, the game they played was far riskier. The color crept up in her cheeks unbidden. I watched the sexuality emerge, some ancient, unspeakable response to her mate. I couldn't believe Raymond didn't pick up on it. The only clue I had about his inner state was the eruption of the tics, which were running once a minute.

Raymond was clearly feeling territorial. Whether he was sensitive to what was actually going on or not, Tate was still a male, not only on Raymond's turf, but in close proximity to his woman. Raymond seemed to swell, trying to engage Tate in a shoving match of boasts and braggadocio, a verbal pissing match. I don't know what, among women, would constitute an equivalent. I tuned out the talk because it was all chest-thumping bullshit, fueled by alcohol and testosterone. I couldn't even begin to compute what Tate's response might be when he found out Bibianna was sleeping with Raymond. The whole situation might have amused me if I hadn't been so eaten up with tension.

Luis was watchful. The usual blank mask fell away and I saw, for the first time, a wily intelligence at work. Behind his dead eyes, a lively animal lurked, all the more dangerous for its cunning at concealment. The spark died. He slouched in his seat, flinging an arm across the back of the chair. He lifted his beer bottle by the neck and drank deeply. By the time he looked at me again, the arrogance was back, the superiority of the male lording it over lesser mortals.

I thought the night would never end. The Spanish music was jarring, either loud and frenetic or emotionally oppressive. The air was cloudy with smoke and the smell of beer. The only thing I cared about was staying very close to Tate, whose sun-weathered face was the only refuge I could see. I made him dance with me, in part to keep him away from Raymond, who was no fool. In the stress of the moment, we all drank way too much. I'd be sick in the morning, but I didn't care at this point. Maybe I could carve out a quiet life for myself on the bathroom floor, head hanging over the toilet bowl.

We closed the place down at 2:00 A.M. Outside the bar, we parted company with Tate. I was just relieved to get out of the situation in one piece, with no fisticuffs, no confrontations, no tears. Luis left the three of us out in front of the apartment, peeling off in the Cadillac. I preceded Raymond and Bibianna up the stairs, waiting while Raymond unlocked the door and let us in. The dog lay in the doorway like a sentinel, lifting his heavy bony head to give me a look as I passed. At least he had the good grace not to growl.

I went into my room and slipped into my nightie, then headed for the bathroom. The door to the master bedroom was closed. I knew from the way Raymond had been looking at Bibianna that his desires were at a peak again. In the interest of keeping peace, she was going to have to submit. I felt for her. What could be worse than making love to someone you didn't want to be with, caught up in a situation that dictated intimacy? I washed my face and brushed my teeth, turned the bathroom light out, and padded barefoot into my room. I opened one of the windows and leaned out, gazing briefly along the street, first in one direction, then the other. No one was stirring. In the quiet of the hour, by the pale wash of moonlight, even poverty can look appealing. The shabbiness is cleansed, all the broken parts made whole. The concrete sidewalk seemed to glow with silver, the street a darker tone. A car passed, driven slowly. Jimmy Tate, perhaps? Was he wild with the notion of Bibianna in bed with someone else? I remembered Daniel, my second ex-husband, whose sexual betrayal had been a source of such anguish once. Later, after love dies, it's hard to remember how it could have ever mattered so much.

From the other room, I heard the muffled thumping as the king-size bed banged into the wall. I lifted my head, suddenly sobered by the realization that this was the perfect time to get some work done if I moved fast enough. I peeled off my nightie and pulled on some jeans. I yanked a

T-shirt over my head and slipped my bare feet into Bib-ianna's tennis shoes, which I tied in haste. I unlocked the sliding glass window and shoved it open, aluminum frame rasping in its track.

The night air was cold and a light breeze whipped across my face. Below, the passageway between buildings looked dark and empty. I could smell smog and briny ocean in a heady mix. I boosted myself up onto the windowsill and scrambled out onto the metal landing between flights of stairs. The alcohol I'd consumed was acting as a sedative for any anxiety I might have felt. My heart was pumping hard and the effect was energizing. I was thrilled to be on the move again, excited to be looking at some action after all the enforced passivity.

17

My tennis shoes made hardly any sound as I eased past Raymond's darkened window. I held my breath, but the closed bedroom drapes were still being flattened rhythmically as the headboard banged against them. I felt my way down the stairs, my footsteps making soft tinking sounds where my rubber soles touched the metal. At the bottom of the steps, I paused to orient myself. I was sheltered in the dark shadow of the apartment complex. It was close to 3:00 A.M., the street deserted, the neighborhood cloaked in silence. Even traffic on the big boulevard half a block away was only intermittent. The moon was full and rode high in the night sky. The Los Angeles city lights projected an ashen reflection across the heavens, blotting out the stars. As my eyes became accustomed to the dark, I began to distinguish the clear, pale light being cast by the moon. I emerged from the gap between Raymond's building and the apartment complex next door. I turned left, clinging to the shadows as I crossed the street, moving toward the auto salvage yard. I touched the fence and felt my way along the perimeter, sometimes traversing the circular glow of streetlights. I chose a spot halfway down the block where a driveway cut through the fence. A cluster of tall weeds and ratty shrubs flanked the gate. By day, the dirt lane was used by the tow trucks bringing in disabled vehicles. At night, when the yard closed, a wide gate was rolled across the opening, looped with a chain, and secured by a padlock. I pushed at the gate, forcing it open as far as the chain would permit. A ten-inch gap appeared. I hunkered, holding to the gatepost with both hands as I slid my right leg through. By pushing back with my hips, I could force the fence post back by another couple of inches. I rotated my shoulders, slipped my head through the gap, and then pivoted on my feet, neatly inserting myself into the yard on the other side.

The chunky mountains of rusted metal were lightly frosted by moonlight. I felt as if I'd entered a charnel house of wrecked autos. Some cars had flipped, their tops squashed flat. Some had been torn in two on impact with trees, bridge abutments, and telephone poles. The roll call of destruction conjured up awesome images of the attendant human suffering: ripped chrome and cracked glass, smashed fenders, splayed and flattened tires, engines rammed through hoods, steering columns crammed up against broken front seats. Every vehicle I saw represented a chapter in somebody's life—sometimes the last—sirens and flashing lights signaling injury and death, the loss of a loved one, or the opening scene in a nightmare of mending and medical expenses.

I waited until my heart had stopped pounding in my ears and then I picked my way down the dirt lane toward the offices of Buddy's Auto Body Shop. The pickup truck I'd seen earlier was no longer parked near the trailer, but Brutus had been left behind to stand guard over the property. I could see him, black and bulky near the single-wide, keeping watch as I approached. I sank down on my heels, calling to him softly, making little kissing sounds in the quiet. He gathered his hind feet under him, launched himself into a standing position, and began to toddle toward me carefully. He seemed to tiptoe, bones creaking, his forward motion fueled by memories of a vigorous youth.

I held my hand out and he sniffed it, making hoarse sounds of joy and recognition. I spent a few minutes with him, assuring him of my benign intentions. When I rose to my feet, he accompanied me to the trailer and watched politely while I removed all the louvers from the window. I stuck a hand through the opening and felt a solid wooden surface, which I guessed was a desk shoved up against the wall just below the window. I stacked the louvers neatly on the desk top inside.

I hoisted myself up, whispering compliments to Brutus, who wagged his tail so hard he nearly toppled sideways in the process. "Back in a flash," I said. I swung my feet through the window and eased myself into the pitch black of the office. I was now sitting on a desk. I could feel an adding machine, the telephone, and miscellaneous office supplies. I replaced the glass louvers in the metal brackets made for them.

I eased down off the desk. I stood there for a few minutes until I got used to the darkness. I usually don't do these breaking-and-entering gigs unless I have my little tool kit in tow: flashlight and lockpicks, adhesive tape, and jimmies. Here, I was empty-handed and I felt distinctly disadvantaged. All I wanted was to check the file cabinets to see if Raymond kept his papers on the premises. Once I established the whereabouts of the records, I was out of here. I was going to have to risk a light. I kept in mind the sign I'd seen, indicating an alarm system. Would Raymond actually have such a system, or was he the kind who thought he could deter all the burglars and vandals by pretending to have security? Hard to say with him. He was so righteous about the law when it suited his purposes.

I felt along the wall until I found the switch. I hesitated for a moment and then flipped the light on. The forty-watt bulb revealed an inner office maybe ten feet by twelve, wall paneled halfway up with sheets of fake knotty pine. Girlie calendars from the last six years were tacked up above a workbench where some front windshields had been piled. Three extension cords were plugged into a socket in the inner office and looped through the doorway to service the outer office. Every surface in the room was a jumble of cardboard boxes and greasy car parts. Two gray metal file cabinets were tucked into the corner on the far side of the room. As I crossed the open door leading to the outer office, I caught a blink of light out of the corner of my eye. The passive infrared "seeing eye" of Raymond's alarm picked up my body heat and set off the entire system.

A horn, probably adequate to announce the end of the world, began a great whooping noise that alternated between high notes and low notes and seemed to include some kind of bell clanging in between. We are programmed from birth to react to sudden loud noises. Of course I jumped and my heart kicked up into high gear. At the same time, I could feel my emotions disconnect as they do in certain emergencies. I wondered belatedly if Raymond's alarm was set up to signal the police. I better count on it, I thought. I glanced at my watch. It was 3:12 A.M. I figured I had about five minutes max before the black-and-whites showed up. Might have been a charitable estimate on my part. Maybe the LAPD didn't even bother with alarms. Maybe they'd respond in their own sweet time. What did I know about the machinations of big-city police procedure? While the alarm system bleated and shrieked and pointed an auditory finger, I crossed to the file cabinet and opened the first drawer. Invoices, car parts. I shut that one and tried the next. More invoices, financial records, correspondence, blank forms. Drawer three was a repeat. I skipped to the next file cabinet and started with the top, working my way down. The bottom three drawers were packed with manila folders full of claim forms. I glanced at dates in haste, noting that the claims seemed to extend back about three years. Outside, Brutus was offering up an occasional hoarse bark, apparently overjoyed that I had hit the jackpot. I closed the file drawers, checked to see that the louvered window was shut, tidied some papers on the desk, and brushed some dirt off the Month-at-a-Glance that was lying there. I walked into the outer office, moved around the corner to the front door, which I opened, ducked back to the inner office, and flipped out the light there, then felt my way in the dark to the front door again. I stepped out and gave the door a hard pull behind me, effectively locking it again. The alarm clamoring against the night air seemed to have aroused no particular interest among the neighbors. I wondered if Raymond could hear it from across the street and two doors down.

I set off at a run, jogging down the dirt path toward the gate, with Brutus bringing up the rear. I could hear him loping along behind me, panting happily as he maneuvered his legs in some dimly remembered sequence. I glanced back. For an old pooch, he was really truckin', determined to keep up with me in my little nighttime ramble. I reached the gate and pushed it, reversing the procedure by which I angled my way in. I heard a car squeal around the corner and looked back just in time to see the black-and-white appear on the scene. I shoved back hard on the fence post and pivoted my way through the narrow opening.

I heard a sound like the equivalent of a canine rebuke. When I looked over I saw that Brutus had his head stuck in the gap between the gate and the fence post. He was yanking backward, his bony head and the thick muscular neck pinched in a vise of fencing. Car doors slammed and one uniformed cop headed toward the front entrance while the second one walked in my direction.

"Oh, God," I said. I jerked the gate forward and pushed the dog's head to free him. Then I plunged into the bushes and crouched down. I was shielded temporarily by a tangle of shrubbery, but the oncoming cop was scanning every inch of the fence with a heavy-duty flashlight. Meanwhile, inside the fence, Brutus had discovered what I was doing. He put his nose against the chain link and made a worried sound, half growl, half celebration of our newly cemented friendship.

The cop down the block near the office gave a whistle and the officer closer to me turned and headed back the way he'd come. I pulled myself to my feet and extracted myself from the bushes, inching away from the squad car as inconspicuously as I could. Brutus began to bark, unwilling to be abandoned just when the game was getting good. There was a line of parked cars at the curb. I reached the first and ducked behind it, using the cars as concealment until I reached the corner. I crossed the street at an angle and doubled back toward Raymond's, cutting into the heavy shadows between apartment buildings. Above me, the window in his bedroom blazed with light. I took the metal stairs three at a time, pulling myself up by the railing. Out of breath, I eased past the bedroom, found my open window, and plunged into the bedroom again. I whipped my shoes off, pulled my jeans down, and stuck my head out the door, squinting at the lights that were now flipped on in the hall. Bibianna, in a silk robe, was just emerging from the bedroom. I could hear Raymond in the living room on the phone with someone.

"What's happening?" I asked.

Bibianna rolled her eyes. "It's the body shop. False alarm. Sometimes the damn thing goes off. Chopper's on his way over, but the cops say it's nothing. Go back to bed."

I closed the door. Sleep was a long time coming.

I woke at nine-thirty to the smell of coffee. I showered and dressed. The door to the master bedroom was open and I caught a glimpse of the broad king-size bed, neatly made. No sign of Raymond or Bibianna. I wandered into the living room to find that Luis was the only one on the premises, except the dog, of course. Luis paid no particular attention to me. He placed a clean mug on the counter and I poured myself some coffee.

"Thanks," I murmured. I sat down at the kitchen table, doing a quick inspection first to make sure it had been wiped clean. "Where's Bibianna?"

"They went off someplace."

"What are you, the baby-sitter?"

He made no reply. A carton of eggs sat open on the counter. In the day since I'd cleaned the kitchen, it had fallen into disarray again. Trash bags were lined up against the cabinets, bulging with beer bottles and discarded paper plates. The sink was piled high with dirty pots and pans, ashtrays spilling butts. Who smoked? I never saw anyone with a cigarette. Luis had pulled out the only clean skillet. He set it on a burner. He began to remove items from the refrigerator: peppers, onions, chorizo. "You want breakfast?"

"Sure, I'd love it. You need any help?"

He shook his head.

It seemed like the perfect opportunity to pump him for information, but I didn't want to start with the fraud ring itself lest I seem too inquisitive. "I hope this doesn't seem too personal," I said. "I thought Raymond would be upset about Chago's death, but he hasn't said a word about it. Weren't they close?"

Luis sliced the peppers into rings and then chopped onions, making no reference to the chemically induced tears rolling down his cheeks. His gaze came up to meet mine. "Chago was all he had. Raymond's sisters kicked him out when he was fourteen on account of his temper. He was on his own after that and he's done okay, considering. Kids in school used to mock him, making fun of his disease."

"You knew him then?"

"Juan told me about it. I kind of wish he'd go to the doctor, get some help for himself, but he won't do it. He thinks Bibianna's all the help he needs."

I watched him, expecting more, but apparently he felt what he'd said should suffice. He used the knife to mound the onions, then walked the blade through the pile, mincing them. He crossed to the stove. I waited as he tilted the skillet, watching a hunk of melting butter circle lazily. He tossed in the onions and peppers. Finally, he spoke up again. "How you know Jimmy Tate? I saw his picture in the papers. He's a cop," he said, rendering the word with venom.

"An ex-cop. From grade school. We were kids together in Santa Teresa a long time ago."

"He's a snitch."

"That's bullshit. L.A. County Sheriff's Department just fired the guy and he turned around and sued. They're not going to hire him to do anything!"

Luis turned, pointing at me with the knife. "Let me tell you something. Tate's got no business with us. He shows up and I smell a snitch. Don't tell me bullshit. I know what I'm talking about."

I could feel myself hesitate, backing up a step. The idea of Tate undercover had crossed my mind, too. In the interview with Dolan and Santos, I'd asked twice if they had a man in and both times they'd been nonresponsive. Tate's suit against the department and his Tuesday night arrest might be part of his cover. If Luis was suspicious, then Raymond would be, too, and every move Tate made would be subject to scrutiny. "What's Raymond say?"

"He's checking out a source."

"Well, that's good," I said. "Then he can find out for sure, right?" My heart did a rat-a-tat-tat from fear. The possibility of a department leak was already a source of concern. If word trickled out about me, I was dead.

Luis retreated again. He sliced into the skin of a Mexican sausage and squeezed out the meat in a gesture surprisingly ominous. Soon I could smell the chorizo sizzling away with the onions and peppers. Luis broke eight eggs into a bowl with one hand, then whipped them into a froth with a fork.

I didn't want to defend Jimmy Tate too vigorously because it might backfire. Somebody might begin to wonder what made me such an expert. Best not to protest too much when you're tampering with the truth. Besides, Tate's cover had to be deep—if, indeed, that's what was happening. Dolan and Santos were both aware of the need for secrecy. I let the subject drop. I had thought to probe for information about the fraud ring. Now, I decided to bypass the quiz. All I needed was Luis turning his steely gaze on me.

We ate the omelet in silence. I'm forced to report it was one of the best I've ever eaten. The few bites I couldn't finish, I put down for the dog. Perro snapped the eggs up in one bite with a jerk of his head that propelled food down his throat. After breakfast, Luis scrubbed the skillet. My job was to fold the plates and throw them in the trash.

"What's the program for the day?"

"I take you to the chiropractor as soon as Raymond gets back."

"How come we have to wait? Can't we do anything on our own?"

Luis said nothing. I decided it wasn't wise to press. Raymond didn't seem to trust him much more than he trusted me.

At noon Raymond and Bibianna returned to the apartment. Her face was haggard, the look she turned on me full of dread. She was signaling something, but I wasn't sure what. In contrast, Raymond's mood seemed expansive, though I noticed the twinkle of a tic in his blinking. Bibianna took her jacket off and tossed it on the couch. There was a Band-Aid across the crook of her right arm. Raymond grabbed her from behind in a bear hug, an odd hostility disguised as affection.

He caught my look, which had touched on the Band-Aid and glanced off. "She had a blood test. We're getting married as soon as the license comes through. Three days max."

"Congratulations," I said weakly. "Really, that's great."

Luis extended his hand. He and Raymond went through some complicated series of palm slaps and grips, signifying great gang joy at the nuptials of another. Bibianna's happiness was so overwhelming that she had to leave the room, a reaction not lost on the ever-vigilant Raymond. I could see the tic pick up, his mouth coming open, his neck jerking back. Luis broke out a couple of beers, ostensibly to celebrate. My guess was he hoped to head off one of Raymond's attacks. "Get her out here. Luis is going to get us some champagne. We'll drink a toast."

"I'll be right back," I murmured, and went into the bedroom. Bibianna was sitting on the edge of the bed, her head in her hands.

I sat down on the bed beside her, watching her without a word. What could I say? She was married to Jimmy Tate. There was no way she was going to end up married to Raymond, too. Finally, I said, "What are you going to do?"

She looked at me bleakly. "Kill myself or kill him." She reached out and took my hand, giving it a squeeze.

"I'll hang in," I said.

"I know that," she replied.

18

Luis parked the Ford in a small weedy lot adjacent to a strip mall that had probably been built in the early fifties judging by the architectural style, which was of the cinder block and glass brick variety. The chiropractor's office was located in a storefront, wedged between a barbecue joint and a barbershop. Dusty beige drapes covered the plateglass windows, protecting the interior from the curious stares of those passing on the street. Not that there was much to see inside. The walls were flat blue, lined with metal folding chairs. A television set in the corner ran a Spanish-language tape extolling the virtues of the chiropractic arts. A tattered illustration on the wall labeled "Chart of the Eye" showed the split circles with radial divisions essential to iridiagnosis, by which one could accurately identify diabetes mellitus, typhoid, aortic regurgitation, and other alarming conditions. The floor was covered in marbled beige vinyl tiles, through which a damp mop had been trailed recently, leaving tracks of yesterday's dirt. A counter separated the reception area from the examining rooms in the rear. There were sixteen people waiting to see Dr. Howard and no magazines. One of the other patients was a fellow I thought I'd seen in Raymond's apartment the day I arrived. I filled out a rudimentary medical history, automatically printing the first three letters of "Millhone" before I caught myself, converting the *i* and *l* to the double *oo*'s of my current alias, "Moore." The form itself took two minutes to complete, after which we all sat and looked at one another while two babies cried and eleven people smoked thirty-four cigarettes between them. The inhalation of passive smoke in conjunction with my boredom was enough to make me want to flee the premises. I checked my watch. I'd been sitting for an hour and a half. I didn't feel I could complain since I was only there to cheat the insurance company. I imagined all the other people, blacks, Hispanics, the elderly, the weekend athletes, being variously cracked, pummeled, pounded, and popped into alignment in the back room while I awaited my turn. People coming out to pay for treatment did appear to be relieved. Their backs seemed straighter, shoulders squared. They moved with more energy, taking with them enormous jars of pills which I assumed were expensive vitamins or calcium supplements. Many soft and crumpled dollar bills were passed over to the bilingual receptionist, a woman in her forties, quite possibly the doctor's wife.

When my turn came, I checked her name tag, but all it said was Martha. She walked me down a short corridor, past the open door of what must have been Dr. Howard's office. I caught a glimpse of a scarred oak desk covered with stacks of charts and small standing picture frames, probably showing him with loving family members, thus establishing his marital status and firmly declaring him off limits to women patients with designing minds. I was ushered into the adjoining examining room, noting with interest the door between the two rooms, which stood ajar. I could see through the doctor's office right back out into the hallway, where a passing patient turned and looked at me with curiosity. Martha opened a cabinet and removed a print smock that seemed to be made of two oblong cotton panels stitched together at the side and secured with elastic at the neck.

"Take your shoes off and strip down to your panties," she said, handing me the gown. "He'll be with you in ten minutes."

"Thanks. Uhm, could we close that other door?" I asked.

"Certainly." She moved through the doctor's office to the hall door, closing it as she went out.

I could feel my fingers start to itch.

My, my. All by myself and the office records of a scofflaw, insurance-defrauding bone cracker not ten feet away. I checked the door to the examining room, which had a thumb button on the knob, which I pressed, locking it. I stripped my clothes off in haste and pulled the gown over my head, then padded barefoot into the doctor's office, locking his door, too. The walls were so thin and so poorly constructed that it wasn't hard to run an auditory check of what was going on around me. I heard the doctor enter the room across the hall, greeting the patient by name as he closed the door behind him. Their murmurs were audible, though the content of the consultation was lost as he proceeded to his adjustment. I kept one ear cocked while I searched as thoroughly as I could in the eight minutes allotted me, uncovering a drawerful of claims that were a cursory match to the insurance forms I'd seen at Raymond's. I heard the door across the hall come open, the doctor's voice growing more distant as he gave a few final words of counsel and advice. I closed the desk drawer and crossed rapidly to the office door, grabbed the knob, and twisted. The button popped out. I was heading toward the examining room again when one of the little framed family photos on his desk caught my eye.

I stopped and squinted, peering at a bridal photo of a young woman I could have sworn I'd seen before. I snatched up the double frame, quickly rearranging the remaining frames to conceal the sudden gap. I eased into the examining room and had just tucked the picture frame in the handbag I'd borrowed from Bibianna when I heard the doctor try the door.

"Just a minute," I called. I popped the lock and opened the door for him with a sheepish smile. "Sorry," I said. "I didn't realize it was locked. Are you Dr. Howard?"

"That's right." He came into the room, closing the door behind him.

I resisted the impulse to shake hands with the man. It seemed inappropriate since I'd just burgled something from his desk. He was in his sixties, very clean looking. He wore white pants and a white jacket, with a snowy dress shirt underneath, starched shirt collar standing up so high it seemed to pleat his neck. His dark hair looked soft on top. His hairline was receding, which left him with a long expanse of unlined forehead. He had cold eyes, a mild brown behind square tortoiseshell frames, a humorless mouth that turned down slightly at the corners. He managed a perfunctory smile with his lips while the rest of his face remained fixed. His gaze was intense, giving him the look of a man capable of seeing straight from his own felonious heart into mine. The fragrance of crushed spices wafted into the room behind him, some faded Oriental blend of musk and sandalwood.

He glanced at my chart. "Miss Moore. What seems to be the trouble? Why don't you hop up on the table."

"It's my neck," I said as I hiked myself onto the table. "I was in a little accident and Raymond Maldonado suggested I have you check it." He crossed to a corner sink and washed his hands with a virulent-looking red liquid soap from a wall dispenser. The gaze he turned on me was brief, but sharply focused. "You should have mentioned that to Martha. We'll need an X ray," he said. "I'll have my assistant take it. You can come back here when you're done." He moved to the door and held it open for me. Instinct told me to take my handbag, which I picked up and tucked under one arm, a gesture of distrust not lost on him.

"Your purse is safe, if you'd care to leave it," he said.

"It's no trouble," I murmured, not volunteering to put it back. I had visions of his searching it in my absence, discovering the photo I'd swiped before he arrived. My memory warbled a little tune, too faint to identify. I was certain I'd seen the woman in the picture, but I had no idea where.

Barefoot, I followed him down the corridor to a makeshift X-ray laboratory, partitioned off by a few temporary plywood screens. The equipment looked like some

I'd seen in a doctor's office when I was a kid: bulky and black, with a cone the size of a zoom lens. I imagined 1950s-style rays, thick and clunky, piercing my body in poorly calibrated doses. The assistant, a young guy with a cigarette bobbing in his mouth, took two views—a full spine and a close-up of the cervical vertebrae. I'm wary of unnecessary X-ray procedures, but again, since I was cheating, it was hard to protest. I returned to the examining room, where I had another long wait, this time sitting dutifully on the paper-covered table. For all I knew Dr. Howard was observing me through a hidden peephole. He returned in due course, snapping the developed film onto a wall-mounted viewer. He explained patiently, in chiropractic terms, how misshapen my spine was. Happily, my neck wasn't broken, but almost every other part of my back was in want of improvement. He put me facedown on the table and did something divine, crunching my bones in a manner that sounded like someone chewing ice. He prescribed a lengthy series of adjustments, writing out his diagnosis with a fountain pen. He was left-handed, wrist curving atop the sentences as he sketched out his recommendations. The pen made a scratching sound as it angled across the page. Even his writing looked expensive, I thought. California Fidelity was going to pay dearly for my ills.

"What's your relationship to Raymond?" he asked without looking up. Something about the nonchalance of his tone sounded a note of caution.

"I'm a friend of Bibianna's, his fiancée."

"Have you known her long?"

"Two days," I said. "We did an overnight together in the Santa Teresa County Jail."

The sharp gaze shifted and I thought I detected a nearly imperceptible pursing of his lips. He disapproved of lowlifes like Bibianna and me, probably Raymond Maldonado, too. "How long have you had your offices down here?" I asked.

"Since my license was reinstated," he said, surprising me with his candor. Maybe I'd misjudged the man. He opened a drawer and took out a number of ink pens, of various types and colors. He passed me a sheet of paper with a series of slots in the left-hand column. "Sign each line with a different pen, rotating them randomly. We'll fill the dates in later when we go to bill your insurance company. Who's the carrier?"

"California Fidelity. I called the office up north and they said they'd send the claim forms down."

"Good," he said. "And what sort of work do you normally do?"

"Waitress."

"Not good. I don't want you on your feet and no lifting heavy trays. File for disability. Nice to meet you," he said. He snapped my chart shut, got up, and left the room. Half a minute later, I heard him entering the examining room next to mine.

It was two fifty-five by the time I left his office. The day was hot for late October, the air perfumed with the yeasty smell of warm exhaust fumes. The neighborhood we were in wasn't much of an improvement over the one where Raymond lived. As I approached the Ford, Luis leaned over and opened the car door. I slid into the front seat. Whatever Dr. Howard had done in the way of adjustments, my hangover was at least gone. I tilted my head this way and that, taking inventory of my neck. Not bad. No stiffness, no more aches or pains.

The interior of the car smelled of fast-food burgers and cold French fries. There was an empty milk shake container on the dashboard and a white paper bag sitting on the front seat. "Oh, goody, for me?" I asked. I peered into the bag, hunger rising suddenly. "Luis, there's nothing in here but trash!"

"I thought you'd ate."

"You thought I'd ate?" I said pointedly.

Luis seemed embarrassed. "Eaten."

"Yeah, well, I eaten the same time you did and I'm starving again." I revised my tone. There was no point in being a bitch about this. "Isn't there any way we could stop and pick up some lunch for me on the way home?"

He started the car, checking the flow of traffic in the rearview mirror. "Raymond said come back as soon as you got done. We got work to do."

"How come we have to do everything he says?"

Luis turned a flat look on me.

I thought about Raymond's temper. "Good point," I said.

When we got back to the apartment, the dog was tied to the railing out on the balcony and the apartment door was standing open. There were six or eight young Hispanics on the premises, most of whom I hadn't seen before. Bibianna sat on the couch, bending over a game of solitaire which she'd laid out on the coffee table. Luis went into the kitchen and fetched himself a beer. I excused myself with a murmur and went into my room, where I removed the stolen pictures from my handbag. I moved over to the window and opened it quietly. The frame was a bifold, two photographs in matte gold, hinged in the middle. I dismantled the frame and tossed it out the window, checking first to make sure I wouldn't be clunking anybody in the head with it. I studied both photographs closely, holding them up to the light. These were formal wedding portraits. The first was one of those group shots taken at the church altar afterward, people lined up in a semicircle with the bride and groom in the center. In addition to the newlyweds, there were six young women in lavender, fanning out to the left, and six guys in gray tuxedos with lavender cummerbunds on the right. Dr. Howard was clearly the father of the bride, whose mother didn't look a thing like the receptionist. I'd guessed wrong there. The second photograph was a full-length shot of the bride herself. She was the woman I thought I recognized. She was standing in three-quarter profile, her eyes lifted solemnly toward the stained-glass window above her head, bridal bouquet held at her waist. The dress was a close-fitting satin with a train that had been spread out around her feet as if the material had melted to form a pool. Her blond hair was pulled back, secured in some kind of netting like a bridal snood. The face was tantalizing, not pretty by any stretch, but she'd clearly hired a team of makeup experts to enhance her every feature. I was sure I'd seen her recently, but not looking nearly as good as this. I squinted, perplexed. It was like seeing your mailman at a cocktail party in fancy dress. I had to shrug and forget it for the moment. It would come to me, probably popping into my head when I was in the middle of something else.

I crossed to the closet, slid the door back, and pulled up a corner of the dark blue shag wall-to-wall carpet. I slipped the pictures under it and pressed the carpet back in place.

I returned to the living room, where Bibianna was studying the run of solitaire she'd laid out. I settled into the chair. I tucked my feet up under me and watched Bibianna play, keeping a discreet eye on the gangbangers, who had formed a rough line near the kitchenette. It must have been payday. Raymond sat at the table, collecting hand-held slips of paper, counting out bills in return. He was all business, conducting transactions in Spanish. Without appearing to pay much attention, I took note of the faces, wondering if I'd be able to identify them later from mug shots, if required. The only two I recognized were Raymond's brother, Juan, and the sulky fellow, Tomas, who'd had so much trouble with his paperwork the day I arrived. Raymond glanced over at me and I dropped my gaze to the solitaire laid out on the table.

I'd watched her set it up so many times by now, I was almost ready to try it myself. This one wasn't the usual red queen on a black king strategy but ran in suits so that if you won, you ended up with only four piles, one for each suit, cards in numerical order from aces up to kings. She went through all the cards in her hand by threes without coming up with a play. She tossed the hand in and pulled the cards together in a pile.

"You want to do my chart?" I asked.

She shook her head. "The stuff's at my mother's and Raymond won't let me talk to her. I tried to call her last night, but he caught me with the phone and nearly beat the shit out of me. What an ass. . . ." She glanced over at Raymond, who had stopped what he was doing so he could stare at her. Bibianna stirred uneasily and glanced at me. She said, "I can read your palm instead. Put your hands on the table."

"Palm down?"

"Yeah. Just put 'em down on the tabletop."

I eased my feet out from under me and leaned forward so I could rest my palms flat on the table as instructed. Raymond must have realized she was into her palmistry and he went back to work. Bibianna's look became intent. She scrutinized the backs of my hands, then lifted both and turned them over. She took my right hand in hers and examined it with care, saying nothing. Her manner was as professional as a doctor's. I don't believe in palmistry, any more than I believe in numerology, astrology, the Easter bunny, or the tooth fairy, but there was something in her expression that piqued my curiosity. "What?" I said.

She ran an index finger across my right palm, took up my left palm, and looked at it again. "You like action. You know how I know that? When you put your hands down on the table, you left a lot of space between. Insecure people put 'em close together. Short nails indicate you're aggressive. No ridges or spots, which is good. Means you're healthy. Skin type is medium, doesn't say much, but look at this . . . how wide the space is between your thumb and the fingers on this hand. You think for yourself. . . ."

Her voice was hypnotic and I found myself listening to her with great seriousness. I'd expected a lot of talk about life lines and love lines, but she didn't have a chance to get to that. The trouble broke out so suddenly, I never knew what started it. I heard a shout, the banging as a chair fell over backward. By the time I looked up, Raymond had Tomas down on the floor. He was clutching the guy by the throat, the switchblade against his cheek. Raymond's face was contorted by rage, his hands shaking as he squeezed his fingers into Tomas's windpipe. Tomas was burbling, his eyes wide as he struggled to free himself. Sweat had beaded his forehead. I saw the blade of the knife slip into his cheek, sinking into the flesh, blood welling up. Raymond seemed almost hypnotized by the process. No one else made a move. It seemed to be one of those moments where retaliatory violence would only jeopardize Tomas's chance of survival.

Bibianna whispered, "My God . . ." She crossed the room, kneeling beside Raymond, where she began to murmur in his ear. I could see him struggle for control. He made a sound like a sob, very tight and ancient, almost a squealing at the back of his throat. Bibianna touched his hand, talking to him earnestly. "Don't do this, Raymond. I beg you. Let him go. He didn't mean nothing by it. You're hurting him. Please . . ."

He lifted the knife. Bibianna extracted it from his hand while his victim rolled away, blood pouring down his face. Raymond seemed to cough and his rage shifted from Tomas to Bibianna. He grabbed her by the arms and hauled her upright, shoving her up against the wall so hard her head banged a piece of plaster loose. He put his face an inch away from hers, the now familiar ripple of tics tugging half the muscles in his face. His eyes rolled up in his head so that he seemed to look at her with the milky, blind slits. His voice was a whisper. "I'll kill you, you ever interfere with me again, you got that?"

Bibianna nodded frantically. "I won't. I'm sorry. I didn't mean to . . ."

He stepped away. The ritual cough and bark began and I could see him jerk his head, rolling his shoulder in its socket. Luis had grabbed a kitchen towel and was pressing it against the cut in Tomas's cheek, issuing orders in Spanish. Blood soaked through instantly. Two of the guys came to Tomas's assistance, helping him out the door. The apartment cleared rapidly. My heart was pounding. Bibianna sank down on the couch, white-faced. She put her head between her knees, close to fainting. I moved over and sat down beside her, patting her and murmuring words of encouragement as much for my own benefit as for hers. Moments later, Luis returned. I gathered that someone was taking Tomas off to the emergency room. In the meantime, Raymond seemed to have regained control. Bibianna composed herself and picked up her cards again with shaking hands. Luis wiped blood off the kitchen floor. All of us understood how important it was to get past the moment. To avoid any further upset, we acted as if nothing had happened, which made us co-conspirators. No reference was made to Tomas or what he'd done to precipitate Raymond's reaction.

Raymond paced the room, snapping his fingers restlessly as he turned to Bibianna. "Hey. Get your jacket. We're going out. Hannah, you too."

I got my jacket. Hell, I wasn't going to argue with the man.

This time Raymond and I took the Ford, while Luis followed us in the Cadillac, Bibianna in the passenger seat. I turned halfway, looking through the back window at the Caddy, which kept pace with us. Luis and Bibianna were only dark silhouettes. "How come she always goes with him on these runs?"

"We fight," he said.

I studied him with interest. He seemed relaxed, his manner open and easy. I was beginning to understand that for a short period of time just after an "attack," he was really rather benign, as if soothed by the outburst. For a brief interlude, he would be completely approachable, even loving. He was not a bad-looking guy. He could probably find a woman who'd care for him if he wasn't fixated on Bibianna.

He caught my look. "What are *you* lookin' at?" His words were belligerent, but the tone was mild.

"I was just trying to figure out why you're so obsessed with Bibianna. Why insist on marriage when she's clearly not that hot for it?" I held my breath, but he didn't seem to take offense.

"She can't mess with me. No way. People who screw with my head have to learn they can't. She hasn't got the word yet."

"About what? You have her back. What else do you want?"

"I have to make sure she stays."

"How can you do that?"

"I did already," he said. "She just doesn't know it yet."

19

That afternoon at the Southern California College of Auto Fraud, I took a "crash" course in "Swoop and Squat," which Lieutenants Dolan and Santos had summarized so neatly in our little jailhouse chat. We drove up into West L.A., on the border of Bel Air, running Sunset Boulevard from Sepulveda to Beverly Glen. Afternoon traffic was hellish and the drivers familiar with that stretch of road seemed to drive with their eyes shut, shifting lanes without notice, exceeding the speed limit by thirty and forty miles per hour.

Once we found a mark, Raymond and I, as the "squat" car, would position ourselves in front of it while Luis and Bibianna would pull up beside us. Luis would "swoop" suddenly into our lane. Raymond would slam on the brakes and the hapless mark behind us, caught by surprise, would plow right up our tailpipe. Luis would speed off while Raymond and I, in our car, and the mark in his, would pull over to the curb, all of us dismayed and outraged by the unexpected turn of events. There was no danger of the mark's turning around and calling the cops, because we all knew the LAPD wouldn't respond to the scene of an accident unless there was bodily injury involved. It was strictly up to us to exchange names, addresses, telephone numbers, and the names of our various insurance companies, after which we'd take off, connect up with Luis and Bibianna again, and go looking for the next vic. We ran the scam four times, with Raymond assuring me we'd racked up maybe thirteen thousand dollars' worth of business.

What troubled me, aside from the fact that I was whipping the hell out of my neck, was a worrisome little shift in my attitude. What idiots, I thought. People deserve anything that happens to them. I was beginning to believe it was all the mark's fault for being gullible and stupid, for not recognizing the game in progress, for being foolish enough to take our assurances at face value. I could feel that secret sense of superiority every con artist must have when the bait goes down and the victim snaps it up. Mentally, I had to shake myself off, though I suppose it never hurts to be reminded that none of us are that far away from larceny. Actually, it's the people who make the most righteous moral noises that I worry about the most.

We packed it in at five after a quick conference in a little pocket park where we'd pulled off to compare notes. Several nannies in uniform murmured together while the toddlers in their keeping cavorted on the play equipment. We sat on the grass, Bibianna with her shoes off, while Luis and Raymond stretched out in the fading sunlight and relived every thrilling moment. It was like hearing men talk about a golf game or a hunting trip, the two of them rehashing the experience in amazing detail. There was a quick debate about whether to try one more quick accident, but none of us were really interested. All I wanted was some aspirin and a trip back to Dr. Howard's office, where I could look forward to a back cracking that would liberate my neck.

Raymond said he had an errand to run, so he and I got back in the car. Luis peeled off in the Caddy with Bibianna while Raymond turned onto Beverly Drive and headed into the heart of the Beverly Hills business district. Two blocks down, he took a right on Little Santa Monica, which runs parallel to Santa Monica Boulevard. As we approached Wilshire Boulevard, he slowed, looking for a parking space. The meters had all been taken. With an expression of impatience, he turned into the entrance to an underground parking garage that serviced a twenty-story office building. We paused at the electronic kiosk, which buzzed, clunked once, and presented him with a ticket. The electronic "arm" shot up and Raymond slid into the nearest parking spot, clearly marked for the handicapped. He left the keys in the ignition and opened the door on his side.

"Wait here. Somebody hassles you, move the car. I'll be right back."

A vertical sign on the wall indicated that the elevators were located through the double glass doors. He walked rapidly in that direction, heels tapping on the concrete, the sound echoing against the ramps sweeping up to the left. What was he up to?

The minute he was gone, I took the keys out of the ignition and slipped around to the rear of the car, where I opened the trunk. It was empty except for the spare tire and jack. Rats. I slid into the front seat again and returned the keys to the ignition. I leaned over and checked the door pocket on Raymond's side of the car, but all I came up with were a torn Los Angeles street map and some discount coupons for a local pizza joint. The pocket on my side of the car was empty, which I knew because I'd checked it slyly while we were driving around. I popped open the glove compartment, crammed with junk. I began to sort through the wad of old gas receipts, defective ballpoint pens, successive years of car registrations, the service manual, work orders from the mechanic who did the routine maintenance. Raymond was conscientious about upkeep, I had to give him that. At regular thirty-second intervals, I checked the underground reception area where I'd seen him disappear. I was assuming he'd gone up in the elevators to one of the executive offices above. I sorted through the mess of papers in my lap, uncovering rags, a beer flip, a moldy Hershey's bar suffering from heat prostration, a foil-wrapped condom. Did we once keep our gloves in our automobile glove compartments? Now, the space seemed to rank right up there with the refrigerator as a resting place for animate and inanimate debris, evidence of a lack of personal cleanliness you'd just as soon your friends never found out about. I returned the odds and ends to the glove compartment, being careful not to be too tidy about it. Frustrating. I'd hoped to come up with something. Oh, well. With snooping, you can't expect to score every time out. An illegal search might net results in four cases out of ten. The rest of the time, it simply satisfies your basic nosiness.

By the time I heard Raymond's heels tap-tapping against the concrete, everything was back in place and I was ratting my hair in the rearview mirror, which I'd swiveled around to face me. This "Hannah Moore" persona was having a distinct effect. My "do" now consisted of some really nifty spikes on top. I looked like a punker, but it was kind of fun, if you want to know the truth. Next thing I knew I'd be getting my ears pierced and chewing gum in public, social sins my auntie had always warned me about, along with red nail polish and dingy bra straps.

Raymond opened the car door and tossed the automated parking ticket on the dashboard while he shrugged out of his jacket and tucked it in the backseat. I picked up the ticket and held on to it for him, taking advantage of my little helping girl impulse to glance down at it casually. On the back, in lieu of parking validation stickers, there was the stamped imprint from the firm of Gotlieb, Naples, Hurley, and Flushing. Attorneys? Accountants? Raymond whipped the ticket out of my hand and stuck it in his mouth, clamping it between his teeth while he started the car and backed out of the space. What was his problem? Gosh, the man just didn't seem to trust me. As we turned left out of the parking garage, I silently repeated the name of the firm, like a mantra, until I'd committed it to memory. I'd have Dolan check it out if I could get a call through to him.

We drove back to the apartment through rush-hour traffic: six lanes of the Indy 500, featuring business execs and other control freaks. I was tense, but Raymond didn't seem affected. External stresses didn't seem to disturb him the same way emotional matters did. He flipped the radio on to a classical station and turned the volume up, treating the cars on either side of us to a sonata that sounded like it was made up almost entirely of mistakes. This stretch of the 405 was flat, a sprawling expanse of concrete, riddled with factories, dotted with oil derricks, power lines, and industrial structures designed for no known purpose. In the distance, an irregular fence of chimneys was silhouetted against the skyline, which had browned down to an eerie sunset of green-and-orange light.

It was after seven o'clock and fully dark by the time we pulled into a parking space out in front of the apartment building. Walking up to the second floor, I was struck by the sounds of apartment life. As usual, many front doors stood open, televisions blaring. Children were running along the balconies, engrossed in a game of their own devising. A mother leaned over the railing and yelled at a kid named "Eduardo," who looked to be about three years old. He was protesting in Spanish, probably complaining about the indignity of an early bedtime.

Luis took the dog and went home soon after we got to the apartment. He'd been baby-sitting Bibianna, making sure she didn't bolt the minute Raymond's back was turned. The television set was on, tuned to a cable rerun of "Leave It to Beaver," which Bibianna watched halfheartedly while she laid out another hand of solitaire. Nobody seemed to feel like fixing dinner since we'd all spent a hard day smashing up cars and cheating California motorists. Bibianna's depression was exacerbated by cramps, and she went off to bed with a hot-water bottle. Raymond conjured up the telephone from its latest hiding place and sent out for Chinese. His tics were back, though they'd ceased to bother me. The guy's personal problems were much larger than the Tourette's, which I suspect other people probably learn to cope with pretty well. His sociopathology was a different matter altogether.

While the two of us sat at the kitchen table, waiting for the guy to deliver the order, Raymond rolled and smoked a joint. I picked up a couple of the half-completed insurance forms I'd seen earlier. Time to make myself useful, I thought. I looked from the first form to the second. "What's this?" I said, a laugh bubbling up again. I can't help it—some spelling errors tickle me. "Suffering from a bad case of 'bruces'?" As I reached for a third form, Raymond snatched the papers away from me.

"Raymond, come on. What's the matter with you? You can't send that to an insurance company. Both of those claims say exactly the same thing." I went ahead and pulled a third claim form from the pile. "Here's another one. Same date, same time. Don't you think they check this stuff? They're going to pick up on that. Here, look. If you want to have those guys fill out the forms, at least use a little imagination. Set up a few different stories. . . ."

"I was going to do that," he said with irritation.

"Let me have a turn. It'd be fun," I said.

At first, I didn't think he'd do it, but his gaze had settled on my face and I could see I'd piqued his interest. Reluctantly, he relinquished the form we'd been wrestling over. I picked up a pencil stub and began to print out the narrative for an auto accident.

"Don't make it sound too smart," Raymond said.

"Trust me."

I proceeded to invent, off the top of my head, several variations of the accidents I'd participated in that afternoon. I had to pat myself on the back. I was really good at this. I'd make a fortune if I ever turned my hand to crime in earnest. Raymond apparently thought so, too. "How you know all this stuff?"

"I'm a person of many talents," I said, licking my pencil point. "Quit peeking. You make me nervous."

Raymond got us both a cold beer and we chatted while I wrote up fictional fender-benders and minor wrecks. Raymond hadn't managed to graduate from high school, whereas I attended three whole semesters of junior college before I lost heart.

"Why'd you quit, though? You're smart."

"I never liked school," I said. "High school, I was smokin' too much dope to do well. College just seemed to be made up of all this stuff I didn't like. I was too rebellious back then. And it's not like I had a 'career' goal in mind. I couldn't see the point in learning things I didn't want to know. Poly sci and biology. Who needs it? I don't give a damn about xylem and phloem."

"Me neither. Especially phloem, right?"

"Yeah, right," I said, laughing on the assumption he was making a joke.

He smiled at me, rather sweetly. "I wish Bibianna were more like you," he said.

"Forget it. I'm a mess. Divorced twice. I'm not any better at relationships than she is."

He cleared his throat. "You know, in my experience?

Women are no fuckin' good. The average woman will take you for everything you got. Then, you know what they do? They leave your ass and walk off. I don't get it. What'd I ever do?"

"I don't know what to tell you, Raymond. Guys have left me and that doesn't make 'em bad. That's just the way life goes."

"They break your heart?"

"One or two."

"Well, now see . . . that's the difference. You get your heart broke like I do, it's hard to trust, you know that?" He stared at his beer bottle, peeling a strip of the label with his thumbnail.

I felt myself go still and I chose my words with care. "I'll tell you what somebody told me once. 'You can't make anyone love you and you can't keep anyone from dying.' "

He stared at me, his dark eyes nearly luminous. There was a silence while he digested that. He shook his head. "Here's what I say. Somebody don't love me? They die."

At eight forty-five, our dinner arrived in six white cartons, complete with tiny flat plastic pillows of soy sauce and Chinese mustard strong enough to cause a nosebleed. I forked up my food with the voracious appetite generated by secondhand marijuana smoke, which was probably fortunate under the circumstances as the dishes themselves seemed remarkably similar. All of them were tossed together in a flurry of bok choy and bamboo shoots, one smothered in a sauce that looked like Orange Crush thickened with cornstarch. Both Raymond and I made little snuffling noises as we ate, polishing off everything except a golf-ball-size clot of steamed rice. The strip of paper in my fortune cookie read, "Your sunny disposition brightens everything around you." Raymond's read, "No two roads ever look alike," which made no sense whatever. He seemed to think it was profound, but by then the whites of his eyes had turned pink and he'd started eating a dope-inspired snack that he had devised—grape jelly scooped up with stale corn chips. I went to bed, but before I turned off the light, I took out the stolen bridal photo and took one more look. Who was this woman? I knew it would come to me. Her identity might also turn out to be unrelated to the investigation, but I didn't think so.

I settled down for the night on my lumpy couch. I longed to be at home in the safety of my own bed. I could feel anxiety whisper at the base of my spine. There was an ancient, familiar physical sensation I couldn't at first identify—some piece of my childhood being stirred up by circumstance. I felt a squeezing in my stomach—not an ache, but some process that was almost like grief. I closed my eyes, longing for sleep, longing for something else, though I couldn't think what. My eyes came open and in a flash, I knew. I was homesick.

My aunt had sent me off to summer camp when I was eight, claiming that it would be good for me to "get away." I see now maybe she was the one who needed the relief. She told me I'd have a wonderful time and meet lots of girls my own age. She said we'd swim and ride horses and go on nature walks and sing songs around the campfire at night.

In dizzying detail, memories passed across my mental screen. It was true about the girls and all the activities.

What was also true was that after half a day, I didn't want to be there. The horses were big and covered with flies, hot straw baseballs coming out their butts at intervals. Their muzzles were as soft and silky as suede with little prickles embedded in it, but when you least expected it, they would whip their heads up quick and try to bite you with teeth the size of piano keys. Nature turned out to be straight uphill, dusty and hot and itchy. The part that wasn't dry and tiresome was even worse. We were supposed to swim in a lake with an Indian name, but the bottom was vile and squishy. Half the time I worried there'd be broken bottles buried in the ooze. One false step and I knew my tender instep would be slashed to the bone. When I wasn't worried about slime and sharp rocks, I worried about the creatures gliding through the murky depths, tentacles trailing languidly toward my pale skinny legs. The first night around the campfire, after we sang "Kumbayah" about six times, they told me about this poor girl camper who had drowned two years before, and one who'd had an allergic reaction to a bee sting and nearly died, and another who broke her arm falling out of a tree. Also one of the girl counselors had been parked with her boyfriend necking when the radio announcer told about this escaped raving maniac and after they rolled the car window up and drove away quick, there was his *hook* right in the window. That night I cried myself to sleep, weeping in utter silence so as not to disgrace myself. In the morning, I discovered that I had all the wrong kind of shorts and I was forced to endure a lot of pitying looks because mine had elastic around the waist. At breakfast, the scrambled eggs were flabby and had white parts this girl in my cabin said were made out of unborn baby bird. After I was sick and got sent to the infirmary, there was a twelve-year-old girl who was bleeding, but they said wasn't really hurt. It was just a dead baby coming out of her bottom every month. At lunch, there was carrot salad with dark spots. The next day, I went home, which is where I wanted to be now. I slept poorly.

20

Early the next morning, the Santa Teresa cops called to say Chago's autopsy had been completed. Raymond went off to the funeral home to make arrangements to have the body brought down. The funeral director had apparently assured him by phone that he could have Chago ready for viewing that evening. Rosary would be recited Sunday evening at the funeral chapel. A mass would be said at 10:00 A.M. Monday morning at Blessed Redemption, with interment following at Roosevelt Memorial Park in Gardena.

When Raymond got back he conferred with Luis, who left soon afterward with the dog. Word was apparently out on the street. The same two girls I'd seen the first day showed up and sat down at the kitchen table, where they began putting together paper booklets with a stapler and some colored marker pens. I could see "R.I.P. CHAGO" in ornate Gothic letters on the front. A stack of Xeroxed photographs were being collated with printed matter. Within an hour, Chago's old homies began to arrive in twos and threes, some accompanied by wives or girlfriends. Most of them seemed too old to be active gang members at this point. Drugs, cigarettes, and booze had taken their toll, leaving bloated bellies and bad coloring. These were the survivors of God knows what turf wars, guys in their late twenties who probably considered themselves fortunate to be alive. The mood of the gathering was one of muted uneasiness, a community of mourners assembling to honor a fallen comrade. All I'd known of Chago was his last inching journey toward a Santa Teresa street corner. In the rain and the darkness, he'd set his failing sights, hunching toward home. I saw no sign of Juan or Ricardo, Raymond's two remaining brothers, but Bibianna assured me they'd be at the funeral home later. I gathered visiting hours would extend through the evening and both of us would have to be there. In the meantime, I was feeling awkward. I hadn't known Raymond's brother and didn't know any of the people who'd come to pay their respects. I was looking for the opportunity to excuse myself discreetly and retire to my room. There was a little flurry by the front door and the priest arrived in clerical black, a hyphen of snowy white collar visible at his neck.

Bibianna leaned close and murmured, "Father Luevanos. He's the parish priest."

Father Luevanos was in his sixties, a spare man with a withered face and a frizzy cloud of white hair. He was small and trim, shoulders narrow, his hands long and thin. He seemed to hold them away from his body, palms facing outward, like St. Francis of Assisi only minus the birds. He moved through the crowd, talking softly to each of his parishioners. He was treated like royalty, people parting to let him through. Raymond crossed to his side. Father Luevanos took his hands and the two murmured together in a mixture of English and Spanish. I could see Raymond's grief surface in response to the priest's compassion. He didn't weep, but his face underwent a curious series of tics that, from a distance, looked like the fast-forward sequence of a man in tears. I gathered Chago had been one of Raymond's anchors, perhaps the only family member who really loved Raymond and was loved in return. Raymond caught my eye. He beckoned me over and introduced me to the priest. "She's from Santa Teresa."

Father Luevanos held on to my hands while we talked. "Nice to meet you. You have a lovely community in Santa Teresa. How long have you known Valensuelo?"

"Who?"

"Chago," Raymond murmured.

"Oh." I could feel my cheeks color. "Actually, I'm a friend of Bibianna's."

"I see."

As if on cue, Bibianna moved forward to greet the priest. She had changed into a black skirt, a white blouse, and black spike heels. She had tucked a red satin rose in her hair. Her face was very pale, makeup looking stark against the pallor of her cheeks. "Father . . ." she whispered. She was close to tears and her mouth began to tremble when he took her hands. He leaned toward her, murmuring something in Spanish. She must have felt an almost overwhelming impulse to unburden herself.

Once Father Luevanos had departed, the mood of the place began to lighten. The afternoon had a lazy feel to it, despite the occasion. The front door stood open and the crowd spilled out onto the balcony. Some of the guys had brought six-packs, chips, and salsa. Conversations were punctuated by the hiss of pop-tops. There was muted laughter and cigarette smoke. Somebody brought a steel-string guitar and picked out intricate melodies. A nine-month-old baby named Ignatio toddled five steps and then sank down on his diapered behind, thoroughly satisfied with the applause his journey had netted him.

At five-thirty, the crowd began to thin. We were expected over at the funeral home early so Raymond could view the body before the others arrived. We headed out for the funeral home at six. Bibianna and I sat together in the backseat. Luis drove. Raymond sat in the passenger seat, silent and distraught, clutching a bundle he'd carried out of the bedroom with him, wrapped loosely in the folds of a white satin scarf. His emotional distress had set off a whole galaxy of symptoms, jerks and twitches that seemed all the more wrenching for the look on his face. In the space of an hour, he'd gone from a vicious hoodlum to a scared-looking kid, overwhelmed by the ordeal that lay ahead of him.

The funeral home was housed in an extravagant Victorian mansion, one of the rare remaining structures from the early grandeur of Los Angeles. The onetime single-family residence was three stories tall, the roofline broken up by towers and chimneys. The face of it was smoke-darkened stone and brown shingle, ancient tattered palms and cedars overpowering the lot, which was flanked on either side by squat concrete office buildings. The facade jarred my sense of reality, placing me for a split second in the year 1887, past and future trading places briefly.

The interior was a cavernous collection of hushed rooms with high ceilings, dark varnished woodwork, textured wallpaper, and indirect lighting. The muted chords of an organ were barely audible, creating a subliminal mood of sorrow and solemnity. The furniture was Victorian, damask and ornately carved wood, except for the metal folding chairs that had been arranged around the "parlor," where Chago had been laid out. The pearly gray coffin rested in a bay at the far end of the room, half lid open to reveal a white satin interior and a portion of his profile. The bier was surrounded by big sprays of white gladioli and wreaths of white carnations, white rosebuds, baby's breath. Raymond had apparently spared no expense.

Luis, Bibianna, and I lingered discreetly near the entranceway while Raymond approached the coffin, bearing his bundle like an offering. I gathered this was the first time he'd seen Chago since his death on Tuesday night. He bowed his head, staring into the coffin, his expression not visible from where we stood. After a moment, he crossed himself. I saw him unfold the white satin scarf and lean close to Chago's body, but it was hard to tell what he was doing. Moments later, he backed away from the coffin and crossed himself again. He took out a handkerchief and blew his nose. He mopped at his eyes and tucked the handkerchief away, then turned and walked the length of the room in our direction. When he reached us, Luis put out a hand and clasped him by the shoulder, giving him a consoling pat. "Hey, man. It's rough," he said his voice barely audible.

Bibianna moved away from us. She approached the

coffin reluctantly, her apprehension apparent. She looked at the body briefly, then crossed herself. She went over and took a seat, fumbling in her handbag for a Kleenex.

"You want to see him?" Raymond asked. His eyes were clouded by a pleading impossible to resist. It seemed like an intimate moment, observing the dead, and since I hadn't known the man, it seemed inappropriate that I'd join his friends and family at the head of his coffin. On the other hand, it seemed insulting to refuse.

Raymond picked up on my indecision, smiling sweetly. "No, come on. It's okay. He looks good."

That was a matter of opinion, of course. I'd actually seen Chago twice: once on Tuesday at the CF offices when he bumped into me in the hall, and again that night at the Bourbon Street restaurant when he'd abducted Bibianna at gunpoint. He'd seemed like a big man then, but death had pressed him flat. He looked like a Ken doll on display in an oversize carrying case. He was probably four or five years younger than Raymond, with the same good looks. His face was smooth and unlined, chin and cheekbones prominent. His hair had been blown into a dark glossy pompadour that made his head seem too large for the width of his shoulders. Raymond's satin-wrapped packet had apparently contained religious items. An oversize Bible, bound in textured white, had been clumsily propped up against the chalky pink of Chago's folded hands. A rosary had been laid across his fingers and a framed photograph of him as a small boy placed on the small white pillow on which he lay. The pillow was satin and looked like the sort women use when they don't want to mess up an expensive salon hairdo. Luis and I studied

Chago as attentively as one watches an infant in the company of a proud parent.

At seven, some of the homeboys I'd seen at the apartment began to arrive. They seemed ill at ease in Raymond's presence, unaccustomed to seeing him in a sport coat and tie. Chago's buddies had all donned specially made up black T-shirts with "In Loving Memory of Chago—R.I.P." on the back and their own names on the front.

I sat down beside Bibianna, the two of us saying little. Occasionally someone would make eye contact, but no one talked to me. Most of the conversations taking place around me were in Spanish anyway, so I couldn't even eavesdrop decently.

The crowd was swelling. There was no sign of either of Raymond's brothers, but I did see three women I took to be his older sisters. They seemed remarkably similar with their large dark eyes, full mouths, perfect skin. They sat in a cluster, beautiful women in their forties, heavy and dark, looking like nuns with their black mantillas and their rosaries. They would exchange occasional comments, but not a word to Raymond, who was making an elaborate show of not giving a damn. In an unguarded moment, I saw him flick a look in their direction. I understood then that Bibianna was just another version of his sisters, exquisite and rejecting just as his mother must have been. Poor Raymond. No matter how many versions of the story he managed to create, he would never win her love and he'd never make it come out happily.

A cluster of three mourners approached Bibianna, Chicanas in their twenties, one with a baby on her hip. I got up and eased toward the door, wondering if there was any way I could get to a telephone. Before I reached the doorway, Luis appeared at my side and took my arm. I leaned close. "Do you think there's a ladies' room upstairs?"

"You're not going anywhere."

"Oh. Well, I guess it doesn't matter then if there's one upstairs or not."

I sat back in my chair and glanced at my watch. It was ten after eight. I was hungry. I was bored. I was restless. I was scared. I'd been living for too long with high doses of fight-or-flight anxiety and it was making my head pound and my stomach churn. Luis stuck to me like a burr. For the next fifty minutes, I squirmed on my folding chair, crossing and uncrossing my legs, fiddling with my hair. To amuse myself, I memorized faces, just in case later I'd have to identify someone on the witness stand. Finally, at nine-twenty the dark-suited staff person assigned to our viewing room made an appearance and glanced pointedly at his watch. Raymond got the message and began to circle the room, saying good night to the last of the visitors.

On the way home, we dropped Luis off at his place. As soon as we reached the apartment, Raymond disappeared into the bedroom while Bibianna and I began to tidy up the place. It's not like either of us cared much, but it was something to do. In the background, without being fully conscious of it, we could hear the rattle of change on the wooden chest of drawers as Raymond emptied his pockets. We tossed empty beer cans in a plastic garbage bag, dumped out laden ashtrays. Raymond emerged from the bedroom and moved into the bathroom usually designated for my use. Moments later, I heard the squeak of the faucets. Pipes began to thunder and water splashed against the shower tiles like a sudden autumn rain.

I glanced over at Bibianna. "How come he's showering in my bathroom?"

"It'll give him a chance to . . ." She made a gesture toward the crook of her left arm.

"He's shooting up?"

It dawned on me first, the significance of the rattle of metal in the bedroom. I felt my head come up. Luis wasn't here. There was no dog at the threshold. She caught my sharp intake of breath and looked over at me.

I said, "Jesus, what's wrong with us?" I moved swiftly into the bedroom and grabbed the car keys off the top of the dresser where he'd dumped them. I hesitated and then jerked open the drawer with the handguns in it. The box was where I remembered it, miscellaneous ID's under it. I lifted the lid. The SIG-Sauer was still there, along with the Mauser and the cartridges. I tucked the SIG-Sauer in my waistband. To hell with being unarmed. I'd just as soon walk naked through an airport terminal. I was back seconds later with the keys, which I tossed to her. The shower had been turned off. Deftly, I transferred the gun to my handbag. We heard the bathroom door open. "Bibianna?"

She was struggling to separate out the keys to the Caddy, attached to the ring on a circle of wire. Her hands were shaking badly, keys jingling between her fingers like castanets.

"Take the whole friggin' thing!" I hissed. "Go!"

The telephone rang and we both jumped, in part because the sound was so unexpected. The instrument sat on the floor under the kitchen table, plugged into the wall jack. I gave her a push toward the door and snatched up the receiver. "Hello?"

On the other end of the line, a woman with a tremulous voice said, "Bibianna, thank God. Lupe told me you were back. I tried to reach you up in Santa Teresa. I've been at the hospital . . . I've been—" She broke down.

"Excuse me. I'm sorry. I'm Hannah, Bibianna's friend. Hold on a sec. She's right here." There was something in the woman's tone that went beyond distress.

Bibianna had stopped midway across the room and was staring at me. I held out the receiver.

She approached like a sleepwalker. I wanted to hurry her, anxiously aware that Raymond must have heard the phone ring, too. She took the phone from me. "Hello?"

I stared at her, mesmerized.

She said, "Mom? Yes . . ."

Raymond appeared in the doorway, his hair still tousled where he'd toweled it in haste. "Bibianna?" He'd pulled on a pair of chinos, hands still busy with his belt buckle. I found myself checking his bare arms for the injection site. He said, "What's going on? Who's on the phone?"

Bibianna turned away and pressed a hand to her ear so she could hear over Raymond's questions. A frown formed and she said, "What?" with disbelief.

The remainder of her mother's message to her was played out on Bibianna's face. Her eyes strayed to the wall of broken mirror tiles, plaster showing through in irregular patches where the glass had been shattered. Her lips parted and a sound escaped. She put a hand up to her cheek. Something in her expression made my stomach churn with dread.

No more than fifteen seconds had passed when Raymond strode across the room, snatched the receiver, and slammed it into the cradle. He ripped the phone cord from the jack and flung the instrument at the wall. The plastic housing cracked, splitting open to expose the internal mechanism. Bibianna's horrified gaze jumped from the telephone to his face. "I know what you did to her. . . ."

"To who?"

"My mother's in the hospital."

Raymond hesitated, sensing from the break in her voice that he was losing control. "What I did? What'd I do?"

Bibianna's lips moved. She was repeating a phrase . . . a mere murmur at first, gradually raising her voice. "You cut her face, you son of a bitch. You cut her face! *You cut my mother's face right here in this apartment!* You cut her beautiful face, you son of a bitch. *You bastard. . . ."*

She flew at Raymond, her fingers curved as claws digging into his face. She plowed into him, the force of her fury driving him back against the table. One of the kitchen chairs tipped over backward with a clatter. Bibianna reached the kitchenette in two steps, caught a kitchen drawer by the handle, and gave it a yank. Raymond lunged and grabbed her from behind. He half lifted her off her feet and dragged her back, Bibianna clinging to the drawer by the handle. The whole drawer was jerked free, a jumble of utensils flying everywhere. Raymond dropped, pulling her down on top of him. She struggled, half turning, kicking at Raymond with her spike-heeled shoes, long legs flashing. He tried to punch her and missed. She caught him in the chest with a kick and I heard the "oof" as the air was knocked out of him. She torqued around to her hands and knees, scrambling back into the kitchenette, where she snatched up a butcher knife that had skittered across the kitchen floor. She swung around, bringing the knife down. Raymond's hand shot out. He locked her wrist in an iron grip, squeezing so hard I thought he'd crush the bone. She cried out. The knife dropped. For a moment, they lay together. His body half covered hers and both were panting hard.

Her face began to crumple, tears welling up in her eyes. "Get offa me, you bastard," she said. Raymond seemed to think the worst of it was over. He lifted himself away from her and extended his hand, pulling her to her feet again. The moment she was upright, she lashed a kick at his groin, the pointed toe of her spike heel making contact slightly off center, but with sufficient force to cause him to grab at himself, hunching forward protectively. The sound he made was a churlish mix of pain, surprise, and fury.

I had lost track of the car keys, which must have sailed out of Bibianna's hand at some point in the struggle. I scanned the floor in haste, spotted them near the wall, and scooped them up. I tossed them to her underhand, a perfect throw. She caught the keys and took off. The front door banged back and she was gone, high heels pounding rapidly toward the stairs and out of earshot. I headed for the door at a dead run myself.

Raymond tackled me from behind. I stumbled, flinging my hands out, and he brought me down. We grappled, making grunting sounds. He pounded me with his fist, venting his fury in a succession of blows, which I warded off with my arms raised in an X across my face. He grabbed me by the hair and hauled me to my feet. He whipped my right arm behind my back and jerked upward, propelling me out the door and along the gallery. All he had on was a pair of pants. His chest was rosy from blows that had been landed on his bare skin. I longed to stomp his bare feet, but I knew he'd break my arm in retaliation.

Out in front of the building, I could hear Bibianna revving up the Cadillac, which peeled out with a shriek of tires. Raymond marched us to the Ford. He popped open the trunk lid with one hand and grabbed a tire iron, pulling me around with him to the driver's side. He smashed backward at the window until enough glass was gone to allow him to reach in and pull up the door lock. He yanked the door open and shoved me into the car. He pulled a set of keys from under the front seat, along with a handgun. He cocked it and pointed it at me, then reached under the steering column with his left hand and started the car.

21

We took off. Bibianna had no more than a two-minute head start. Raymond placed the handgun between his thighs. At fifty miles an hour, he really didn't have to worry that I'd bolt from the moving vehicle. He jammed down on the accelerator, pushing the shimmying Ford to sixty, sixty-five. Streetlights streamed by. I hung on for dear life, my eyes pinned to the road with all the horrified fascination of a funhouse ride. Judging from the consternation of the drivers on all sides of us, Bibianna must have been cutting through red lights at the intersections just ahead.

Raymond didn't seem nearly as concerned as I was with the cars or pedestrians, with the niceties of stoplights or the sanctity of crosswalks. People were diving out of his path, a string of honking horns and curses flying up in our wake. He picked up the car phone and held it against the steering wheel so he could punch in a number with his thumb. He listened for one ring, two. Someone picked up on the other end.

He said, "'Ey, Chopper! Bibianna just took off in the Caddy and I need some help. . . . Right. She'll hit the 405 northbound at Avalon. If you miss us at the Harbor, try Crenshaw or Hawthorne."

There was obviously a question being posed from the other end.

"I'll leave that up to you, man," Raymond said. He hung up. He set the phone down and retrieved the gun from the fleshy holster of his thighs, holding it in his right hand while he steered with his left.

We were still on Avalon Boulevard, screaming toward the freeway. By the time we reached Carson, the light was green and we sailed through. Raymond had eased back to sixty miles an hour, squeezing out a lane of his own between parked cars and the moving vehicles crawling toward the on ramp. I braced myself, one hand on the dashboard, one hand clutching the seat back. I could see drivers in cars just ahead spotting us in their rearview mirrors—first the casual glance, then the double take as they calculated our speed, realizing that we would shortly be climbing up their rear bumpers. Some cars would speed up, crowding left to allow us room to pass. Some would take the first avenue of escape they could find, squealing into driveways, up onto the sidewalk—anything to avoid the inevitable rear-end collision. I found myself gritting my teeth in silence, then warbling out a cry of fear and distress as we overtook each car and managed, somehow, to get past.

Raymond's face was totally composed, his concentration intense. I could see now that his pupils had been reduced to pinpoints, but he showed no other signs of heroin intoxication. Maybe he had his doses so carefully calibrated that he could function normally even with his veins full of smack. He sideswiped a parked car and I shrieked involuntarily, my head jerking back as the impact bounced us into the oncoming traffic. He corrected our course. If he was aware of my vocalization, he gave no indication of it. The irony wasn't lost on me, that in this situation of high stress, I was exhibiting all of Raymond's symptoms. Maybe in his neurological makeup, some part of him was forever reacting to high-speed chases and phantom crashes, narrowly averted disasters from which he saved himself with quick action and spontaneous yelps of horror, dismay, and surprise.

We careered to the right, up the on ramp to the 405, northbound. I had no idea how he knew she'd be there, but I spotted Bibianna just ahead of us in the black Caddy the moment we merged with freeway traffic. It was late Saturday evening, so we weren't looking at the usual jam and crawl of the rush hour. I kept my eyes glued to the road, praying mutely for her safety. She probably thought she was free, not realizing he was already there behind her only eight cars back. He tucked the handgun between his thighs again and picked up the car phone, punching in the number with his thumb. He spoke rapidly to Chopper, giving our coordinates. I could hear them calculate the projected point of interception. My heart was still pounding and I watched the Caddy fearfully, scanning the freeway for some sign of the CHP.

We had just passed the on ramp at Rosecrans when I heard the chirp of a car horn next to us. I looked over at the next lane. The car was a Chevy, dark blue. Chopper was driving. Raymond pointed at the Caddy and then sliced his index finger across his throat. Chopper grinned and gave Raymond the thumbs-up. Raymond eased his foot off the accelerator, dropping back to normal speed, while the guy in the Chevy eased into our lane and sped up. The last I saw of Bibianna, the Chevy was just beginning to overtake her. That's when I caught a glimpse of the vanity license plate. A chill puckered my scalp and rippled down my spine, the cold wedging like a pillow in the small of my back. The plate read PARNELL. Raymond must have had Parnell Perkins's car ever since his death, probably using it to collect phony damage and injury claims.

Raymond spotted a black-and-white in the southbound lane. It was possible somebody'd called the cops to report his erratic driving because the officer gave the Ford a quick startled look as we passed. Raymond cut over two lanes to the right and took the nearest off ramp. Even if the cop circled back, we'd be gone. He found a darkened side street, pulled over to the curb, and parked. He sat back and expelled a breath of air.

I had started to shake, from fear, from relief, from visions of Bibianna's fate and bloody images of Bibianna's mother, whom I'd never even laid eyes on. I thought about Parnell facedown in the parking lot with a bullet in his head. I pressed my hands between my knees, teeth chattering, my breath coming in gasps.

Raymond was looking at me with puzzlement. "What's the matter with you?"

"Shut up, Raymond. I don't want to talk to you."

"I didn't do nothing. What'd I do?"

"You didn't *do* anything? I don't believe this. . . ."

"Chick stole my car and I chased her. What'd you expect?"

"You're crazy!"

"*I'm* crazy? Why? Because I won't let that bitch take me for everything I'm worth? You better believe it."

"What's going to happen?"

"Beats me."

I sat up, irritated with his attitude. "Don't play dumb, Raymond. What's Chopper going to do to her?"

"How do I know? I'm not a fuckin' psychic. Don't worry about it. It's got nothing to do with you."

"What about her mother?"

"What do you care? Quit acting like this is *my* fault."

I looked at him with astonishment. "Who's fault is it, then?"

"Bibianna's," he replied, as if it were self-evident.

"Why is it her fault? You're the one who cut the woman."

"Who, Gina? She's alive, isn't she? Which is more than you can say for Chago. I got a brother dead, and who do you think did that?"

"Not her," I shot back.

"That's my point," he replied patiently. "She didn't do nothing. She's innocent, right? Just like him. Tit for tat. It says so right in the Bible—an eye for an eye—and that's all this is about. Lookit, I could have killed the bitch, but I didn't, did I. And you know why? Because I'm a good guy. Nobody gives me credit. Bibianna has to learn not to fuck with me, I told you that. You think I like this? She'd done what I said to begin with, we wouldn't be here."

"Which is what?"

"Quit horsing around and get serious. She shoulda married me when I asked her. I'm not stupid, you know. I don't know what's going on, but I've been as patient as I'm gonna be. And that goes for you, too. You got that?"

I stared at him, at a loss for words. His view of the world was so skewed there was no reasoning with him. He really seemed to see himself as innocent, the victim of a circumstance in which everyone was responsible for his behavior except him. Like every other "victim" I've known, he clung to his "one-down" position as justification for his abuse of other people.

Raymond picked up the car phone and punched in a number. " 'Ey, Luis. Raymond. Put some clothes on, we're swinging by to pick you up." He glanced at his watch. "Ten minutes. And bring the mutt."

He started the car then and pulled out, hanging a left onto a main artery as we headed south again. I glanced out the window. Raymond was driving at a sedate forty miles an hour. We were now on Sepulveda, not far from the airport. Not a wonderful neighborhood, but I thought I'd be safe until I could get a call through to the cops. I opened the car door. Raymond speeded up.

"Please stop the car. I'm getting out," I said.

He picked up the gun again and pointed it at me. "Close the door."

I did as I was told. He turned his attention to the road again. In the glow from the streetlights, I studied his profile, hair still damp from the shower, the tousle of curls, dark eyes, long lashes, the dimple in his chin. He was bare-chested, barefoot, his skin very pale. I could see the faint scarring in the crooks of his arms. My guess was that after the intensity of the chase and the rush of adrenaline, the euphoric effects of his shooting up were beginning to wane. His ticcing had returned. The mysterious connections in his neurological circuitry were touching off a series of reactions, as if he were enduring tiny jolts of electricity. His mouth came open and he jerked his neck to the right. His body jumped with the same irrepressible response I've felt when a doctor pops with his rubber hammer on my patellar reflex. In that quick tap, there isn't any way to prevent my foot from flying out. Raymond seemed to live with the constant assault of invisible rubber hammers, which rapped him randomly at all hours of the day, testing every reflex . . . little elves and fairies tapping on him like a boot. If his gun hand jerked the wrong way, he was going to plug me full of holes. My own adrenaline had seeped away, leaving me depleted.

"Oh, God, Raymond. Please. I just want to go home," I said wearily.

"I'm not going to let you out here. It's too dangerous. You wouldn't last a block."

I wanted to laugh at the absurdity of his concern. There he was, holding me at gunpoint, probably willing to kill me if it came to that, but he didn't want me out on the streets in a questionable neighborhood. Raymond punched in another number. He really reminded me of some high-powered business exec.

Someone answered on the other end.

"Hey, yeah," he said. "I got a problem. Somebody just stole my car. . . ."

I slouched down on my spine, knees propped against the dashboard, listening with wonder as Raymond availed himself of city police services in the matter of his missing Cadillac. From his end of the conversation, I gathered he was going to have to go over to the 77th Division and file a stolen vehicle report, but he was the soul of cooperation, Mr. Righteous Citizen rallying the forces of law and order to his cause. He hung up and we drove in silence as far as Luis's place.

We pulled over at the curb and Raymond gave a quick beep. A moment later, Luis appeared with Perro at his side. Raymond pulled on the emergency brake and got out on the driver's side. "You drive," he said to Luis.

Luis put the dog in the front seat between us and got behind the wheel. "Where we going?"

"Police station."

Luis took off. Perro leaned against me, panting bad breath. I could tell he would have preferred the window seat himself so he could hang his head out and let his ears flap in the passing breeze.

Luis watched Raymond in the rearview mirror with guarded interest. "So what's happening?"

"Bibianna stole the Caddy. We gotta file a report."

"Bibianna stole the Caddy?"

"Yeah, can you believe that? After all I've done for her? I called Chopper and sent him after her. I don't have time for that shit, you know what I'm talking about?"

Luis made no comment. I saw him slide a look in my direction, but what was I going to say?

We reached the 77th Division police station. Luis parked on the street and got out of the car, peering into the backseat while Raymond gave him instructions about the stolen Caddy. "What about the registration?" he asked.

"It's in the car," Raymond said irritably.

"You want me to give 'em your telephone number?"

"How else are they going to notify me when they find the car?"

"Oh."

"Yeah, 'oh,' " Raymond said.

Luis disappeared.

"Guy's a fuckin' pinhead," Raymond said to himself. He kicked the back of my seat. "I still got a gun on you," he said. "I ain't forgettin' it was you helped Bibianna get away."

I waited in the car with Raymond, pinned in place by Perro's weight, wishing a cop would saunter by so that I could scream for help. Several patrol cars gunned past us, but no one seemed to realize that this tacky-looking Anglo was Nancy Drew in disguise. I stared out at the police station not fifty feet away.

Luis came back to the car and got in without a word. He took a quick look in the rearview mirror. I turned around and looked myself, realizing belatedly that Raymond had nodded off.

Once we reached the apartment complex, Luis had to help Raymond up the stairs. I went up first, with the dog bringing up the rear. Raymond was awake but seemed groggy and out of it. When we reached the apartment, Luis unlocked the door. For a moment, the exterior lights fell on Raymond's bare back and I saw that his skin was crisscrossed with scars, like a webbing of white diamonds. The old cuts had healed but had never entirely gone away. The even spacing suggested quite methodical work.

Inside the apartment, I scanned the living room, searching for the handbag I'd left behind earlier. I spotted it on the floor, shoved halfway under the upholstered chair. It had apparently been kicked to one side during the struggle with Raymond and the top was now yawning open. Luis held Raymond's gun and he motioned me toward the couch. I took a seat. From that angle, the butt of the SIG-Sauer was clearly visible in the handbag. I willed myself to look away. I didn't dare make a move for it for fear Luis would catch sight of it. Raymond staggered off to bed.

I was forced to sleep on the couch that night. Perro guarded the front door while Luis dozed in the chair, keeping watch over me, Raymond's gun in hand. The kitchen bulb glowed like a nightlight. Now and then, Luis and I would stare at each other across the dimly lighted room, his dark eyes devoid of any feeling whatsoever. It's the same look you get from a lover when he's moved on to someone new. Whatever moments you might have shared get buried under layers of hostility and indifference.

I was jolted awake at eight by a banging on the front door. Perro started barking savagely. I swung my feet off the couch and got up, automatically moving toward the door. Luis beat me to it. He had the dog by the collar. He opened the door and I saw Dawna on the threshold in a nifty black suit. Oh, great. This was what Dolan and Santos called "Don't worry about Dawna, we'll keep her out of circulation." Raymond emerged from the master bedroom, pulling his shirt on. He was still barefoot, wearing his wrinkled chinos from the night before. "What's happening?" he asked.

"It's Dawna," Luis said.

As Raymond moved to the door, I leaned over the upholstered chair and eased my handbag out from under it, closing the flap across the butt of the gun.

Luis had turned. "Sit down."

"I'm sitting," I said irritably. I took a seat in the uphol-stered chair, feigning boredom while Raymond and Dawna went through murmured greetings. Her face had crumpled at the sight of him. Raymond put his arms around her and rocked her where they stood. Wait till she got a load of me. The only comfort I had was the handbag, which now rested to the right of the chair, just beyond my fingertips. Luis had moved into the kitchen and he was leaning against the kitchen counter, rolling a joint with complete absorption. Stoned on Sunday morning. Just what we all needed. Dawna sat down on the couch, still crying into Raymond's handkerchief.

Her face was Kabuki white, her mouth a pout of bright red. Her hair had been newly bleached to the color of typ-ing paper, standing up in spikes as if somebody'd folded it in quarters and cut it with a pair of scissors. The effect was of an albino rooster. Where her suit jacket gaped open, I caught sight of a thickly padded gauze bandage, secured with adhesive tape. She didn't look so hot and my guess was her injury had taken its toll. I could see Perro lying on the floor near the couch, staring at the juicy part of Dawna's leg. I studied her with dread and anxiety. Once she regained her composure, she was going to notice me. There was a fair chance she'd remember me from the CF offices, but what was I going to do?

22

The tricky part of any lie is trying to figure out how you'd behave if you were innocent. I couldn't act like I didn't know Dawna Maldonado at all. We'd both been there Tuesday night when Chago was killed. Should I treat her as a friend or foe? Under the circumstances, it seemed wise to keep my mouth shut and let the scenario play out as it would, like improvisational theater. As there was no escaping, I tucked the handbag under my arm and moved over to the kitchen table. I sat down, placing the bag casually near one leg of my chair. I picked up Bibianna's ragged deck of cards. I shuffled the cards, trying to remember how Bibianna set up the solitaire she always played.

Meanwhile, conversation between Raymond and Dawna had turned to the shooting. It was just at that point that Dawna finally caught sight of me. "What's she doing here?"

Oh, well, I thought, here we go.

Raymond seemed startled by her reaction, which had a distinctly hostile tone to it. "Oh, sorry. This is Hannah. She's a friend of Bibianna's."

Dawna's eyes were ice blue, lined with black, her gaze calculating. "Why don't you ask *her*? She was with 'em that night."

"*She* was?"

"She was there at the restaurant, sitting at the table with 'em when I got off the phone."

Raymond seemed confused. "You're talking about Hannah?"

"God, Raymond. I just got done sayin' that, didn't I?"

He turned to me. "I thought you met Bibianna in jail. I thought you said you were cellmates."

I started laying cards out like this was no big deal. Seven stacks, first card up, the other six facedown. "I never said that. We got thrown in the slammer together, but I'd met her before that, at a singles bar. I figured she'd told you or I'd have said something myself."

Next round, skip the first pile. The face-up card went on the second pile, the other five facedown. Just playing solitaire here, casual as all get-out. Luis was eavesdropping, being careful not to call attention to himself lest Raymond take off after him.

"What the fuck were you doin' there with her and Jimmy Tate?"

Ah, he'd figured out it was Tate, probably from the description Dawna'd given him of the guy. "I wasn't doing anything. We'd just gone next door for a bite to eat when those two showed up."

"Bibianna was with Jimmy Tate?"

Dawna snorted. "Jesus, Raymond. What's the matter with you? You sound like a parrot." Out of the corner of my eye, I could see how much she was enjoying herself. In her family dynamic, she was probably the kid who puffed up her self-importance by tattling on all her siblings.

Raymond ignored her, focusing on me. "How come you never told me she was with him that night?"

"Jimmy Tate was with me. We ran into Bibianna at the bar and asked her to join us for a bite to eat. What's the big deal?"

"I don't believe it."

I stopped dealing out the cards. "You don't believe me?"

"I think you're lying."

"Wait a minute, Raymond. I've known you all of five days. So how come I'm suddenly accountable to you for my behavior?"

Raymond's eyes were glittering, his voice too soft to suit me. "Dawna says Tate was the one killed my brother. Did you know that?"

Oops. Actually I did know that. I said nothing, wondering why my mouth was suddenly so dry. I couldn't think of an adequate response and for once the glib lie didn't spring that readily to mind.

"Answer me," he said. "Tate killed my brother?"

I picked my way through the possibilities, not wanting to commit myself to a course of action just yet. "I don't know," I said. "When the shooting started, I hit the pavement."

"You didn't see Tate with a gun?"

"Well, I knew Tate had a gun, but I don't know what he did with it because I wasn't looking."

"What about Chago? You knew he was hit. Who you think did that?"

"I have no idea. Honestly. I didn't have a clue what was happening. All I know is Tate and I run into Bibianna, we go next door for a bite to eat, and next thing I know these two goons show up and take Bibianna off at gunpoint. Shooting breaks out, cops show up. Bibianna and I are hauled off to jail. . . ."

I was on slightly safer ground here because I knew Dawna had disappeared about the time Chago was hit. I was working on the assumption that she didn't have any idea what had gone on after that. Actually, I wasn't as nervous about the current subject as I was about the possibility of her remembering she'd seen me at the California Fidelity offices.

She'd been studying my face, her brow furrowed with one of those quizzical looks that indicate a marine layer blanking out memory. Any minute now the fog might begin to lift. "She's bullshitting you, Raymond."

"Just let me handle this," he said irritably. He turned away and lit a cigarette, watching my face as he took the first drag of smoke.

The phone rang. The four of us turned and stared. Luis moved first, picking up the receiver. "Hello?" He listened briefly, then covered the mouthpiece with his right palm. "Cop on the line says they found the car."

Raymond took the phone. "Hello? . . . Yeah, this is him. . . . Anybody hurt? Oh, really. Well, I'm sorry to hear that. Where is that? Uh-huh . . . yeah. Where's the car now? Yeah, right. I know the place. . . . Huhn, he did? Hey, that's too bad."

Raymond got off the phone with a glance at Luis. "Bibianna had an accident up in Topanga Canyon. Chopper pushed the Caddy off a cliff, from what this guy says."

"No shit," Luis said.

I could feel my heart beating in my throat. "What happened to Bibianna? Is she okay?"

Raymond waved dismissively. "Don't worry about it. She's at St. John's. Get a jacket, baby-doll. We got work to do." He flashed a grin at Luis. "This is great. Caddy's totaled. We're talking twenty-five hundred bucks." He caught sight of my face. "What are you lookin' at? I got a legitimate auto claim here," he said self-righteously.

"What about me?" Dawna said, protesting.

"You can come with us if you want or you can stay here and sleep. You look beat. We'll be back in an hour and then go over to the funeral home."

She stared indecisively, then conceded. "You go on. I'll grab some rest."

Raymond drove way too aggressively for traffic conditions. I was sandwiched between him and Luis in the front seat, one hand braced on the dashboard, making small involuntary sounds each time Raymond changed lanes without warning or pushed the Ford up within a few feet of somebody's back bumper before he pulled out and around, passing them with a dark backward scowl. His jaw was set, his tics almost constant, and everything in life was someone else's fault. Even Luis began to react, murmuring, "Jesus," at one of Raymond's hair-raising near misses.

The two talked across me as if I were empty space, so it took me a moment to realize what they were saying.

Raymond said, "Stupid bitch must have got off the 101 at Topanga. God, how dumb can you get? That's the middle of nowhere. You know that road?"

"Hey, that's rugged," Luis said.

"The worst. Mountains sticking straight up. Sheer drops off the sides. She should have stayed in the populated areas and found a cop. She's not going to get any help out there. All Chopper had to do was wait till she hit one of those hairpin turns and *boom!*" Raymond gestured his contempt. "Cop says he must have rammed into the Caddy's rear end and got himself hung up but good." He made a diving motion with his hand.

I glanced at Raymond. "*He* went off, too?"

Raymond gave me a look like I'd suddenly started speaking English. "What do you think we've been talking about? Chopper's dead and she's not that far from it. Serves her right. You didn't figure that out? Bibianna's in whatchacallit . . . intensive care."

"Oh, no," I said.

"What is it with you? You gonna make that my fault, too? Bibianna steals my car and totals the fuckin' thing and *I'm* to blame?"

"Oh, for God's sake, Raymond. Take responsibility. This is all your doing and you know it."

"Don't push your luck, bitch. I didn't do nothin'!" Raymond's face darkened and he drove in stony silence. I could feel anxiety seeping into my chest wall, squeezing my digestive system.

We got off the 405 at the Santa Monica Freeway,

heading west as far as the Cloverfield exit, which we took and then turned right. I'd been to St. John's some years ago, and by my recollection, it was not far away, somewhere around 21st or 22nd Street, between Santa Monica Boulevard and Wilshire. It was ten-thirty by now. Hospitals are rigorous about visits to ICU, but Raymond would no doubt bull his way in.

We parked in one of the visitors' lots and crossed to the main entrance, passing under an arch. A fountain lined with blue-green tile splashed noisily in the center of a brick-paved court. Beyond the fountain was a bronze bust of Irene Dunne, the first lady of St. John's. The place was massive, cream-colored blocks that had probably once been a fairly straightforward chunk of concrete. Now a portico jutted out in front, two wings flanked the building on either side, with a multistory addition looming up in the rear. It looked like most of the available land had been devoured by new construction, surrounding properties annexed as the space needs of the hospital grew. The rest of the neighborhood was a modest assortment of single-family dwellings, 1950s style. An ambulance passed us, emitting an occasional short howl. Its yellow lights were flashing, sirens off, as it headed for the emergency entrance.

Wheelchair ramps swept up to the front on either side of the main entrance with a central staircase. We moved up the center steps and into the lobby with its muted maroon carpet and the spicy scent of carnations. To the left, an entire wall was devoted to listing the names of those who'd made significant financial contributions to St. John's, the range extending from benefactors, to patrons, to fellows, to donors too miserly for categorization. On the far side of the wall, Admitting was dominated by a large oil painting of a curly-haired person looking heavenward in torment.

Raymond inquired at the Patient Information desk for the whereabouts of ICU. I comforted myself that she must have been conscious when they brought her in or the cops never would have found out who she was. As far as I could tell, she'd had no identification with her.

Behind me, I overheard a fragment of conversation. A woman said, ". . . so I says to this chick at the sheriff's department, 'What business is it of yours? If he ain't been charged with nothing, how come you're talkin' to his probation officer about it?' That's like a violation of his civil rights or something, isn't it? . . ."

Two wires connected in my brain, completing a circuit. I made the kind of "oh" sound that escapes your lips when you spill ice water down your front. I knew who Dr. Howard's daughter was, the bride in the photograph. She was the civilian clerk who'd given me such a hard time at the S.T. County Sheriff's Department when I was trying to get Bibianna's address. Oh, hell, I had to get to a telephone. No wonder Dolan thought he had a leak!

Raymond marched us to the elevator, which we took up to the second floor. When the doors opened, we turned right, passing the maternity ward, where a recently delivered mother, in robe and slippers, proceeded at half speed, touching the wall gingerly as she walked. Raymond was on his best behavior, moving quickly, his gaze front and center. I could see Luis's eyes flick into an occasional empty room. I did likewise, unable to resist, though there wasn't that much to see. The air already smelled of lunch.

The wing designated 2-South housed Intensive Care, Coronary Care, the Cardiac Surgery Unit, and Intermediate Care behind closed double doors. A sign said AUTHORIZED PERSONNEL ONLY, with a wall-mounted telephone nearby. Apparently, you had to call in and get permission to enter the department itself. Four women sat in the adjacent waiting room, variously conversing and reading magazines. I could see a public pay phone, a magazine rack, a color television set. In the hallway, there was a water fountain and, in a niche, a statue of a male saint supporting baby Jesus by his bare bottom. The floor was made up of polished marble chips in squares with thin metal seams between.

Luis took a seat on a beige leather bench, his knee jumping. A lab tech walked by with a fat tube of dark red blood. Luis got up and moved to the wall, where he studied three lines about the visiting hours. It was the first time I'd seen the two of them in a situation they couldn't handle with machismo.

Like Luis, Raymond was apparently one of those people made uneasy by illness. He was subdued, respectful. The ticcing had started up, the head jerk reminding me of the sort of startle reaction I sometimes experience when I'm on the verge of sleep. Hospital staff, catching sight of him, seemed to diagnose him in passing, thinking no more about it than I did at this point. From Raymond's manner, I had to guess he'd been hospitalized as a child, subjected to medical processes that had left him edgy and alert. Almost imperceptibly, he slowed, shoving his hands in his pockets while he decided what to do next.

He was just picking up the telephone when the double doors opened and a nurse emerged. She was a redhead, in her thirties, white pants suit, thick-soled white shoes, wearing a nursing school pin but no cap. "Can I help you?"

"Yeah, uhm, I got a . . . my fiancée was brought in last night. She was in this automobile accident? The cops said she was here. It's Diaz, the last name . . . I was just wondering, you know, if I could see her."

She smiled pleasantly. "Just a minute, I'll check." She moved on to the waiting room, where she stuck her head in, beckoning to one of the visitors. The woman set her magazine aside and followed the nurse back through the double doors. I took the liberty of peering through the glass, but all I could see was an extension of the corridor and, at the far end of the hall, a glass-enclosed room furnished with monitoring equipment. The patient was barely visible and there was no way of knowing if it was Bibianna or not.

Luis was shifting from foot to foot, fingers snapping softly. "Oh, man, I hate this. I'm going down to the lobby. You can pick me up on the way out. Maybe I'll find the coffee shop and get me something to eat."

"Do it," Raymond said.

Luis crossed his arms and hugged himself casually. "You want me to get you some coffee, something like that?"

"Just get outta here, Luis. I don't give a shit."

"Maybe I'll come back in a while," he said. He glanced at me and then walked backward for a few steps, waiting to see if Raymond had any serious objections. Raymond seemed to be fighting his own inclination to bolt. Luis turned and headed toward the elevators.

As soon as he was out of sight, I touched Raymond's arm. "I think I'll look for a ladies' room, okay?"

The nurse returned. "It'll be a few minutes. The neurologist just left, but I think he's still in the hospital. Would you like to have him paged?"

"Uh, yeah. Could you do that?"

"Of course. You can have a seat, if you like," she said, indicating the waiting room.

"She going to be okay?"

"I really couldn't say," the nurse said. "I can have Dr. Cherbak talk to you about her condition as soon as he gets here. Your name is?"

"Raymond. I'll just wait. I don't want to interrupt nobody. . . ."

"There's a vending machine if you want to have some coffee."

"Can you tell me where the restrooms are?" I asked. God, couldn't I think of any more imaginative way of getting away from these guys?

The nurse pointed toward the corridor. "First door."

I went into the waiting room with Raymond. As soon as he sat down on the couch, I said, "I'll be right back."

He could hardly pay attention, he was so uneasy by then. I walked away from him, trying to control myself, trying not to break into a run. I passed the restroom and kept going, looking for a place I could have a little privacy and the use of a telephone.

2-South segued back into 2-Main without any noticeable shift in floor covering or the wall colors, which were pale blue and pale beige, with a pattern of cattails or full-foliage trees in silhouette. I became aware that I had moved from near death to near birth, the signs on the wall pointing to Labor, Delivery, the Newborn Nursery, and the Fathers' Waiting Room. I was looking for a pay phone, fumbling aside the gun in my bag for loose change, feeling panic mount as the seconds ticked away. Once I got the relevant information back to Dolan, I was out of there.

I passed the desk on 2-Main. There was a counter to my left with wall-mounted monitors that showed green lines I assumed were vital signs.

A black nurse coming out of a room marked "Staff Lounge" nearly bumped into me. She was wearing an ankle-length white gown that tied in the back, a mask pushed up on the middle of her forehead like a pale green hump. She was in her forties, slim, with dark eyes and a clear, unlined face. "Can I help you?"

"I sincerely hope so," I said. "This is my situation and you just have to trust me on this. I'm a private investigator from Santa Teresa. I'm working undercover on an auto insurance fraud case and I'm here in the company of a thug who's going to start looking for me any minute. I have to get a call through to Lieutenant Dolan up in Santa Teresa. Do you have a telephone I could use? I swear it won't take long and it could save my life."

She looked at me with the blank contemplation of somebody assessing information. It must have been something in the tone I used, pure desperation overlaid with "earnest." It certainly wasn't anything in the way I looked. For once, I was telling the truth, using every cell in my being to convey my sincerity. She listened, brown eyes intent on my face as I spoke. It's possible the tale I told was so preposterous she just didn't think me capable of making it up. Without a word, she pointed toward a telephone on the desk behind the counter.

23

I went through the hospital operator, placing a person-to-person call to Dolan at the number he'd given me. While I waited for the call to be patched through, I read the bulletin board, which seemed devoted in equal parts to medical cartoons, notices of classes coming up, and menus for neighborhood fast-food restaurants offering free delivery. I was starving to death.

When I heard Dolan's voice, I closed my eyes and put a hand on my chest, patting myself with relief. "Lieutenant Dolan, this is Kinsey Millhone. I'm calling from St. John's Hospital and I don't have long."

"What's up?"

I started talking, my mind racing ahead, trying to organize the information as I spoke. "First of all, Bibianna Diaz is in ICU down here. She was run off the road last night—"

"I heard," Dolan interjected.

"You know about that?"

"One of Santos's men called me the minute the report came through. Hospital has orders to be polite to Raymond without letting him get anywhere near her hospital bed. They know what to do."

"Well, thank God for *that*." I filled him in quickly on the situation to date, including the file I'd seen at Buddy's Auto Body Shop. "I think I've figured out who the leak is up there." I told him about Dr. Howard, the chiropractor, and the photo of his daughter. I had no idea what her married name was, but I gave him an accurate (though acid) description of her. As a civilian clerk working for the county sheriff's department, she was in a perfect position to funnel information to her father, and through him to Raymond. The minute Bibianna was first arrested in Santa Teresa, Raymond would have known her whereabouts. A sudden thought occurred to me. "Lieutenant, do you know anything about the gun Parnell was murdered with? Raymond's got a thirty-caliber broomhandle Mauser. I saw it in his dresser drawer."

Dolan cut in. "Forget Parnell for now and do me a favor. I want you to hang up and get the hell out of there."

"Why, what's happening?"

"Tate's probably already on the premises. Hospital notified him late last night and he took off, heading south. If Raymond finds out he's there, they'll have a showdown for sure."

"Oh, shit."

Behind me, a woman doctor came into the nurses' station, wearing surgical greens. She pulled off her cap and shook her hair out wearily. She paused to study me, hair rumpled, lines of exhaustion weighting down her face. I couldn't tell if she wanted the telephone or the chair.

Dolan was saying, "I got somebody down there who can help you out. Hold on. I got a call coming in. . . ."

I saw Raymond pass the desk, heading toward the elevators, probably in search of me. I couldn't wait for Dolan. "I gotta go," I said into dead air, and hung up. Every brain cell in my head was screaming at me to get out, but I couldn't leave Jimmy Tate here without backup. I left the nurses' station and trotted down the hall behind Raymond, finally catching up with him.

I tapped him on the shoulder. "Hi, where did you go?"

He turned and looked at me irritably. "Where the hell have you been? I'm off lookin' for you."

"I went over to the nursery to see the newborns," I said. "What for?"

"I like babies. I might want to have one of my own someday, you know? They're really cute, all tiny and puckery. They look like Cornish game hens—"

"We ain't here for that," he said gruffly, though he seemed mollified by my explanation. He grabbed my arm and turned me, walking us back down the corridor toward ICU.

"Why don't we take a break and get some coffee," I said.

"Forget that. I'm jumpy enough as it is."

We reached the ICU waiting room and Raymond sat down again. He took a magazine from a nearby stack and flipped through it with an air of distraction. The pages made little snapping sounds in the quiet of the room. Two women seated at the other end of the room stared at him, frankly curious about his tics.

Raymond glanced up, catching them in the act, and

stared back at them until they broke off eye contact. "Jesus, I hate it when people stare at me. They think I like doing this?" He gave me an exaggerated jerk, glaring darkly at the two women, who were stirring with self-consciousness.

I said, "How's Bibianna doing? Has anybody said?"

He shifted restlessly. "Doctor's supposed to show up any minute and talk to us."

I had to get him out of there. A color television in the corner, sound off, was tuned to one of those nature films where they show half of one species being eaten by another.

Raymond leaned forward. "Jeez, what's *taking* them so long?"

"You want some lunch? Why don't we go down to the coffee shop and find Luis. I'm starving."

He hung his head, shaking it, and then looked over at me, his expression bleak. "What if she doesn't make it?"

I bit back a retort. I couldn't think of an answer that didn't seem quarrelsome. I revised my reaction. On reflection, it seemed perfectly in keeping with the depth of his denial that he'd now be worried sick about a woman he'd tried to have assassinated less than twenty-four hours before. If Raymond found out Jimmy Tate was here, he'd bring the whole place down.

I said, "We're both going to go crazy if we hang around here. It won't take long. We can grab a quick lunch and come right back up. The doctor might not be back on the ward for an hour."

"You think?"

"Come on. Get a cup of coffee, at least."

Raymond tossed the magazine aside and got up. We

moved into the corridor and he slowed his step. "Maybe I should tell the nurse where we are in case he shows."

"Or I can do that if you like. Why don't you go ahead and buzz the elevator for us?"

Two Hispanic nurses approached from down the corridor.

There was some activity in the hallway and both of us looked over. A doctor appeared from the Rehab wing, heading for ICU. He was wearing a calf-length white duster over a gray suit. He had his full name stitched above his pocket in blue script. A stethoscope coiled up out of his pocket like a length of narrow-gauge garden hose. He was in his fifties with closely clipped gray hair, rimless glasses, and a limp. His right foot was strapped into a walking cast that looked like a ski boot. He noticed my glance and smiled apologetically, though he offered no explanation. I pictured a sports-related mishap, which might have been his hope. He probably tripped on a sprinkler head while he was pinching suckers off his roses. "Can I help you folks?"

Raymond said, "I'm here about Bibianna Diaz. Are you the doctor?"

"Absolutely. Nice to meet you, Mr. Tate. I'm Dr. Cherbak." He reached out to Raymond and the two of them shook hands. "Nurse said you were here. Sorry it took me so long. . . ."

Raymond's smile slipped a notch. "The name is Raymond Maldonado. What's Tate got to do with it?"

Dr. Cherbak blinked with uncertainty and then checked Bibianna's chart. "Sorry. She asked to have her husband notified, and naturally, I thought . . ."

From where I stood, I could see the big pink notice reading PC, protective custody, affixed to the front. Raymond seemed to spot it about the same time I did.

"Her husband?" he repeated. He stared at the doctor, who must have realized he'd committed an egregious error.

I touched Raymond's arm, murmuring, "Raymond, there's been a misunderstanding, that's all. Maybe she has a head injury. Who knows what she might have said? She might be hallucinating—"

Raymond jerked away from my touch. "Shut up!" he said. And then to the doctor: "She told you that? Jimmy Tate's her *husband*? That's bullshit. I'll rip your fuckin' face off, you say that."

The two nurses, in conversation, were suddenly attentive, watching the encounter as if it were a soap opera. I could feel the dread suffuse me like a fever. "Let's come back later. . . ."

"How's she doing?" Raymond asked. He was being pugnacious, jaw working with tension.

"I'm not at liberty to—"

"I asked you how she's doing. You want to answer me, you dick?"

Dr. Cherbak stiffened. "I can see I've made a mistake," he said. "If you're not related to the patient, I'm limited in the amount of information I can give you. . . ."

Raymond gave him a push. "Fuckin' A you made a mistake! I'm going to marry this woman, get it? Me. Raymond Maldonado. You got that straight?"

Dr. Cherbak turned on his heel and moved toward ICU at a brisk clip, pushing through the double doors. I heard him on the other side. "Get Security up here. . . ."

Raymond banged through the doors after him and grabbed him from behind. "Where's Bibianna?" he screamed. *"Where is she?"*

The doctor stumbled off-balance and one of the duty nurses started to run. A second nurse picked up a phone to call Security. Raymond pulled out a gun and pointed it at her, his arm stiff, his intent murderous. She lowered the phone. He swung the gun back and forth as he made his way down the hall. I pulled out the SIG-Sauer, but the doctor was in my way. Hospital staff seemed to be everywhere.

I screamed, *"Tate!"* I started running.

Bibianna was in the second room. Tate was on his feet, his gun out. Raymond fired. I saw Tate go down.

Raymond doubled back, heading right at me.

I held the gun with both hands and yelled, "Stop!" but he knew I wouldn't fire under the circumstances. There were too many people in the vicinity to risk shooting. He shouldered me aside and took off at a dead run, his heels clattering as he plowed through the double doors and down the corridor. He still had his gun, but he was moving too fast to take aim or fire with any accuracy. I banged through the doors behind him and pounded down the hallway after him. Heads appeared in doorways, people attracted by all the commotion, disappearing again quickly when they spotted the guns. Raymond reached an Exit sign and grabbed the knob, flung the door open, and headed down the stairs. I caught the door as it swung shut and forced it back with a crash. I could hear Raymond's descent, his footsteps echoing rapidly in a spiral below me. I was jumping down three steps at a time, trying to cut his lead, when I heard him reach the exterior door below. His exit set off an alarm bell that began to peal shrilly.

I doubled my pace, hitting the door with one hand, the SIG-Sauer in the other, nearly recoiling at the sudden blast of bright sunlight in my face. I could see Raymond tearing across a stretch of lawn just ahead of me. We'd emerged from one end of the hospital, close to Arizona Avenue in an area of small stucco houses with an occasional three-story medical building. Raymond ran toward the street, feet flying, arms pumping. I was vaguely aware of someone running behind me, but I couldn't afford to look. I was narrowing the gap, calling on the last of my physical reserves. I had to be in better shape than Raymond, but I could feel myself wheezing, lungs on fire. Six days without exercise had taken the edge off, but I still had some juice.

Raymond took a quick look behind him, gauging the distance between us. He got off a shot that smacked into a palm tree to my left. He tried to goose up his pace, but he really didn't have it in him. I was close enough now that the sound of his heavy breathing seemed in concert with mine and the heels of his shoes nearly touched my pumping knees. I had a tight grip on the gun. I reached out and pushed him hard in the back. He stumbled, arms flailing as he tried to regain his balance. He went down in a sprawl and I landed, knees first, in the middle of his back. His breath left him in a *whoosh* and the gun flew out of his hand. I was up and on my feet, panting heavily. He turned over as I raised the barrel of the gun and placed it between his eyes. Raymond had his hands up, inching away from me. For ten cents I would have blown that motherfucker away. My rage was white hot and I was out of control, screaming *"I'll kill your ass! I'll kill your ass, you son of a bitch!!"*

Behind me, I heard, *"Freeze!"*

I whipped around.

It was Luis.

The gun in his right hand was pointed directly at Raymond. In his left hand was a badge. He was LAPD.

Epilogue

By the time I got back upstairs, the emergency room crew was already working on Jimmy Tate, who was whisked into surgery within the hour. The bullet had caught him in the abdomen and he'd apparently suffered a ruptured spleen. Bibianna wasn't in much better shape, but both survived. Whether they lived happily ever after or not, I really couldn't say, as all this happened just three weeks ago. I made it back to Santa Teresa in time for Vera's wedding on Monday night, which was Halloween. Naturally, as I hadn't had time to shop, I was forced to wear my faithful all-purpose dress, which in my opinion suited the occasion to a T. Vera was urging me to bring a date, so I took Luis with me, Donald and Daffy Duck arms and all.

Raymond Maldonado has hired himself a top-notch attorney. At this point the charges against him range from murder one, in the case of Parnell Perkins, to grand theft, insurance fraud, mail fraud, all the way down to petty larceny. I gather that certain cases involving individuals with Tourette's syndrome present a serious challenge to the criminal justice system. My guess is he'll work out a deal, naming some of the other key figures in the fraud ring including three attorneys from the law firm of Gotlieb, Naples, Hurley, and Flushing.

The cops never did come up with my black leather jacket. Somebody in the restaurant probably lifted it the minute my back was turned. I'm tellin' you, people are crooks! And it's not just the ordinary man in the street. I haven't been paid for all the work I did. I billed the Santa Teresa Police Department for services rendered. Dolan tells me he forwarded the invoice to the LAPD, who'll probably turn around and try to lay it off on the Department of Insurance. I'll give those turkeys ninety days to "process" my money and then I'm calling my attorney.

The only other matter that needs clearing up has to do with Gordon Titus and that's simple enough. The sucker fired me.

THE #**1** *NEW YORK TIMES* **BESTSELLING AUTHOR**
SUE GRAFTON

A IS FOR ALIBI

"Bright, brisk, and
thoroughly engaging."
—*The Washington Post*

A KINSEY MILLHONE NOVEL

St. Martin's Griffin